VENGEFUL PROPOSAL

SIDEROV BRATVA
BOOK 1

BROOK WILDER

INTRODUCTION

This series is a prequel story to two existing series - the *Barinov Bratva* trilogy and the *Starukhin Bratva* duet.

While you don't need to read those series in order to understand what happens in this series, but reading them will make for a richer experience.

If you'd like to check them out, you can do so here:

BARINOV BRATVA
Deceitful Vows
Deceitful Lies
Deceitful Bond

STARUKHIN BRATVA
Unforgiving Sinner
Unforgiving Saint

1

EMILY

If there's one place that I would call hell, it would be baggage carousel number six at Naples-Capodichino Airport.

Especially when your flight arrived two hours later than it was supposed to, and it feels like the air conditioning in the entire airport is broken.

Heck, there's not even a single fan on!

"Sorry, I mean—scusa! Scusa!" I say as I push myself through the large crowd heading in the same direction as me while doing my best to ignore their annoyed eye rolls.

Is scusa *the right word? I should've paid more attention to that YouTube language guide.*

Whatever, it's already too late for that. I need to hurry if I want to check into the hotel in time to do my last-minute maid-of-honor duties for my best friend Nadia's bachelorette party.

I pick up the pace, ducking low to avoid a large backpack suddenly swinging in my direction from a couple of guys talking excitedly about their hiking trip to Mt. Vesuvius.

... and come to an abrupt stop when I collide with something right in front of the carousel.

No, scratch that.

Some*one*.

"Oof!" the sound bounces out of my mouth as I slip and fall to the ground.

"Are you alright?" A lightly accented voice—deep and crisp—rumbles in my ear.

A massive hand extends out to help me. I look up, and feel my heart skip a beat.

Oh my.

He has to be the hottest man I've ever had the pleasure of being face to face with. I sit there on the ground, and crane my neck up to gawk awkwardly at him.

His mahogany hair is thick on top, textured with a fade that tapers toward his long, tan neck, the perfect complements to his ice-blue eyes.

The gray slacks and sienna dress shirt can't hide his powerful muscles. There's a lopsided smile on his face that makes the tiny mole below his right eye shift upward. My eyes are drawn to his lips—soft and full. For a single reckless moment, I want to confirm my hypothesis.

It takes me a moment to realize that I'm staring, and another moment for me to take hold of his offered hand.

A searing warmth instantly rushes through me upon touching his skin, piercing me all the way down to my core, where a delicious fire is stoked between my legs. The heat grows as he pulls me effortlessly off the ground like I'm weightless.

"Sorry, I'm in a hurry and I should've looked where I'm going and—"

"It's alright." He interrupts me, the smile never leaving his face. "First time in Naples?"

"First time in Italy, actually," I laugh nervously. *Ugh! His voice is like ear chocolate.* "And wouldn't you know it, I'm already running late."

"That would mean you're actually early," he replies. "By Italian standards, of course."

"Unfortunately." I spread my hands. "The maid of honor can't be late."

"Destination wedding?"

"Bachelorette party, actually." I correct him, and then in another reckless moment, I add. "In the Amalfi Coast."

"A lucky coincidence," he muses. "I'm actually headed there myself."

"Really? For what?" I ask as I scan the carousel, searching for the familiar bright pink Hello Kitty bag tag on my bag handle. "Destination wedding?"

His laugh is warm and it sets my face flushing. Suddenly, I'm glad that the air conditioning doesn't work here.

"Work, actually," he says. "And if you'll believe it, my flight happened to have arrived two hours *early.*"

"Sounds like you're really early," I tell him. "By Italian standards, of course."

"You could say that." He laughs again. "If you're willing to wait a bit, I can give you a ride. Free of charge."

"I wish I could," I tell him apologetically, my heart plummeting. "But like I said, I'm already late. But maybe I'll see you out there?"

"Maybe." His smile widens ever-so-slightly, and my heart skips another beat.

I turn and take another glance at the carousel.

There it is!

The black luggage is identical to a number of bags going around the belt, but the bright pink Hello Kitty tag on the handle is unique—a gift from my sister Olivia right before she left home for good.

Seeing it is also a punch to the gut. My hand hovers in the air briefly, almost as if it doesn't want to touch the bag.

But it starts to circle out of reach on the carousel. I close my fingers around the handle and yank off at the last second.

"Well, good luck with everything!" I tell the handsome stranger.

"Have fun," he replies. "And try your best not to run into anyone else while you're out here."

You're the only one I want to run into again. But for some reason, the words don't leave my mouth.

Rolling my bag through the exit, I walk away from him, sparing him one last look as sweat slowly starts to dampen my white shirt. He never breaks eye contact with me, and for the third reckless moment of the day, I almost want to run back towards him to tell him that I *will* take up his offer for the ride.

But maid of honor duties beckon, and I can't just duck out on my responsibilities. So, giving the handsome stranger one final wave goodbye, I walk past the doors and emerge into the blistering hot sun as a cacophony of voices erupts around me, beckoning me to choose one of the myriads of taxis lined up at the arrivals gate.

"Need a ride, signorina?"

I stand quickly to face the man speaking to me. He's dressed in a loose-fitting tan shirt with a deep V-neck.

"Do you take credit cards?" I ask, realizing I haven't had a chance to exchange any money.

He looks me up and down, then opens my door for me. "Sure."

I get in, wrinkling the bridge of my nose as the smell of sweat and stale cigarettes assaults my nostrils.

"Where to?" he asks.

"Amalfi Central Hotel?"

"Ah!" he nods. "Three hours. If we're lucky, two and a half!"

"Is it actually that far?"

I'm pretty sure the route I looked up only said an hour and a half.

"Lots of traffic, today, signorina," he answers with a toothy grin. "Can't go any faster, I'm afraid." I blink, and he fans his fingers by his face. "Unless you prefer to wait for someone else."

If you're willing to wait a bit, I can give you a ride. Free of charge.

My hand reaches for the door handle but I stop myself.

I'm late enough as it is without indulging in unrealistic fantasies about hot strangers in Italy. So, with a resigned sigh, I click my seat belt in, tug it extra tight, and offer up a weak smile knowing that I'm about to get hustled.

"Three hours will be fine."

Sighing, I sink into my seat, rolling my shoulders in an attempt to get comfortable. My body is rigid, and my mind flies backward to the moment two weeks ago when everything fell apart.

2

EMILY
TWO WEEKS AGO

I WAS RUSHING BACK TO THE STUDENT HOUSING TO GRAB AN extra tampon when I noticed my boyfriend Phil pacing just outside the building. He caught my eye, then dashed over to grab my wrist, telling me he needed my help.

It wouldn't be the first time he needed my help. This was a practiced ritual that Phil had drilled down to perfection. He'd tell me his problem of the week and I'd sit down with him, reassure him that everything would be okay, and then propose a solution.

Most of the time, the solution meant I stuck my neck out for him.

So, I thought nothing of it when I took his hands in mine and told him that whatever it was, I'd be happy to help.

He told me that the campus police had found his stash in our room. I knew he had a jar of weed there. Not the best look for someone whose dad was one of the biggest donors to the university, but not entirely illegal either. It was just something against the code of conduct in the dorms. The university wanted to talk to him, probably to reprimand him. But he couldn't risk his father finding out.

Which was where I came in.

I had no criminal history, he told me. The university was just looking for someone to blame, he told me. The cops wouldn't even press charges, he told me. So, please, please, please, just take the fall, he begged. After all, with my perfect reputation and excellent grades, I would get no more than a slap on the wrist after a hearing with a disciplinary committee.

Please, Emily. Just this once.

But it was never *just this once*, was it? It always turned into *just one more time*.

I should've told him that.

But instead, I agreed to cover for him, go before the disciplinary committee, and tell them it was a mistake. That the stash wasn't his, but mine.

And only at the hearing did I find out that the stash they found wasn't his jar of weed. It was cocaine and Adderall— enough that they could involve law enforcement if they really wanted to.

To make things worse, there were plenty of undergrads who pointed the finger that *our* dorm room was where they bought the drugs from.

They gave me a choice: voluntarily ask for my expulsion from vet school, or the university could escalate this to law enforcement.

There was no debating my fate at that point.

When I went to Phil after the dust settled, he apologized profusely and made empty promises that he'd make it up to me somehow. I hated how he said that ... Like it was possible to soothe me with some sweet words. That was always his method when he did something wrong: crawl to me with sugary smiles and a shiny gift.

He did that when he crashed his car and asked me to say

I was driving. I did, and suffered his parents' scowls every time I walked into their home for dinner.

I should've recognized that he was using me to get what he wants.

That he had *always* just used me to get what he wants.

The signs were all there from the start. I should have seen them. Maybe I did and ignored them.

But not anymore. Never again.

The only satisfaction I got out of this mess was the look of shock on his face when I finally broke up with him.

3

EMILY
PRESENT DAY

WHAT WAS SUPPOSED TO BE A THREE-HOUR LONG RIDE TURNS out to be more than five.

But it's hard to hate how long the drive is when the view is beautiful. The sapphire Mediterranean Sea gleams below us as the wide highway slowly gives way to narrow single lane roads. Mountains rise up—seemingly right up to the sea—and I can't help but marvel at the brilliant white houses clustered above on the cliffside, decorated in dazzling red barrel clay tiles of varying hues.

The taxi pulls in front of a cobblestone plaza and I recognize the large fountain carved into a fifteen-foot-high wall of the Amalfi Central Hotel. Pavers are green with damp moss. Angelic faces—worn away by weather—jut from the fountain. Water bubbles from their cracked lips, the soothing sound relaxes me.

"Here we are," the driver says as he passes a credit card reader over to me.

What little sense of relaxation instantly turns into panic when I spot the bill.

Three *hundred* Euros!

What the actual fuck!

But there's nothing I can do now except insert my card into the reader, and agree to pay him for this highway robbery of a ride. At least he's still willing to help me with my bags when I exit the car. With another toothy grin, he gives me a wave, steps back into the driver's seat, and peels away.

I swear I can hear him laughing as he disappears out of sight.

The Amalfi Central Hotel is a medium-sized building with a skinny balcony surrounding the second level. Yellow paint coats its outer walls, making it stand out from the otherwise white buildings of the town.

It looks like a lemon, and since the air is heavy with the scent of the fruit, it's all I can picture it as.

Nadia loves the smell of lemons, so this hotel was a no-brainer.

It takes about ten minutes to check in, haul my suitcase up the narrow steps to the suite, and reach the maroon door with a golden 8 on it. By the time I open the door, my shirt—already damp from the Italian heat—is drenched in sweat and sticking to my chest and stomach.

I need to change into something clean, I think as I push my way inside.

But as eager as I am to put on something dry and non-sweaty, I take a moment to appreciate the room.

There are two large beds with tall wooden posts that rise to the ceiling. Mint-green wallpaper with a white diamond pattern extends over every surface, including the floors where the lavender rug doesn't hide it. I peek into the bathroom; the sink is shaped like a seashell, and the soap smells like the lemons on the trees outside.

I did my best to find a place where there are reminders of the beach all around us.

But the best part is the balcony. I spent hours on the phone, squeezing out every little detail Nadia wanted. Somehow, in every phone call, she'd tell me that she wanted to sit on a balcony on the Amalfi Coast with a glass of wine in hand, the salty sea breeze in her hair, digging into a plate of freshly made tiramisu in front of her.

I push the glass door aside, letting the warm air into the room. It's still hot in the bright sun, but the salty sea breeze wafting off the waves directly into my face offers just a tantalizing hint of relief.

I hurry over to my bag. There's still one more thing to do before Nadia arrives: set up the balloons. The special-ordered lavender, glitter-filled balloons arrived just in time before I left for the airport.

Popping my bag open, I reach inside, moving clothes around to find the balloons.

Wait, hold on.

Since when did I pack a black and silver button-down? Or a cobalt blue tie? Or a pair of Prada lace-up black shoes in a men's size twelve?

"What the hell?" I whisper.

There's a sharp knock on the door. *Oh shit, is Nadia here already?* I thought I had more time!

Still casting confused looks at my bag, I open the door and my eyes bulge even wider when I spot the last person I expected to run into in the world.

Familiar mahogany hair, ice-blue eyes, gray slacks and sienna dress shirt, and a tiny mole just beneath his right eye that shifts up when he smiles.

It's him!

The handsome stranger that I ran into at the airport five hours ago.

Before I can say something, he holds up a black bag.

"I believe there's been a mix-up." His voice is just as crisp and deep as I remember. But my attention is drawn towards the pink Hello Kitty bag on the handle. It's the same as the one I have on what is clearly not *my* bag.

"Is that mine?" I ask. "Wait. How ... No, *why* do you have a pink Hello Kitty tag? More importantly, how the hell did you find me here?"

His grin grows wider, and my heart swells right along with it.

"I did what anyone does after arriving: open my bag to change out of my clothes ... only to find things that were decidedly not mine."

Yep, that checks out.

"From the dresses to the heels to the *scandalously* tiny swim suit in there, and based on a conversation I had with a woman who insisted on not taking a free offer, I assumed that the owner of this bag must've been on her way to a bachelorette party."

I fight to keep the blush from searing further up my face.

Guilty as charged.

"Since this is one of the *most* popular hotels for bachelorette parties, and I happen to know the owner ... I figured it didn't hurt to ask if a beautiful woman with chestnut hair and blue eyes recently checked in." Chuckling, he sets my bag on the floor. "How'd I do?"

"Pretty damn good." I pause, and add hopefully as my heart skips a beat. "Are you staying here then? Since you happen to know the owner and all?"

He laughs again, and this time, I *know* I can't hide myself blushing anymore because my whole face—no fuck that, my whole body—feels like it's on fire. He looks me over, those beautiful ice-blue eyes lingering a moment before they meet mine. The slight, knowing smile—like he's holding a secret he can't wait to tell me—grows on his beautiful lips, and sends another surge of heat shooting through my core.

"Not here. But close by. You should visit Salerno if you have the time. The views of the sea are stunning."

The views here are pretty great too. I ogle his long legs as he walks into the room toward his bag. He bends over to close it, and I can't help but sneak a look at the firm ass that's barely contained in his gray slacks. Trailing in his wake, like a whisper beckoning me to lean in for more, is a hint of light soap and aftershave.

"Thanks for finding me." I feel another drop of sweat rolling down my side as he stands up. Suddenly, I'm aware of just how close we are to each other, and just how closely I'm studying every detail on his handsome face. "You really saved my ass there."

He leans down, and my mind is suddenly filled with the image of his full lips crushing against mine. His powerful hands pulling me close into his muscular body. The warm sea breeze caressing our bodies as he trails kisses down my body and ...

I *really* need to turn on the A/C.

"Maybe I'll see you around." He flashes me another smile and walks past me.

I almost shout *Don't go!* But instead, my tongue sticks to the roof of my mouth until I finally I blurt out, "Yuppers!"

Fuck. Yuppers? Who the hell says yuppers?

With a final quick glance from his seductively curious eyes, he vanishes down the stairs, the bag rolling gently by his ankles. The light scent of soap and aftershave trails in his wake, tempting me to follow.

I almost do.

Shutting the door reluctantly, I jump straight up when the knock comes. *He's back?* I yank the door wide open, excited by the prospect of Mr. Sex-on-Legs returning so fast.

Instead, I see Nadia standing in the hallway, her orange plastic roller case at her side, and her attention straight down the hall where the hot, sexy stranger was just a moment ago.

She whips her head toward me so quickly it sends her blonde hair flipping and her gold sunglasses sliding off her forehead to the floor.

"Emily." Her lips open into a big, knowing smile. "Who. Was. *That?*"

"Nobody," I assure her.

Oh God, why am I blushing? It's not like anything happened.

"Oh my God, you're such a terrible liar!" Sliding her bag inside, Nadia bumps the door shut with her hip. "First of all, you go, girl. And second of all, if I weren't getting married, I'd be fighting you for a chance to see what he's packing!"

"Careful now, you don't want me to tell Lawrence."

"Oh please, as good-looking as Mr. Tall and Sexy might be, I still lucked out with Lawrence. I mean, it's not every day you have a guy who's got a footlong—"

"Okay!" I hold out my arms to stop her before she gets going and won't stop. "Hi! How are you? How was the flight? How was the drive?"

She practically throws me straight to the floor as she hugs me. "Ahh! We're here, Emily! We actually made it!"

"Happy to see you too," I giggle, straining in her grip. "But you're choking me."

Her response? Hugging me even tighter.

"Oh my God, that drive! It was ah-may-zing! And the

people? And the *buildings?* Did you see that fountain right out front? We have to get photos there with the other girls!" She's rambling now and not even giving me a chance to respond. "Emily, this is wonderful! I know this must've been hard, what with you breaking up with Phil and all."

And even though I know she doesn't mean to, but the mere mention of Phil is like a splash of cold water on my face.

She doesn't even know the reason for the breakup.

She has no idea what Phil did.

For a moment, I have a powerful desire to just ... spill my guts. *Don't. Don't bring the mood down! You can tell her later, after everything is over and we have to go back to face reality.*

She stares down at me with her bright green eyes. Some of her hair has gotten tangled in the peacock feather earrings she has on.

"I think both of us need this," I tell her. "Actually, I'm not sure who needs it more."

"I know, right?" Kissing my cheek twice, she helps me to my feet. "Now that that's out of the way. Spill the tea, bitch. Who. Was. That. Man? And if you say nobody again, I swear to God, Emily, I'm going to find him and march him back here for some real answers."

"Good luck with that, because it's the truth," I reply. "We bumped into each other at the airport, and grabbed each other's bags by accident."

I sure as shit would like *to know him, though.*

"I think he's into you."

Snorting, I roll my eyes extra dramatically, making sure she sees. "Okay, relax."

"Look, I'd be into you too if I were a guy who just got a good look at what your momma gave you." She points at my sweat-soaked shirt.

Shit! It's almost transparent! Fresh heat runs up my face. Did he see? Of course he saw! There's no way he didn't see! Suddenly I remember his gaze lingering for a moment before he looked me in the eye.

And that knowing smile.

Yeah, he definitely saw.

"I can't believe that happened!"

"Don't sweat it, Emily." Nadia winks. I fight the urge to roll my eyes at her pun. "If you're not giving hot strangers in Italy a show, then what are we even doing here?"

"I have to change."

I quickly make my way over to my bag, unzip it, and start looking for something proper to change into. On top of my crumpled clothing is a small slip of paper. The handwriting is neat, tidy, and decidedly not my own.

I promise I didn't look through your belongings too closely. But if I did, I would tell you that the lavender dress will drive every man in this town crazy.

Be careful when you go out in it, Kitty Cat.

"Emily, are you smiling?"

I shake myself and try to tuck the note in my suitcase under some jeans before Nadia notices. "Am I?"

"Oh my God," she squeals when she sees the corner of the paper peeking out. "Did he write you a *note?* Come on, show me! I want to know what Mr. Tall and Sexy said that's got you grinning from ear to ear!"

"Nadia, stop it," I say. "I'm here to make sure you have a fun time. The last thing I want is to have you wondering about random guys ogling me."

"And the last thing I want as your *bestest best friend* is for you to duck out on fate." She's standing with her arms akimbo, watching me. "Or to miss out on good dick."

That gets a rude laugh out of me. "That's just a coincidence and nothing else. I'm not chasing strange tail on this trip, Nadia. Guys aren't on my mind."

"Because of Phil?"

My back tightens up at the second mention of Phil.

"No, but ... Maybe it should be. God, I wish I never dated that guy."

For so many reasons...

"Emily," she says. "I'm not asking you to find the love of your life here. Just parachute into a bed with a hot stranger, have some fun, and break a few hearts of your own. Anything's better than moping over that loser."

"I guess. But wouldn't it be great to go back in time and change things?"

"I know you don't want to talk about what caused the break up." Nadia searches my face. Shutting her eyes, she releases a long exhale. "But you can't fix a past that refuses to be changed. You've gone out of your way to take care of other people—whether it's me, your parents, your sister, or that asshole Phil." I start to argue but she holds up a pointed nail to stop me. "Be selfish, for once in your life."

"I just ... Sometimes I feel like there are things that happened in my life that I could have changed if I was smarter ... or kinder ... or a lot of things I'm not."

And might never be.

Coming closer, she lifts my hands in hers, holding on like I'm about to drop off a cliff. My heart is racing like I'm about to.

"You are the smartest, kindest, most considerate person I know in my life," she says. "Forget the past. Just focus on doing something about your future," she says solemnly.

Yeah ... About that.

I can't tell her.

If I do, she'll just want to give me an even bigger pep talk when this weekend should be about her, and not me. So, despite my own heavy heart, I reach out and squeeze her hands tight. My smile is the only thing holding back tears—but whether they're tears of appreciation or something else, I don't know.

"Thanks, Nadia."

"You're welcome." She returns my smile, wrapping me in a hug. Her voice is a singsong in my ear. "Which is why I'm making you a promise."

I tense up with a nervous laugh. "Oh no."

"You have my blessing—no, fuck that—my *order* to abandon any and all maid of honor duties if you have a chance to hook up with a hot guy." She smirks and jerks her head toward the door. "Especially *that* hot guy. I mean, he's already got a preview. It'll be a *damn* shame if he doesn't get a taste of the main course. Know what I'm saying? What was his name, by the way?"

I open my mouth ... Then I stop.

My heart gives a tiny thud as it drops into the pit of my stomach.

"He never told me."

4

EMILY

Nightfall doesn't do a thing to alleviate the humidity, and I'm thankful that the inside of the Zebra Club is at least air conditioned. Or as air conditioned as it can be with the number of bodies packed in its tight space.

The six of us in matching lavender dresses—me, Nadia, Meghan, Clara, Jennifer, and Heather—make our way to the dance floor. Red lights shift to blue, and the undertones of our outfits change to match it. Slowly, everyone in the room becomes the same saturated color.

I don't recognize the song playing, but it doesn't matter; it's got a good beat and that's all I need. Nadia catches my eye, her teeth glowing in the lights as she dances. We've worked up a sweat when a woman flags us down. She's wearing a pair of black shorts and a white crop top bearing the club's name across the front.

"Your table is ready!" she yells.

"What?" Nadia yells back.

"Your table—"

"We didn't get a table!" I cut in. I originally wanted to, but it was way out of my budget.

The woman jabs her painted nails over to our right. "Someone did!"

Pursing my lips, I follow the woman to an area just off the dance floor. There are a number of booths here, their black surfaces glossy as wet tar. The round table in the center hosts a huge ice bucket with several dark glass bottles sticking out.

"Holy shit, someone bought us bottle service?" Clara asks.

I'm the closest to the table, so I spot the note before they do. Picking up the matchbook-sized square of paper, I read it with wide eyes. It's the same neat and tidy handwriting as the note that was left in my bag.

I knew that dress could drive a man crazy. Sometimes I hate being right.

And then to top things off, there's a Hello Kitty's face drawn at the very bottom of the note.

"Holy shit," I breathe.

It's from *him*.

Nadia snatches the note from my fingers, reading it an inch from her nose. Laughing, she smacks me on the arm with it. "I *told you!* He's got it bad for you, Emily!"

"Nadia ..."

"Ladies." She faces the other four girls with her hands on her hips. "Back me up."

Meghan lifts a bottle from the ice. "I mean, if a guy bought *me* Dom Perignon, I'd take that as a hint he liked me."

"Did you girls know that I caught that guy coming out of our room when I landed? And Emily here *insisted* that they weren't doing anything even though she was soaked in sweat and her hair was a mess."

A chorus of overlapping voices rises, and I do my best not to sink into the couch. I can't muster an argument. I don't want to.

"And believe me," Nadia continues. "That man was F-I-N-E. *Fine!*"

"Emily, you *have* to go thank him for all of this!" Clara yells as she gestures at the couch and the table and the bottles of champagne.

"I don't—"

"Yes, you do." Nadia holds her hand up. "He must be around here somewhere. Hey, do you think he owns this place or something?"

"I have no idea."

"Well, go find out, then!" Meghan interjects.

Nadia collects the glass flutes, passes them around, and gestures at Meghan. "Pop the cork! We're celebrating my maid of honor getting *laid* tonight!"

"I thought we were here to celebrate you getting married in six weeks?" I remind her as my glass is filled.

"We can do both. Besides, we have three whole days ahead of us to celebrate me! Right now, you have a mission." She holds her glass high. "Remember my order?"

"I'm trying my best not to."

Leaning close, Nadia clinks her glass on mine. "Too bad! Because I'm *ordering* you as the bachelorette to thank him and then climb him like a goddamn tree!"

My stomach folds in half as the other girls echo Nadia's words. Each of them is grinning at me excitedly. The pressure to agree to Nadia's terms is overwhelming. They've allowed themselves to become invested in this silly scenario where I end up in bed with a hot stranger who buys private tables and a whole bucket of Dom Perignon like it's nothing.

It's absolutely ridiculous.

What's the worst that can happen?

With their eyes on me, I tip my glass to my lips, drain it, and stand up to the sound of their cheering.

***

MOVING through the club is like trying to wade through sand. The numerous bodies bounce me back and forth, not noticing me, or not caring. Sucking in stale air, I push toward the first opening I spot. It's a gap near the service door and bathroom. Men in stained white wifebeaters run in and out with new trays of glasses to stock the bar, avoiding the long line waiting to get into the stalls.

Standing on tiptoe, I put my hands up to my face, squinting through the strobe lights that are determined to leave me disoriented. Every face is the same reddish shade, so I can't pick apart features or clothing. *It's impossible. I'll never find Mr. Sex-on-Legs in this madness.*

"Hi," I wave at the bartender. "Who can I speak to about table services?"

A crisp, familiar voice suddenly rises behind me. "Was one bucket not enough?"

I don't *have* to look to confirm, but I'm already turning. Mr. Sex-on-Legs is standing just a foot away. He's dressed in an expensive-looking tan jacket over a blue shirt, the sleeves rolled up to expose his muscular forearms. If possible, he's *more* attractive than I remember.

His eyes fall on me, and I swallow as I stand up straighter.

"Fancy seeing you here, Kitty Cat."

Ugh! Somehow, a stupid-sounding nickname like *that* manages to sound sexy coming from his perfect lips.

Before I can say anything, he raises two fingers to get the attention of the bartender.

"Another two buckets for the bachelorette party," he says. "On me."

"Right away, Mr. Siderov."

My heart is doing a tango as I turn to him. "Should I also call you *Mr. Siderov?*"

"Konstantin is fine."

"Konstantin," I repeat, just to feel the letters on my tongue. *I like the way that sounds.* I extend my hand. "I'm Emily."

He takes my hand in his, and I'm overwhelmed by the same warmth that I felt at the airport when he helped me up from the ground.

"I think I prefer Kitty Cat," he says.

I do my best not to imagine those fingers pressing against my thighs, or fantasize how good it'd feel like to have them push my legs apart while those gorgeous eyes look at me from below.

Jesus, calm down! Just thank him and be on your way.

"Do you own this place or something?" I ask him. "Is that why you're here?"

"No," he replies. "I happen to know the owner."

"That sounds familiar," I muse. "Do you happen to know the owner of every establishment here?"

His smirk is like a crescent moon. "Not *every* one of them, Kitty Cat. But close enough that it doesn't matter."

"So why are you here? And I don't mean here in this club. I mean the Amalfi Coast."

"I told you." His smile dips slightly, but doesn't fully leave his face. "Work."

I wonder what kind of work he does. But before I can ask, someone suddenly bumps me hard enough to send me stumbling to the floor.

I spin around, ready to tear into the asshole, but Konstantin is already standing between us. He's not looking at me, but at the man who just knocked me down.

"Apologize." Konstantin's voice is hard as iron, audible even over the pounding bass reverberating through the club. "Now."

The man curls his lips, ready to say something foul. At the last second Konstantin shifts his body, like he's adjusting his jacket. The guy freezes, glancing down at something I can't see. The knob in his neck flexes before he looks over at me.

Even in the club's odd lighting, I can tell his face is pale.

"I'm sorry," he stammers. "It was an accident! I swear!"

He backpedals before I can respond.

Weird.

"So, Kitty Cat." Konstantin smooths the front of his jacket. "Were you looking for me?"

Yes.

But I won't let him win this easily. So, I cross my arms, cock my hip, and smirk. "That's bold of you to assume."

His lip curls into a heart-stopping smile.

"My mistake, then," he says. "I'll leave you to it." He starts to push through the crowd. "Enjoy the Dom."

"Wait!" I try to keep the desperation from my voice and fail horribly.

He stops, giving me a side-eye and that sexy smile of his widens, sending butterflies fluttering in my stomach. *Climb that man like a goddamn tree ...*

"Yeah, okay," I admit. "I was coming to find you. I wanted to say thanks for the table."

"Happy to help your bachelorette have a good time."

"Well, she's loving it."

"And you? Are you having a good time?"

I spread my hands. "That bottle of Dom is the best thing so far."

"Is that your drink of choice when you go clubbing?"

"Not a fan of clubs, actually, if you can believe that. But what the bachelorette wants ..."

"The bachelorette gets." He rubs his sharp chin, considering me like I'm a fascinating flower he just discovered. "If clubs aren't your thing, I happen to know somewhere that's more suited to your tastes. Come."

My jaw drops at the audacity. He doesn't ask. He doesn't wait for my permission. Instead, it's like he's issuing a command that I'm expected to follow. Somehow, I get the feeling Konstantin Siderov has never heard anyone tell him *no.*

My feet stick to the floor. Peering over my shoulder at the table, I search for Nadia. *I don't want to leave her behind. But if I tell her I thanked Konstantin and have nothing to show for it ...*

"Well, Kitty Cat?" He extends his hand to me, lips curling up in a playful smile that sends a shiver of excitement down my spine.

Fuck it.

I unlock my knees. "Lead the way."

5

EMILY

THE SECOND WE EXIT THE CLUB, I PULL IN A HUGE BREATH OF refreshing air. The sea breeze that circulates along the coast is rejuvenating. There's a line of people snaking by the front door of the club. I marvel at it, thinking again that we were lucky we got inside at all.

Konstantin is someone important, that's for sure.

A part of me really wants to know more about him. It's a stupid thing to want. Because odds are good that once I leave, I'll never see this guy again.

"Down here," he says, stepping carefully over the cobblestones of a sharply curving street only wide enough for a moped. The walk is short, and I hear music long before I see the small bar. The front of it is covered in greenery. Potted plants hang from twisting ropes or grow from clay basins. Konstantin enters first, waiting for me just inside the doorway. I don't see a sign with a name anywhere.

I gasp in delight when I enter. A live band is performing on a low stage. Five men play various instruments. I recognize three kinds of guitars and some bongos, but the metal canister that's being rubbed up and down with a stick is new to me. The tables have been pushed to the edges of the room, allowing the main floor to be used as a dance area.

They're all paired up in couples. Whether man or woman, everyone is shaking their hips sensually. It's hypnotic, and I can't stop staring.

Konstantin doesn't waste time. He leads me through the bar, which smells like saffron and white wine, until we're smack-dab in the center of the floor.

"What is all this?" I ask.

"Bachata."

"It looks like salsa to me."

Konstantin laughs in the base of his throat. "It's similar, but there are a few differences."

"Like what?"

"Well, salsa is lighthearted. Energetic." He offers his hand. "Flirty, even."

I stare at his fingers and fight the urge to bite my lip. It's no longer about Nadia's rules. I sure as hell *want* to be here with him.

"And bachata?" I ask as I tangle my hand in his.

"Slower." His other hand rests against the small of my back. "More intimate." A small tug and I find myself pressed close to him. The smell of soap and aftershave—light enough to tease and tantalizing enough to draw me in further—tickles my nose. "And *far* more sensual."

"Is that right?" I breathe, fighting the pounding in my heart.

"Let me show you, Kitty Cat." His hand squeezes mine, and my body warms all through my center.

I could *really* use a cold drink right now.

"I don't know the steps."

"Just let me take control and you'll be fine."

He faces me, and I see my own flushed reflection in his

ice-blue eyes. It's the first time I've noticed how much taller he is than me. I *knew* he was bigger—most people are—but this closeness emphasizes how his chin is half a foot over my head. His back is broad enough that someone standing behind him wouldn't be able to see me. "You sure you want to do this in the middle of the room? There's lots of space on the sidelines," I say.

"People can see us better like this."

"You mean they'll see you get embarrassed by me a lot easier."

He dips his head, and for a single dizzying moment, I imagine him pressing his full lips against mine. But instead, he chuckles as he whispers—breath hot and sultry against my ear, "Nothing you do can embarrass me, Kitty Cat."

My heart wriggles up my throat. *Oh yeah. I'm in trouble.*

Konstantin squeezes my fingers, his shoe sliding back an inch. "Just follow. I'll lead."

"I'll do my best," I whisper.

He moves his arms in gentle swerves, his knees bending, hips rocking. It's like he's the living embodiment of the sea that surrounds us. The entire time he dances, his eyes don't leave mine. I'm less graceful; I have to constantly glance at his feet just to keep up.

We pace in a small square to the beat of the music. Konstantin goes further than that, tapping his feet *between* the beats.

He doesn't just break the rules, he bends them to his will.

I laugh. "How are you so good at this?"

His eyes flash, as do his teeth in his wide smirk. Pressing closer to me, he tugs my arms, causing our bodies to touch. I gasp, partly from shock, and partly from something else stirring inside of me.

"A man needs to be nimble on his feet," he replies. "It's rude to step on someone's toes."

"What about women? Do I get a pass?"

"For tonight? Yes." He grinds his hips forward, and my inner heat simmers as my hips move to match his movement. His hand on my back tugs me just a little bit closer. And for a moment, I dare to pretend that it's just the two of us here.

"Music, movement, the pull of the rhythm, and how they shape the flow of our bodies ..." he says as our hips sway as one. "These are the differences between simply living and being alive."

My hands loosen in his for a moment. Konstantin notices and holds on tighter. He swings me around, erasing the tiny grim voice that was ready to whisper in my ear. His insistence that I keep up with his quick movements is helping me focus on *this*—on the moment.

He can't be doing it on purpose, but it works just the same.

The band hasn't taken a break for the entire two hours, and neither have we. My feet are throbbing; there's sweat up and down my back. The thin material of my dress sticks to my skin and leaves nothing to the imagination.

But somehow, with Konstantin, I don't want him to imagine.

I want him to see.

The only time we slow down is when a giggling waitress with thick red hair holds out a tray toward us. On it are several tiny glasses of clear liquid.

"Limoncello," Konstantin says, grabbing one. "Try it."

"I've had limoncello before."

"But not *this* limoncello. It's made from Sfusato Amalfitano lemons. They're only grown here."

I've been smelling lemons since I arrived. Curious, I take a glass, sniffing it. The citrus makes my nose burn. When he takes a sip from his, I chug mine down. The tingles ripple through my throat.

"Holy shit! That is *strong!*"

Konstantin takes my empty glass with a smile while he downs his. "That's why you're supposed to sip. But no matter, come."

He takes me by my waist, fingers working into my lower back just above my butt. His touch demands my attention and I obey without question. We're pulled back to the dance floor by the music, fueled now by the tart buzz of limoncello. It feels amazing to dance like this, to pant from exertion, and trust him as he guides me through the motions until my muscles turn deliciously sore against him.

His thigh wedges between my legs, and I bite my lip as I ride the hard bands of muscle through the thin fabric of his pants. Pressure grinds along my skin and rushes up beneath my dress. A slow dampness fills the space between us, and a new breed of *sore* wakes up inside of me.

In a great swing of his arm, he yanks me in a circle until my stomach lines up with his. My hands bury themselves in the front of his shirt, clinging to the immaculate fabric as I drive my hips into his thigh, feeling my heart pounding between us. His breathing is heavy, matching the sounds I'm making too.

The yellow glow of the lanterns dangling from the ceiling dazzles his smooth skin and his half-parted lips.

My eyes lock with his, and I want him to do more than see.

I want him to lay me down, peel the sweaty dress off, and trace the outline of my body with his kisses. I want him to push my legs apart and whisper all sorts of dirty things in my ear while his powerful fingers explore me.

I want to feel the weight of his muscled body against mine, to lose control as he fills me up until I can't take anymore.

I want him to fuck me until I forget everything—from my name to my worries to the awful reality waiting for me when I leave Italy.

I can't catch my breath, and it's not from the dancing.

Konstantin dips his head toward me. My heart races as the scent of soap and aftershave—so light that I could convince myself that I'm imagining it—invades my nostrils

I don't have to move to meet him as he closes the distance like an avalanche. The pressure and warmth between us rise, inevitable as the tide. Our mouths crush around each other and I lose myself in the kiss.

His lips are soft ... just like I thought they'd be.

Trembling from the rush of heat that takes over my body, I open my mouth further, and feel his tongue sweep in. My heart flutters and my knees go weak. His hand rises to cup my face and take hold of my chin as his tongue explores each corner of my mouth.

His other hand on my back pulls me closer to him. My heart thunders at my throat, and a soft moan escapes from my throat for him to swallow.

I close my eyes, imprinting the kiss in my memory forever as the music swells to one final crescendo before it suddenly comes to a stop all around us.

We break apart just in time as the other dancers let out a loud collective groan of disappointment. They start gathering their things, and head for the exit, arm in arm.

"Looks like our time here is up, Kitty Cat." he says.

"Oh." Disappointment overwhelm every one of my

senses. My hands are still clinging to him, my leg is still hooked around his thigh, and my eyes are still searching his for confirmation that maybe this isn't over.

Slowly, we untangle ourselves from each other. *No, don't go!* But just like at the hotel, the words never take shape in my throat.

As his warmth drifts further away, I'm desperately searching my mind for something to say.

Something to tell him—and me—that this *can't* be how it all ends.

I stare at him, chewing my lower lip as I contemplate what I can say.

Running a hand through his thick hair, he nods toward the door. "But that doesn't mean the night has to be over. Not yet."

My heart skips.

The last thing I want as your bestest best friend is for you to duck out on fate ... or to miss out on good dick. I can hear Nadia's voice. *I'm not asking you to find the love of your life here.*

"You're serious."

"Always." He smiles like it's a joke, but I have a feeling it isn't. Konstantin has a gravity to everything he does. He's charming ... arrogant ... And all of it is wrapped in just the right amount of danger.

I know he's a man who's used to getting his way.

Just parachute into a bed with a hot stranger, have some fun, and break a few hearts of your own.

Konstantin extends his hand toward me, and I know that if I take it, there's only one way this will end between us.

Forget the past.

I put my hand in his, feeling the surge of heat and electricity shooting through every fiber of my being.

And for the second time tonight, I tell him ...

"Lead the way."

6

EMILY

It's my first time being in a Lamborghini, and I'm *furious*.

Not because the car is bad—God, no. It's because all I can think about is how much I want one, and that I'll never be able to make that happen.

Konstantin takes a sharp curve along the edge of the cliff, making it seem like we're going to swing straight over the cusp and into the sea below. The stars and moon create a luminous blue shimmer on the water. I crack the window to let the salty wind inside, not caring how my hair whips in my eyes and mouth.

"They don't drive like this in Wisconsin!" I laugh.

"Why not? Isn't it all big empty fields?"

"How dare you." I give him a scathing look. "We *also* have corn."

"But not the sea." He nods. "And certainly not me."

"Has that line *ever* worked?" I ask.

Konstantin throws back his head, laughing with such force that his throat flexes. I'm enamored by the angles of his face. A professional sculptor couldn't make edges that sharp.

"Here we are," he says as he pulls up a steep driveway that branches off the main road. We've only gone a few miles. I wish he lived further away just so the drive wasn't over with. I was enjoying the purr of the engine.

Climbing out of the car, I trace my fingertips over the door. "How long have you had this car for?"

"A little after I met you at the airport." He runs his hand over the glossy surface. "I think it matches your hair."

Goddamn, he's good.

I blink up at the two-story house with its crisp white trim and light blue paint. "So, you mean you don't live here?"

"I told you, I'm here for work."

"Then where do you live? Like, for real?"

"I move around so much it doesn't matter." It feels like he's dodging my question, but I decide not to press. He doesn't bother to lock the car. Either he's not worried someone will try and steal it ... Or he knows nobody will dare.

Following him to the front door, I keep a hand's-width distance between us. I'd *like* to get closer, but I don't want to be too obvious about it.

The lights turn on from hidden motion sensors as soon as we enter. His front room has polished wooden floors, and the wide room allows a view into the open kitchen with its double-door steel fridge and massive stove. The main room has two long couches that form a V-shape. A clear glass table rests between them, the base made from pale driftwood.

There's a simple elegance to the space. It takes me a few looks to realize that nothing here has a brand label.

It's all custom-made. Which means it's all expensive as hell.

Makes sense for a guy who can buy a Lamborghini right after he lands.

"Make yourself comfortable," he says.

"Shoes on or off?"

"Up to you. I imagine your feet are sore from the dancing."

He's right; my toes have been throbbing for a while. Slipping my purple heels off, I tuck them beside the door. "This place seems big for just you."

"I like being able to have people over."

Please don't say you throw sex parties with half a dozen women at once. Please, please, please. He's been perfect so far. And I'd hate for that to be ruined.

"Like people you work with?" I ask.

"Something like that." Konstantin peers at me while he hangs his jacket on a hook.

He walks around to the kitchen. He's tall enough that I can see the top of his belt even with the counter in the way. When he bends over to open the fridge, his pants cling to his muscular legs and I feel my thighs squeezing together again at the view.

I clench my jaw and swallow. *Easy, girl, calm down.* "So, what are you cooking for me?"

"How hungry are you?"

"Very, but I'm not picky."

"Good, because I don't have a ton of ingredients."

"Perfect, because I'll eat anything."

Konstantin glances over his shoulder at me with a raised eyebrow. He doesn't say anything, but the look makes my heart flutter and my face heat up. I turn away to gather myself.

The circular stairs leading to the upper floor catch my eye. They're the kind where one wrong step, and you risk breaking your neck. "What's upstairs?"

"My bedroom."

I press my hands tighter in my lap. "Oh."

Cool. Cool. Cool.

A loud popping noise makes me yelp. Konstantin holds up a corkscrew with a cork stabbed on the end of it. He waves a black-labeled bottle. "Wine to go with our food?"

"That depends on what you're making."

"Does it?" he chuckles. He plucks two tall glasses with fat round bottoms from the slats above the sink, where they hang like bats. Turning them over, he fills both to the rim with ruby-red liquid. "Wine is more about the mood than the meal."

"I don't know. Hard to imagine drinking this stuff with sweet and sour chicken."

Does he even know *what sweet and sour chicken tastes like?*

"Never know until you try." He motions for me to take the glass. When I do, he taps the rim of his against mine. The sound is clean and clear, like ice cracking in a river. "Will a ham and cheese panini work?"

I give my wine a swish. "Now you're speaking my language."

Parking myself on one of the tall stools at the counter, I set my elbows on the marble top. I have a perfect view of Konstantin as he navigates the stove. His movements are similar to his dancing at the bar. His shoes click, ankles and knees pivoting, one hand stuffing ingredients into slices of bread while the other turns the panini grill on.

He slathers butter on the bread and throws the thick focaccia bread onto the grill. The metal top coming down and sizzles deliciously. My mouth is watering. It has to be nearly four in the morning—when did I eat last?

My empty stomach is causing the wine to go to my head. Or maybe I'm drinking it too fast. Because when I look at the bottle again, it's half gone. But hey, I'm hungry, and it's all I've got to calm my grumbling belly.

He arranges the hot sandwiches on two white and blue plates, and hands one to me. "Let's go upstairs."

I nearly drop my plate. Upstairs? Where his bedroom is?

"What for?" I ask, my voice high and tight.

"Sun's coming up soon." If he notices my freak-out, he doesn't act like it. "And I'd hate for you to miss the sunrise from the second-floor patio."

Air exits my lips shakily. On one hand, it's not a blatant invitation. But on the other hand ...

At the thought of Konstantin bending me over the railing of the second-floor patio, his fist in my hair as he fucks me in the sunrise ... my heart starts racing again.

KONSTANTIN PINCHES the bottle of wine under his arm, sipping from his glass as he walks. Following him up the steps as carefully as I can, I reach the second floor. There's a room to my left, the door cracked slightly. Inside I spot a king-sized bed covered in a blue duvet. Next to it is the black luggage with the Hello Kitty tag.

It's weird to see it again.

It reminds me of Olivia. I haven't heard her voice in ...

Well, who's counting these days?

I should call her. She probably won't answer. But it won't hurt to try.

Heck, I can probably do more than try. Maybe I should go to her apartment in New York and knock.

I have all the time in the world now.

I can try harder to reconnect with her. Our distance isn't all her fault.

Some of it is mine.

And like every memory involving Olivia, I start thinking about my parents. *They're going to be so upset with me when they learn I got expelled.* I can picture the scowls dragging their jaws low, their eyes hard as obsidian and just as black.

I can hear them already: *Do you have any idea how much all of this costed us?*

The reality waiting for me back in America is bleak.

But those thoughts are chased away when we step around a corner and through a set of glass doors. Salty-sweet air with the heavy scent of lemons rushes over my bare shoulders. Straight across from me is a glistening streak of sapphire water. A tall cliff dotted by numerous painted houses juts out into the water before curving away into the distance.

"Wow," I whisper.

"You like it." It's not a question. "Sit. I promise the view won't change, only your comfort."

I hadn't noticed the round table with two woven-back chairs before. I was too enamored by the incredible view. "You're lucky."

Konstantin stiffens at that, and I wonder if I said something wrong.

In the glow of the sharp moon, his eyes are less ice-blue, and more silver. Slipping his arm over the back of his chair, he brings his wine to his lips. His glass is mostly full, unlike mine, but he's brought the bottle.

I pick it up to refill mine and he grabs my hand.

"Let me."

I don't let go of the bottle. I can't, or I don't want to. I'm frozen with his fingers wrapped around mine, our eyes locked, my heart trying to escape from my mouth.

He pulls slightly, the bottle lifting away. My hand dangles in the air for a moment before I yank it into my lap. I'm flushed all the way across my chest. I can't fucking help it.

Unsure how to act normal, I pick up my sandwich and sink my teeth into it. The explosion of savory caprese and salty ham, followed by the mouthy feel of olive oil and butter leaves me dazed.

"Oh my God!" I'm speaking through a mouthful of food. "This is delicious."

"It's nothing special," he says. "Just some spare ingredients that was lying around."

"Well, it's *incredible* to me!"

His lips drop open. He seems surprised at my reaction, but the way he starts to smile, I'm sure he's pleased. "I'll have to remember the recipe for next time."

"Do you say that to all the other girls?" I tease.

He stares straight at me. "I meant next time with you, Kitty Cat."

I drink some wine to keep myself from choking on the next bite of sandwich. This guy is smooth—it's almost too much. A thorny branch winds through my guts.

"I wish I could stay in Italy forever."

"Just convince your friend to have her wedding here too," he says.

"Nadia's already set that stuff in stone. She's been planning her wedding since she was a kid."

"I get it," he chuckles. "You have a whole life back in

America waiting for you. I don't actually expect you to uproot yourself and stay here."

A whole life back in America ...

He's trying to console me, but he doesn't know the first damn thing about me. How can you comfort someone when you don't know what's caused them harm?

"If I could, I would." I drain the last of my wine. "But I don't want to go home."

"Why? What's back there?"

The sky is tinting red where it kisses the sea. Dawn pries apart the sky with rosy fingers. But the moon hasn't yet fled from the approaching sunrise. I hold my glass up until the silvery sliver is inside of it.

"Reality."

I hear his chair scrape on the patio as he moves closer. "The reality of what, Kitty Cat?"

I grab the bottle, refilling my glass. "Nothing. Forget about it."

"Did someone hurt you?"

More than you can ever know.

His eyes drill into mine, unblinking, and I see something flicker behind them. Something that walks the knife edge of protectiveness and danger.

Something that screams: *tell me their name.*

If I mentioned Phil and what he did ... What would Konstantin do? He barely knows me. Yet I swear, he'd hunt Phil down and punish him for me.

As tempting as the idea may be, I can't agree to that.

"I didn't come here to wallow in self-pity," I say as casually as I can. I even manage a smile before filling my mouth with more wine. It was sweeter before. But it tastes sour now.

He folds his hands over his lips, never taking his attention off me. There's half a panini on his plate, but he ignores it. He's feasting on me.

"I understand."

I draw my chin to my chest with a blink. "You do?"

"I know what it's like to not want to go back to reality ..." A faint smile passes over his face, and he turns to look over the sea. "You're not alone, Kitty Cat."

A hundred questions flock into my brain. *How can a guy who can afford a Lamborghini on a whim and stay in a place like* this *want to run away from reality?* Konstantin drips money. His confidence is worn as comfortably as his bespoke clothes. The base of my neck is itching as I stare hard at him while trying to make sense of his comment.

"You're in town for work. What sort of work?"

He shrugs casually. "I'd bore you talking about it."

"It can't be that bad if you get to travel to Italy." I glance at the glass doors, thinking about what I saw in his bedroom. "You always take that same suitcase with you on your trips?"

"You're wondering about the Hello Kitty bag tag, aren't you?"

"Can you blame me? It's not exactly what I'd expect from someone like ..."

"Like me." His smile is dangerous. "I get it. If it wasn't for my sister, I wouldn't have it at all."

Sister ...

The thorns from before are back. They slither through my veins, cutting me up as they go. "It's hers?"

Shaking his head, he begins to talk in a softer voice. I have to lean closer to hear him over the crash of the waves below.

"I bought it for her. She loves Hello Kitty." He stops talk-ing, as if he's working through a lump in his throat as he says it. "But they only sell the tags in pairs. I gave one to her, and she insisted I use the other. So, I do."

"Same for me, actually," I tell him. "Except, it's my sister who bought it for *me* before she left home."

For the second time, I wonder about her. About how she's doing.

Does she still have her Hello Kitty bag tag?

Does she think of me like I think of her when she sees it?

Konstantin tilts his head at me. His pupils are bottomless, sucking me in. He's reading my pensive mood. I wish I was better at hiding it. I'm a damn open book with my emotions.

He leans in closer, and my heart races as his lips part.

"I—" I try to protest.

Just then, a ringing noise blasts from his pocket. His face contorts, every wrinkle deepening as he hits the ignore button.

But whoever is on the other end is insistent. Not a second later, the phone rings again.

"I think you should pick it up," I tell him, even though every fiber of my being wants him to do the exact opposite.

He nods and checks the caller's name. That's when his eyes widens and he shoves the device to his ear. When he speaks, it's a language that I don't recognize. A rough one filled with shushing corners and rough edges.

His expression changes with every word. The handsome lines of his face contort into something else.

Something dark.

Something dangerous.

When he hangs up, he folds his fingers together as he looks out at the brightening sky.

"Is something wrong?" I ask.

"Yes." Rising, he adjusts the front of his jacket, then pulls down his cuffs to his wrists. He's clear-eyed and calm. Every hint of our relaxed hangout has been erased. "I need to go."

I frown slightly as my heart falls. "Oh, okay."

"Don't misunderstand me, Kitty Cat." He stiffens, looking at me with fresh interest. "I *will* be back. Stay and make yourself comfortable. You can use my bed if you'd like."

I would, in fact, like that.

"Okay. I'll see you soon."

Not long after he's out of view, I hear the car roar to life below. Peering over the patio, I catch the twin headlights as they illuminate the road. In the rising sun, the Lamborghini looks like a bolt of dark fire streaking through the streets.

Propping my elbow on the table, I drum my fingers on the metal surface. The tapping reminds me of the bachata music. I stop myself by making a tight fist.

The clouds over the sea are thick as fresh cream. A few birds glide over them, breaking up the pure white surface with their dark bodies. The world is waking up. *And here I am, already wide awake. I haven't slept a wink.* I glance at the glass doors again. *I could go to sleep and wait for him in his bed.*

Would he like to find me there when he comes back?

Will he wake me with kisses? Will he keep calling me Kitty Cat as he fucks me?

Placing my glass to my lips, I go to take a drink but find the wine is all gone. The bottle still has some left in it. I tip it over and fill my glass with the final drops, then I grab Konstantin's glass and dump the rest of it in too.

As I'm debating stripping down and slipping into his bed to wait for him, that's when my phone begins to vibrate.

My first thought is it has to be Nadia making sure I'm alright.

But then I see the word MOM flash on my screen.

My throat narrows.

Oh no. This is it. My parents have found out about what happened. I bet Phil got to them first, telling them that what happened wasn't his fault. I knew I should've told them ...

I glance at the sky slowly growing brighter by the second.

What time is it over there in Wisconsin? It must be after midnight. They're usually asleep by now.

I'm tempted to hit ignore like Konstantin did. But I know that there's no way Mom is calling for no reason. So, I hit answer and bring the phone up to my ear.

"Mom?" I say quickly, my voice trembling. "What is it?"

"Emily! Thank God you picked up."

She doesn't sound angry. But I don't relax, not yet.

"What's going on?" I ask.

Her sigh is long and deep, like she's straight-up exasperated. "Your father and I need your help."

Bit by bit, my fingers unclench my phone. I allow myself to sink into my chair, and immediately switch into problem-solving mode for them, like I've done for years since the day Olivia left.

At the same time, a guilty giddiness blooms inside of my chest.

They don't know yet ...

"Yeah, of course, Mom. What do you need?"

"Do you know anything about your sister's life insurance policy?"

What? The question throws me for a loop. They've *never* bothered to talk about Olivia in the years since she left, except maybe to use her failures to scare me into doing what they want.

But even then, they never mentioned her name.

It's usually always *that junkie*, and when they feel charitable, *your sister*.

A ringing in my ears starts, the pitch rising until I can barely hear my own breathing. When I don't respond, Mom continues.

"Dad and I have been trying to find out more, but we don't know where to look."

I work my tongue in my mouth, the thickness of it forcing me to form each word deliberately and patiently.

"Why do you need to know? What's going on?"

There's a beat of silence. I've never lived through so many years in a handful of precious seconds.

It's as if my brain is doing all it can to protect me in anticipation for the moment my whole world will be irrevocably changed.

"That junkie is dead." Mom's voice is flat, cold, and emotionless when she replies. "She killed herself a week ago."

7

KONSTANTIN

I'M FUCKING PISSED.

Ever since Emily grabbed my luggage by accident at the airport, I couldn't stop thinking about her long shapely legs, her sapphire eyes that seemed to be hiding some great secret, her lips that should be wrapped around me, and her dark chestnut hair that shone like silk under the fierce Italian sun.

After I found her so easily at the Amalfi Central Hotel, in her shirt soaked with sweat and leaving nothing to my imagination, I knew that I wanted her—no, needed her—in my bed.

When I saw her after I'd walked out of the backroom at the Zebra Club, where that fucker Augusto Ferrata looked me in the eyes and told me himself that we would be redrawing the lines of our territories here in southern Italy, I knew that it was a sign that she'd be mine tonight.

She'd been unafraid of me. And from the way she had looked at me at the bar of the Zebra Club, I could tell that there was an undeniable wildness inside of her. When I pulled her close to me, inhaling her scent of honeysuckle and brown sugar at that nondescript little dance bar, I could *feel* that wildness come to life.

I knew that she would have been one unforgettable fuck the moment my lips touched hers. If that bar hadn't been so packed, I would've fucked her right then and there.

I knew she wanted the same thing from me by the way she was grinding her hips against me, by how *soaked* her pussy became against my thigh on the dance floor, and by how readily she agreed to come back with me.

She was supposed to be the perfect ending to a perfect trip. I had planned on fucking her as the sun rose, and then again after breakfast, and then I planned to keep fucking her until the sun rises again and my cum is leaking out of every one of her holes.

I wanted her to scream, to break, to shatter into a million pieces.

And then I would slowly piece her back together, one kiss and stroke at a time, and do it all over again.

I wanted to *ruin* her for every other man out there.

But instead, I'm forced to leave her behind while my mood darkens with every passing second. My balls grow heavy and painful with the need for release—release that has to wait now.

Because I've just found out my little sister Alisa had been fucking *kidnapped* in New York.

Kidnapped ... the word echoes in my head like a curse.

"What the fuck happened?" I bellow into the speaker-phone as I step harder on the accelerator. The Lamborghini's engine roars in response, and gravity shifts as I take a turn harder than I should.

"I don't know, Kostya," Sima, my avtoritet and best friend, answers. "The only thing I know is that it happened about two weeks ago."

Two weeks ago? Fuck!

I knew it was suspicious when the last time I spoke with my sister Alisa was roughly around that time. I assumed it was just because she didn't want her overprotective big brother checking in on her at every hour of the day and ruining her eighteenth birthday.

At the time, I reasoned that as long as her Instagram kept updating with photos and videos of her time in New York, it meant that she was alright.

How could I be so fucking stupid!

"Who did you hear this from?"

"Matteo Zampa," he answers.

I pound my fist against the steering wheel.

Out of all of the people that we've managed to turn to our side within the Ferrata Mafia, Matteo Zampa is the only one of them that I trust. He'd come to our side about ten years ago. And over those ten years, he's provided us with sufficient information for us to wrest control of the ports in Taranto and Bari from under Augusto's nose.

If Zampa says it happened, then there's no way in hell that it's false

"What else did he say?" I ask.

"He knows about as much as we do," Sima replies. "But he can only say that the order came from the fucking top. Which means it's part of some big plan they got going on."

"What the fuck?"

None of this made any sense. Why would Augusto torpedo the peace deal like this?

No, I think viciously.

Not Augusto.

His piece of shit son Domenico.

The young heir of the Ferrata Mafia has never believed

that their side could ever *lose* this war, even after I'd broken both his legs when we were sixteen.

"I want you to call Augusto right fucking now," I order. "And if he's not at the Zebra Club to explain to me how the *fuck* this could've happened by the time the sun is up, I'm going to burn this whole fucking town to the ground."

"Got it, my pakhan. You want me there too?"

"I do." I nod. "Come armed and bring one for me as well. One way or another, someone is going to fucking *die*."

I can practically see the smile breaking out on Sima's face as he answers. "With pleasure."

8

EMILY

DIED.

What an ugly-tasting word.

It fills my mouth, tainting the flavor of the entire evening.

I fight the urge to rush to the patio railing and vomit over the side.

"A week ago?" I croak. "Why didn't you tell me sooner?"

"We didn't want to bother you with something like this," she says dismissively. "And honestly, we wouldn't have under normal circumstances."

Something like this? I want to scream.

The wineglass tips over as if a small earthquake has hit the table, but it's only my leg banging up and down as disgust ratchets through my blood. I grab the glass before it can fall and shatter.

"This can't be real."

Her voice is strained—the way you'd talk to a toddler. "We all saw this coming. That junkie's bad habits weren't a secret. I know it's hard for you to accept this, sweetie, but this was inevitable."

I want to throw the glass. My mind is racing, tearing itself apart at my mother's blunt, detached commentary.

Bad habits.

Inevitable.

Mom has a natural talent of being so effortlessly cruel and callous with her words.

But I refuse to believe that Olivia had relapsed. The last time I heard from her, she was still clean. But then again, that was more than a year ago.

Maybe ...

No, I tell myself. I refuse to believe that. She *promised* me that she was clean.

She never broke any of her promises to me.

In the background of the phone, I hear my father's annoyed voice. "Did you ask her?"

"I *am* asking her, Sam," Mom grumbles quietly, then directly into my ear, "Anyway, can you find out for us? About that policy? Maybe the paperwork is in her apartment?"

"I don't know if I can," I say.

"Are you sure? Can't you take a couple of days to just go check her apartment? For us, sweetie?"

Reeling from the onslaught of ghastly news, as well as my parents' callous focus on *money,* I bite my tongue until it stings.

Is the money all you care about?! Olivia is *dead,* and the only thing you want to know is if you're getting money out of it? She was your daughter! She's my sister! I loved her more than either of you ever did. Why don't you *care?*

"Emily?" Mom's voice jolts me back to reality. "Are you there?"

I blink and taste blood as I open my mouth, inhaling the salty sea breeze.

I didn't say a single word ... I imagined it all in my head.

"Mom," I begin.

"I know, I know." She sighs in a great heave. "We shouldn't bother you with news about that junkie. I know you've got more important things to worry about."

"Yeah?" It comes out in a gritty whisper.

"Your father and I are very proud of how well you've been doing. Our little girl, soon-to-be veterinarian. Well, it makes up for our other failures, doesn't it?"

The whiplash of this conversation is overwhelming.

Phil hasn't been in touch with them. At least I'm certain of that now.

But the knowledge no longer leaves me giddy.

How will they react when I tell them that I've been expelled because of him? Will I be as good as dead to them, just like Olivia?

Years and years of their scowls being aimed at Olivia will finally be directed full-force towards me.

And Olivia won't be there to stand up for me anymore.

"I'll let you know what I can find." My tone is cold as a Midwestern winter, only without the bite.

Bit by bit, the backbone that had started to grow melts away. I'm a pathetic piece of garbage. I don't have an ounce of courage to tell my parents how cruel they are. How upset I am.

"Thank you, sweetie. We really appreciate it. I know it's late. But give us a call when you can. Love you."

"Love you," I echo mechanically.

When was the last time they ever said that to Olivia?

The call disconnects and I slump in the chair, arm dropping into my lap. My neck cranes back until I'm staring at the stars fading into the pink smear of sunrise. They looked so beautiful earlier tonight.

Everything did.

But now ...

Olivia is dead. A week ago.

And I didn't know.

Rising out of my chair, I bolt down the stairs. It's a miracle I don't break my neck. I finish calling an Uber before I'm on the street. People, tourists and locals alike, are starting to wander the sandy shore nearby. It must be wonderful to feel the waves tickling your feet before the sun fully rises.

Konstantin really is lucky.

Konstantin.

With his name firm on my mind, I glance back at his place. *I told him I'd stay and wait for him.* I hate breaking promises, but this is an emergency.

I wish he'd given me his phone number so I could tell him I'm sorry. It hits me that I *could* leave mine if I just go back in and—

The beep from the midnight blue Taurus that rolls up startles me. The driver waves at me through his cracked window.

"Emily Sullivan?" he asks.

Hesitating with a final look at Konstantin's building, I climb into the car. "Yeah, that's right."

I'm sorry, Konstantin.

I can't delay any further. I have to get to New York. The feeling is so pressing I begin fidgeting in the back seat of the car. My nails scrape over my naked knees, twisting the lavender hem of my dress until it begins to fray.

9

EMILY

WHEN THE CAR STOPS OUTSIDE THE AMALFI CENTRAL HOTEL, I sprint up the steps. They left me gasping earlier this afternoon—has it even been twenty-four hours since I arrived?—but it doesn't matter now.

Nothing can slow me down.

I'm moving so fast I bump into the door of my room. I drop the key and it takes me a few more tries before I finally enter.

Calm down. You don't want to wake up—

"Em?" Nadia yawns, sitting up in her bed, flicking on the lamp beside her. She scrubs her eyes. She looks like she just got back from Zebra Club a little while ago.

Blinking blearily at me, she runs her attention from my heels to my dress, then back to my face.

A smug-ass grin spreads on her face. "Did someone have a *very fun* and exhausting night?"

My belly forms two separate knots. One of them drops into my guts. The other begins to rise in my throat and choke me.

I can't tell her why I'm back here. I have to lie to her. I

can't ruin her bachelorette trip like this. Just nod and smile and agree, then go into the bathroom and wash up, get changed, plan my escape, then boom. Home free.

But I can't.

Nadia's expression morphs from devious to concerned.

"Emily, what's wrong? You look pale."

I suck in a rattling breath and feel the sting of tears at the back of my nose. *Don't you fucking do it! Do. Not. Cry.* I have to keep myself together if I want to drop the news without ruining everything for her.

"I have to fly back to the States."

"What? Why?" She jumps up, hurrying to me, her eyes flushed with worry. "What happened? You look as bad as Clara did before she barfed all over the fountain out front. By the way, photos there are *canceled.*"

My mouth opens, then shuts. I don't know how to begin.

Nadia searches my face, then she puts her hands on my shoulders, leaning in cautiously as a protective fire starts burning in her eyes. "Did that guy do something to you?"

"Konstantin?" I give a blank face, thrown off by her assumption. "No, he didn't do anything."

"Then why are you leaving?" She lowers her voice. "Emily, what's wrong?"

I start shaking my head, and then suddenly, I can't stop.

"My sister is dead," I whisper, like talking softly can help make it not true. "She died a week ago and I just found out."

It's wild that I'm not crying. It's as if the backs of my eyeballs have been sealed by hard wax that refuses to break.

"Emily, oh my god!" Nadia crushes me in an embrace that threatens to snap my spine. I wish she'd hug me even harder. The pressure is the only thing keeping me together. "I'm so sorry. I'm so fucking sorry. Do you know what happened?"

"No," I say honestly. *Mom was talking about Olivia's habits, but I refuse to believe that she went back to using.*

"I just can't believe it," I whisper into Nadia's hair. "I'm still in shock."

"Of course you are! Who wouldn't be?"

"I feel terrible for having to leave, but—"

"No, don't explain. You don't have to justify this to me or *anyone*. Okay?"

My heart swells with immense love for my best friend. "Nadia ..."

She guides me to the bed, sitting me down before standing in front of me, her eyes somber, but not unkind. "First, breathe. Second, you need to book a flight."

I bob my head in agreement. I'm exhausted, burned out, and a hundred other things that on their own would be overwhelming. With Nadia's help, I pop open Google and search for flights to New York.

It's nice to have someone guiding my hand.

And instantly, any good feelings that dared to seep into my mind dissolve away as I face reality again.

Not a single flight is under two thousand dollars.

I can feel my heart thudding in my molars. My thumb scrolls through the list, faster and faster, my panic rocketing higher at every new ticket price.

"I can't afford any of these. What am I supposed to do?" I purchased a round trip already, and that nearly wiped me out.

Why didn't I think about how expensive this was going to be? And I can't wait three days to go back. I just can't.

Nadia yanks my phone out of my grip. I'm too stunned to react, and I watch in disbelief as she taps the screen and walk over to her purse. By the time she whips out her credit card and enters the numbers, I realize what she's about to do.

But before I can say anything, she taps the screen, and my phone vibrates as the confirmation email comes through.

"Done," she declares.

"Nadia!" I shout, jumping off the bed. "No! You can't do that!"

"The hell I can't!"

"This is too much! I don't deserve—"

She jabs a finger at me to shut me up. "Don't you *dare* finish that sentence."

I swallow the words down, choking on them. "It's too much money."

"Nothing is too much for you, Emily." Offering my phone back to me, she cocks her head and smiles. "You worked your ass off to plan me the best bachelorette party in the entire world. You didn't have to do that, but you did. Because you care about me, right?"

"Right," I admit weakly.

"Then accept that I care about you too. More than anyone else." Slipping her hands over mine, she stares into my eyes. "What you're going through is serious, and I can't help with the grief you're about to face. But I can still send you home to face it."

The tears are harder to fight than ever before. "Thank you. I swear I'll pay you back as soon as I can."

"Pay me back by taking care of yourself," she urges me warmly. "Promise me."

"I will." Giving her a firm hug, I hold my face against her shoulder a moment. I really don't think I deserve this act of kindness, but I also need it. I'm desperate for it. Gathering myself, I rush toward the bathroom. "I need to change."

"I'll help pack your bag," she calls after me.

At the large, shell-shaped sink, I rinse off my hands and face. The soap I scrub myself with smells like lemons. I fight back a wave of sadness and instead replace it with something worse:

Hope.

Maybe I'll cross paths with Konstantin again someday.

I'm a pathetic dreamer. But thinking about him reminds me of something.

"Nadia," I say as I exit the bathroom, "let me leave your trip itinerary for you. I had a lot planned. I still want you to do all of it."

"I'll be sure to take a disgusting number of photos for you," she says.

I pull out my sheet of notes. It details everything over the next three days. She's going to love the light blue Fiat I ordered to be dropped off at the hotel tomorrow.

Yet all I can think of is Konstantin's dark Lamborghini.

With a pen, I scribble new instructions at the bottom of the page.

Someone told me Salerno has great views of the sea. And try the limoncello. They make them with the local lemons, Sfusato Amalfitano. Just remember to sip them, because they're strong.

NADIA ACCOMPANIES me on the three-hour long trip to the airport with me, even though I tell her she doesn't have to. The flight won't leave for another eight hours.

I've changed into cropped tan joggers with a matching hoodie, my ponytail pulled through a yellow baseball cap. I need to do all I can to be comfortable when I'm facing a ten-hour plane ride.

"Have a safe flight, Emily."

"I will. And please, have as much fun as you still can on this trip without me, okay?"

She clutches me tight, and I wonder if she'll ever let go. Finally, she releases me, putting her hand on the hood of the taxi waiting to bring her back to the hotel. "Text me when you land."

"Like you won't just creep on my flight details online," I smile.

Nadia's smile smooths as it hovers between becoming a frown. "Just do it, okay?"

"I will," I assure her.

Hooking my hand on my bag, I drag it through the airport. My eyes zero in on the Hello Kitty bag tag, and I feel tears threatening to pour from my eyes again.

Don't cry. Don't cry. You can't cry right now.

———

THE FLIGHT IS PACKED, and boarding becomes a blur of bodies and multiple voices overlapping each other. I'm in my own world, acting on instinct as I make my way to my seat.

"*Mama! Aspetto!*"

A bell-clear giggle shakes me from my stupor. Across the way, in a row of three, is a small girl with her face pressed to the window. Her curly brown hair is pulled into two space buns, but the slightly older girl beside her has left hers wild and loose. They look so much like each other.

Their mother, in the aisle seat, leans over to peer out the

window. She smiles at both of them and says something in Italian. Whatever it is, it has both girls laughing with her.

She leans over and kisses them both on the forehead. Across the row from them, her husband leans over and musses both girls' hair.

I can feel their love from where I sit. But it doesn't make me smile the way it does the little girls. Watching a family together like this, happy and thriving and whole, is killing me.

Olivia and I never saw our parents like these little girls do.

I brace myself as if the plane is already in the sky. My muscles tremble with such violence I bite down in a desperate search for stability. The engines begin to turn, and the girls cheer. They get louder when their mother reaches over to wrap her arms around them both in a hug.

Don't cry. Don't cry.

But I can't stop myself anymore.

Wet droplets fall onto my joggers. I scrub at the damp marks, but the floodgates have opened and can't be closed again.

Everything that was sealed away starts bursting through.

The two little girls turn silent as they watch me. Their wide, curious, ever-innocent eyes remind me too much of a time when I still had my sister in my life.

Olivia and I would have done the same: gawk at the strange woman sobbing on the plane. We would have felt bad because she was sad ... and she was alone.

I don't want their trip to be marred by my misery. Turning away, I lean into the window, curling on myself with my hood over my face. My tears stain the fabric, remaining wet against my cheek as a constant reminder of what I've lost.

And what I'll never get back.

10

KONSTANTIN

Sima is waiting for me outside of the Zebra Club by the time I arrive. The neighborhood around the establishment is quiet now that morning has come. And to my mounting fury, there's not a goddamn person to be seen.

Without bothering to kill the engine, I step out of the Lamborghini and slam the door shut.

"My pakhan," Sima greets me with a quick bow and hands me a submachine gun along with a belt of grenades.

"Where the fuck is he?" I demand as I chamber a round. "Did he even pick up the fucking call?"

"No," Sima replies grimly. "But not long after I called him, I got this."

He holds up his phone, and my heart practically stops when I see it.

It's a screenshot from a security-camera of my sister, hands bound in a tiny room. She's still wearing the dress that she was wearing two weeks ago. Her hands and ankles are bound with silver tape. Her eyes, normally full of clever humor, are wide with terror. They're puffy from crying and there are knots in her thick hair. On her upper arms, I spot the tell-tale green of old bruises.

Alisa! My grip around the submachine gun tightens as rage overtakes me.

"I'm going to peel the skin off every single fucking Ferrata man I get my hands on," I growl.

"Then you're in luck, because I think that's them right now." Sima tilts his head towards the direction behind me, I turn and see several cars pulling up in the distance, and each one filled with men of the Ferrata Mafia.

A feral smile spreads on my face as I pull the pin from a grenade.

Oh, I'm going to enjoy this.

THE SHOOTOUT WAS SHORT, violent, and quick. Exactly like how Sima and I operate. By the time it's over, most of the Ferrata hitmen sent out to kill us are dead.

All except one unfortunate bastard.

And in the basement of a butcher shop, where the owner was more than happy to accept a fat stack of Euros in exchange for looking the other way, I have my victim hanging up on meat hooks for the past hour.

Sima and I have spent that hour taking turns breaking every bit of his body that we can.

Once upon a time, he might've been a proud made-man of the Ferrata Mafia who's used to speaking with his fists. Now he's shirtless and pathetic, head hung low, with bruises dappling from his chest to his abdomen, and blood running down his legs.

"I'll ask you again." Flexing my fingers, I shift the

pocketknife to my opposite hand. "Who gave the order to kidnap my sister?"

To the man's credit, he doesn't say a word. Instead, from the single eye he still has left—I'd already removed his other one—he gives me a baleful glare of defiance.

"I suggest you answer me." Tracing the tip of the knife under his left ear, I whisper. "You're starting to run out of things for me to break. And when that happens, I'm going to start *taking* things."

He swings his head to the side, looking at my knife not with fear, but indifference. I know this bastard would be tough. All of these Italians are. Unlike them, I've never once underestimated my enemies.

But this is starting to get absurd.

I'm tempted to pull out my gun, but I know he is waiting for the sweet embrace of death.

Not like the fool who was stupid enough to knock into Emily back at the Zebra Club.

A savage thrum rushes through me at the unexpected thought of her.

Kitty Cat.

And just like that, I feel an uncomfortable tightness in my pants.

I shake my head. Why the fuck am I thinking about her right now? But now that I am, I can't get her out of my head. Those sapphire eyes. Her dark chestnut hair.

Her wet pussy grinding against my thigh.

Fuck!

My mood grows blacker and I approach my victim and push the knife between his legs until they're resting against his balls. Slowly, I let the tip dig forward, and he raises his head.

"Was it Augusto?" I press the cutting edge along the seam of his balls. "Was it his son? Or was it both?"

The man goes still as stone and holds his breath, waiting for my next move.

"Last chance, *mudak*."

Across the room, Sima watches me with fascination. He plays with his metal lighter, flipping it open and shut as if to keep time. The flame glows bright before snuffing out each time.

"Have it your way, then." I start sawing through the thin skin. Blood gushes and with a single practiced stroke, I remove one of his testicles and hold it up in front of him.

He can't control himself any longer. This time, he *screams.*

"Sounds like it's both." I toss the useless piece of flesh aside, and grab the man by his meaty jowls. "Was killing me part of his plan too?"

He continues to groan in pain, and I wrench his head back, forcing him to look at me.

He's wheezing, his pupil dilating to the point of invisibility. Finally, I see a speck of fear in his eyes.

I curl my lip and dig the knife against his remaining testicle. A tear leaks out of his single remaining eye and mixes with the blood running over his bruises.

"Fuck you!" he gasps.

"Refusing to talk isn't going to do you any good." I let go of his hair. "Why keep doing this to yourself?"

The man rolls his neck, gazing at me with some of his earlier defiance. He licks his chin, smearing crimson all over his teeth and lips. Then he dares to *grin.*

"Because talking won't save me, you Russian fuck." He spits out another mouthful of blood. "You can skip the theatrics and just get this over with."

"Well, we seem to be at an impasse." Gliding my thumb over my knife's handle, I sigh. "Because I have no intention of getting this over with *until* you talk. And if you do, I'll let you die *half* a man."

"We're getting nowhere with this, Kostya." Sima says in Russian.

"I'm not giving him an easy exit." I snap.

Sima clicks his lighter open, the flame dancing in his earth-brown eyes, and sighs. The burn scars on his fingers stand out on his pale skin. "There's no reason to keep torturing him."

"Yes, there is."

My victim's single eye bulges from his skull as I approach. His resistance feeds the part of me that's lashing out, searching for a way to reassert control.

"Why go back on this deal?" Wedging the tip of my knife against his remaining testicle, I give it a hard tug and feel the soft organ detach.

The man screams again until his voice cracks. And through his broken vocal cords, two words emerge.

"Marriage!" He chokes out. "Inheritance!"

I smile savagely back at Sima. "See, Sima? They all break eventually."

I turn my attention back to my victim, but his head droops down and he's limp. "Wake up." I dig my knife through his shoulder. Blood leaks steadily from the fresh wound, but there's no reaction.

Sima places his hand gingerly on my shoulder. "He's dead, Kostya."

Angling the dead man's head back, I gaze into his blank expression—mouth drawn agape and single eye unblinking.

"*Yob tvoyu mats!*" Motherfucker!

"What do you think he meant by that?" Sima asks.

Marriage. Inheritance.

The gears are turning in my head, and it doesn't take long before I figure out exactly what those two words mean.

"They're going to force her to marry Domenico," I whisper. "That's why they called us here to Italy for this meeting. They never intended to agree to a peace deal. They wanted me *here* so they can kill me. And once I'm dead ..."

"Alisa Yurevna becomes the sole heir." Sima nods. "This is so stupidly simple that it's almost brilliant. But Alla Antonovna won't just release the inheritance, will she?"

The mere mention of my grandmother sends a look of disgust on my face. "Under normal circumstances, no," I reply. "But if Alisa is the sole heir, she won't have much of a choice."

Roaring in frustration, I plunge the knife into the corpse's face again and again until it becomes a red ruin.

Panting, I turn back to Sima. "Torch Zebra Club and send the demand to Augusto that he returns Alisa to me safely. In the meantime, rally every brigadier here in Italy with orders to kill every Ferrata man they see."

Sima wrinkles his brow. "What about your grandmother?"

"I'll figure out something about Alla. But I want the kill orders out *now*."

Augusto will take me seriously with this. He has to.

I run water in the large sink nearby. Blood swirls down the drain as I scrub my hands clean, making sure to get beneath my nails.

"And get the jet ready."

"Where are we going that we can't fly commercial?" he asks tensely.

"New York." I glare at him. "If there's even a sliver of a chance that Alisa is there ..."

"No way in hell they'll keep her there." He squints at me like I've lost my mind. "And at any rate, New York is off-limits for you."

"There *are no limits,*" I growl, whirling on him. "Not anymore!"

"The Americans won't be happy about this," Sima stands firm. "Especially not Emilio Lanzzare. He may have his own feuds with Augusto, but he's not going to allow you to bring *your* war to his doorstep."

"I don't give a fuck what Emilio Lanzzare thinks."

Sima stares at me, thoughts turning in his head as he thinks through the consequences. But I know he'll come around to agreeing with me. He cares about my sister as much as I do. He understands the pain I'm in.

Taking a deep breath, Sima stands over the corpse and sighs. "It'll take about three hours for the jet to get ready, and another ten until we land. What are you going to do in the meantime?"

I check my hands again to make sure that there's no blood left. "I'll meet you at the airport."

Without another word, I walk away and leave Sima to his task. Anger rages like a hurricane my mind, and when I emerge into the sunlight, the brightness of almost blinds me.

In my blindness, a singular vision appears in my head.

Dark chestnut hair. Sapphire-blue eyes. Full red lips and freckled skin.

My cock strains against my pants again as dark vicious thoughts swirl around my mind.

THE DRIVE back to the house goes by in a blur, and my cock is rock hard by the time I open the door. But the moment I walk in, I know that something isn't right. The house is silent and still.

Too silent.

I storm my way up the stairs towards the bedroom and when I arrive, I find two empty wineglasses on the patio. The bed is untouched.

But most importantly, Emily is nowhere to be seen.

The only thing that tells me she was ever here is the imprint of her lipstick on the rim of one of the glasses.

I'm too late.

Slowly, I walk over and pick up the glass and clench my fist around it.

A crack appears in the glass from the pressure, but I don't release my grip. And when it shatters, embedding my palm with shards, I relish the pain it brings.

Put her out of your mind. I tell myself. *There are more important things to worry about.*

I'll go as far as I can, be as cruel as I must, in order to get what I want.

I'll make them rue the day they crossed the Siderov Bratva.

And after, I'll find Emily, and teach her the consequences for daring to run away from me.

11

EMILY

WHEN I WAS LITTLE, I BURIED A TIME CAPSULE.

It was just a plastic Easter egg I'd stuffed with a note to myself and some stickers I thought were cool. My plan was to dig it up in ten years and compare it with all the new things I accumulated during that time and see the difference. Mostly I remember being thrilled at the idea of how it would feel to come across something frozen in time.

But now that I'm standing in one, I'm anything but thrilled.

Olivia's apartment hasn't been touched since her death a week ago. Well, eight days now. There's an old plate of apple slices, green from mold, on the coffee table. Clothes are piled randomly on every piece of furniture. The potted plant in the window is nothing but a wilted twig.

I turn the apartment key over and over in my hand, thumbing the rough edges.

The teeth of the key cut into my fingers, but I don't care. It's been almost a full twenty-four hours since I learned that Olivia was dead.

And the entire time, the same thought keeps rushing through my head

They should've told me sooner.

When the police officer handed the key to me, I could tell he wanted to ask why no family came for eight whole days. I almost wished he did. Because I would've told him what I've known my entire life.

My Mom and Dad didn't give a shit about her, I would've said. *They just care that she might finally be able to repay them for all their troubles over the years now that she's dead.*

Useless. I can hear the Mom and Dad in my head. *Ungrateful. Worthless.*

Junkie. Junkie. Junkie.

I squeeze my eyes shut and clench my fists tightly around the key. It hurts, but the pain can't silence my parents' voices.

They didn't care. They *never cared.*

The key came with a few other things that belonged to my sister: her ID, a wallet with nothing in it but maxed-out credit cards, and a phone that I can't unlock.

She had been my selfless defender when I was a kid— always standing between me and our parents whenever they started yelling. And whenever she did that, they would always turn their attention on her.

No matter what they were mad at me about, the moment they saw her, their anger would grow tenfold.

And they made sure their words *hurt.*

Useless. Ungrateful. Worthless. Why are you still here?

She'd take their verbal abuse without so much as a blink, even when I could see the hurt written in her eyes. She would stay strong until it was just the two of us, and only then was I allowed to see her cry.

Only then would she allow me to hold her like she held

me whenever I was bawling my eyes out. Only then would she nod through the sobs when I promised her what she promised me—that everything would be alright.

And the only time I managed to be there for her was the night when she overdosed.

It was the first and only time I *did* save her.

And in the aftermath, she asked me why I bothered to bring her back.

Because you're my sister, I told her. *And sisters have each other's backs.*

That night still haunts my dreams.

In dreams, Mom and Dad would walk over to Olivia's hospital bed and apologize to her for being the reason why she ended up there. They promise that they'll do better than before, that they'll start to give a shit about their daughters instead of worrying about how much money we cost them. That they'll do whatever it takes to keep us all together as a happy family instead of asking when we'll start doing our fair share.

Then I wake up to reality, where they did the exact opposite, and I have to remind myself that it's just a dream.

And dreams always die.

"Stop it, Emily," I tell myself. "You're doing nobody any favors."

Slowly, I make my way to the kitchen, and I'm hit by the smell of decay. The sink is full of dirty dishes—unwashed since her death. There's a small pot with water stagnating in it, and the bottom is all rusted out.

Weird.

Olivia was never much of a cook, which makes the number of dishes feel wrong.

Either she left them for days without caring, or she was feeding multiple people.

She told me she lived alone. The apartment is tiny, to put it politely. There aren't many places to search. With a wary hand, I nudge her bedroom door inward. My hand hesitates when it makes contact with the rough wooden surface. My eyes refuse to look ahead, preferring to focus on the cheap vinyl tiles lining the floor.

Not yet. I can't yet.

But I must.

The door swings and bounces off something behind it— a purple suitcase with frayed corners. I know if I try to extend the handle, it will jam before it reaches full length. Dangling off the handle is a bright pink Hello Kitty bag tag, the same as mine.

The same one as Konstantin's.

And just like that, my heart feels a pang of regret. But at what, I'm not sure anymore.

I look at the bright pink bag tag and I can still hear Mom's words in my head when the door slammed shut behind Olivia years ago.

We should thank her for throwing out the trash for us. Let that junkie be a problem for whatever cop finds her. Maybe she'll finally do something good when she's dead.

Instinctively, my hand reaches up to my cheek. I can feel the sting of where Mom's palm struck me all those years ago after Olivia had left. I can still hear Dad bellowing that if I ever talked back like that again, he'd teach me a lesson I wouldn't ever forget.

Mom's words have come true in the worst possible way.

And I'm the one who has to pick up the pieces.

Sighing, I force myself to look at the twin bed with its disheveled green blankets and checkered sheets. There should be crime scene tape here. NYPD clearly decided that there was no need.

In the autopsy report they handed me, it said that my sister's death was a suicide by heroin overdose.

And like my parents, they were quick to judge who she was.

But the more I look in the apartment, the less I believe that she overdosed.

So far, I haven't seen a single needle. There are also no elastic bands, no burnt spoons, and certainly no tiny dime bags.

In short, I haven't seen a damn thing to support that she *was* using.

I look back at the bed. Even though the stark yellow tape isn't here, I know in my heart that this is where she died. I swear I can still see the impression on the mattress from where her body was.

It's so damn easy to imagine her *here*.

Suddenly my phone buzzes in my hand. I look down, expecting something from Mom. But instead, I see a text from Nadia. When I open it, another comes in.

Nadia: HOLY SHIT!!

Nadia: There was a shootout at the Zebra Club, and someone fucking burned it down!

My blood runs cold. *What is she talking about?* Opening Google, I quickly begin to search. It's not long before the first news article pops up. Reading it sends my pulse racing:

A deadly shoot-out took place outside of a bustling nightclub in the Amalfi Coast in midday, with several casualties...

I stop breathing. I have to sit on the bed before I collapse.

I tuck my phone back into my pocket, and just like that, I'm thinking about Konstantin again. I've tried not to think about him since I left Italy. Only a minor fantasy here or there as the plane took off. A dream or five before I landed.

But with this news, grim as it is, I'm pinwheeling back through the intoxicating memory of my time with him.

Is he still there?

He must still be. *Is* he okay?

It doesn't matter. I need to get a grip and get back to why I came here.

The front door to Olivia's apartment suddenly squeaks opens. It startles me so hard I bite my tongue.

Who's there?

I peer out from the bedroom just enough to get a glimpse of a man standing in the living room close the front door behind him.

His face is all rectangles. Long black hair is pulled back into a ponytail that enhances the grooves of his cheekbones and chin cleft. With his polished leather jacket and his hands behind his back, he reminds me of a snake searching for its next meal.

The hair on the back of my neck rises and my heart pounds like a drum. Slowly, I begin backing away into the bedroom.

Every part of my body is screaming at me to hide.

But where?

The only place I *can* hide is under the bed, and this stranger is already turning his unblinking gaze towards me.

There's no time.

Then his unsettling stare catches me, and I freeze.

Shit!

"You're not supposed to be here," he says quietly, voice so low that I almost don't hear him over the sound of my pounding heart.

My stomach drops away as his arms move out from behind his body.

And in his hand is a knife.

Shit! Shit! Shit!

Without another sound, he rushes towards me, closing the distance in three quick steps.

Shrieking in the hopes that someone will hear me, I try to slam the door shut. But he's faster than me. In a blur, he crashes through the thin door and knocks me down onto the bed.

The musty odor of Olivia's sheets rises up to choke me, and long thin fingers close around my throat to silence my cries.

I grab his wrist with my left hand to no avail. He's just too strong.

Kicking and struggling under the weight of his body, I swing my right hand—still closed around the key to the apartment—towards his face. My left hand extends for anything I can reach, and grab nothing but empty air.

The man snarls. The knife rises.

In that moment, two things become crystal clear:

One, Olivia didn't kill herself.

Two, I'm about to join her.

12

KONSTANTIN
MINUTES EARLIER

"YOU SURE ABOUT THIS?" SIMA CRANES HIS NECK IN THE driver's seat to look up at the apartment.

In the few short hours I've landed in New York, I've already tracked down a number of Ferrata men.

Unlike the stubborn fool in the Amalfi Coast, these were *much* easier to crack.

And even though they were clueless to the full details, they've provided enough information to tell me that this rundown walkup in East Bushwick is the last place that Alisa was taken to.

I squint through the tinted windows in the back seat at the building.

Its brick facade is chipped and stained by questionable liquids. There's nobody outside, almost as if people know better than to walk around this area alone.

But the part that concerns me the most is just how close it is to the airport.

It's less than a twenty-minute drive.

Sima might be right. There's no way they'd keep her here.

But I have to be sure.

"This is the place." Feeling for the comfort of the gun in my jacket, I open the car door. "Stay here."

"I should come with you." Sima taps his fingers on the steering wheel rapidly. "You don't know what you'll find in there."

"I'm more afraid of finding nothing," I reply. "Stay here and discourage the curious. *Eto moi prikaz.*"

"*Konchecno.*" He nods.

Stepping out from the car, I walk quickly over the cracked sidewalk toward the front steps of the apartment.

This place looks like shit.

The windows on the bottom level are protected by rusted bars. Trash bags are oozing on the curb.

My fingers wander to the gun in my jacket as my mind is lured into one of my many vengeful fantasies. I picture screams, explosions, and dark smoke that chokes hordes of my rivals. I see myself walking across their broken bodies on my way to take out Augusto and his son.

I imagine the old man falling on his knees and begging me not to kill them both.

I run my tongue over my teeth.

I'll make every single person who had a hand in my sister's disappearance pay.

With interest.

The front door isn't fully closed, and as I climb the stairs, someone cracks open their door. A single wary eye gawks at me before the door slams shut. The tell-tale click of a bolt locking fills my ears. I keep my hand on my weapon.

The residents here might be Ferrata informants for all I know.

Surely, word will have spread that I'm in the city by now, especially with the trail of corpses in my wake. There will be consequences, that much is for sure. But if I can find more clues as to where Alisa is ...

Or better yet, if I can find her here.

It's nothing more than a fool's hope, but I cling to it regardless.

I freeze on the landing of the second floor. In front of me is a reddish door with the faded number 28 painted on the surface. The pervasive stench of mold permeates everything. Beneath the strong odor, I can smell my own eager sweat.

With one hand on the gun's trigger in my jacket, I reach into my pocket, pull out a handkerchief, and grab the doorknob to avoid leaving any fingerprints.

Just then, I hear a startled shriek. My grip tightens on my gun.

What the fuck?

It's not Alisa. But it sounds *familiar.*

Tucking the handkerchief back in my pocket, I kick the door open and immediately spot the open bedroom door. A man in leather jacket is face down on the bed, and that's when I spot something else:

Cropped tan joggers. A pale fist punching uselessly at the man from underneath.

Something glints and I see the knife in his hand rise up in the air.

Without hesitation, I aim my gun at his hand and pull the trigger.

13

EMILY

MY EYES SQUEEZE SHUT AS THE KNIFE DESCENDS, BUT somehow, the pain never comes. Instead, a banging sound—so loud that it leaves my ears ringing in pain—overwhelms the tiny space. My would-be murderer screams. The grip around my neck loosens and something falls off to the side.

The knife!

Adrenaline and the animal instinct to survive take over.

I pick up the knife in my left hand and, screaming, stab into the man's face.

He shrieks and rears back up away from me, just in time for his head to explode in a shower of pink mist.

He collapses to the floor.

Dead.

Panting as my heart races at a million beats a second, I prop myself up and stare at disbelief at the person in front of me.

Familiar mahogany hair, thick on top and turning into a fade that tapers towards his long, tan neck. Ice-blue eyes. A tiny mole below his right eye that's no longer shifting up.

He's dressed as sharply as he was when I last saw him.

White sleeves peek out from under his suit, and a heavy gold watch clings to his wrist.

Konstantin.

He quickly closes the distance between us, wrench the knife out of my left hand, and pull me up on my feet until his ice-blue eyes are the only thing I can see. The warmth of his touch leaves my knees feeling weak.

All I can do is look up at him, asking myself silently if I'm not already dead.

But he is no longer the charming man who danced with me in a hidden bar with the scent of lemons in the air.

He looks like a different man now.

A dangerous man.

All at once his eyes narrow in a mixture of fury, recognition, and something else.

Something that makes my stomach loop in anticipation and warmth pooling between my legs.

His hand tightens around my wrist, and when he speaks, that familiar deep rumble of his voice—like chocolate to my ears—wakes me up to the fact that this is real.

He really is standing here in front of me.

"Fancy seeing you here, Kitty Cat."

14

KONSTANTIN

EMILY IS AS BEAUTIFUL AS WHEN I LAST SAW HER. THE shadow of a sunburn tinges her pale nose and shoulders with a light pink hue. She's let her hair drift loose, and one of the strands sticks to her forehead, begging for me to brush it away.

A thousand emotions roll through me at once. Trying to catch them is as pointless as collecting every drop of rain.

What the hell is *she* doing here?

I kick the knife away from both of us and glance around the tiny bedroom, searching for signs of danger, or even another person.

Other than the dead man beside us, she's alone.

And judging by how quickly she grabbed the knife to stab that man, she definitely came alone.

But that doesn't calm my pulse.

If she's alone, then that means she came to this apartment by choice.

Which means ...

Is she connected to this place? To Alisa's kidnapping?

She took my suitcase in Italy. She snubbed me that same

night. She'd been alone with me with so little effort. I force myself to tear my gaze away from her intoxicating sapphire-blue eyes to the bloody knife on the floor, and an unsettling realization congeals in my stomach.

She could've killed me.

And now she's here? Where Alisa's trail ends?

I don't believe in coincidences.

Not after this.

"What are you doing here?" she asks.

Her trembling voice brings my attention back to her and I can't help take in just how close she is to me. Her familiar scent— honeysuckle and brown sugar—fills my nose and I feel my cock springing to life in her presence.

She slips her foot an inch backward, as if trying to run away from me.

I tighten my grip around her wrist to keep her close.

"I should ask the same of you," I demand. "Tell me right now. I'm not playing games with you."

"Games?"

"Whose apartment is this?" I growl.

Emily crinkles her nose and stays silent. Right away, I know she's not going to tell me anything. A police siren wails in the distance, growing louder with every passing second. Errant Ferrata soldiers aren't the only problems facing me right now.

Who knows how many cops are working for them?

Who knows if *Emily* is working for them? I can't risk staying here to find out. So, say the only thing I can say in the moment.

"You're coming with me."

"I'm not going anywhere with you," she says curtly.

"You don't seem to understand, Kitty Cat," I tell her as I step closer. "You don't have a choice anymore."

As my grip tightens on her wrist, she suddenly spins and swings at my face. I snatch her wrist, but I'm too slow— something she's holding slashes across my cheek. It's a shallow cut, but it fucking *hurts*.

Kitty Cat has some claws. I don't know why, but the idea that she's even capable of hurting me leaves me feeling *excited.*

I tuck my gun into my back pocket and wrench at the offending hand that hit me. She yelps, and a key tumbles to the ground.

She had a *key* to this apartment? Who the fuck is this girl?

"Stop fighting!"

"Let me go!" She screams, and I cup my palm over her mouth to muzzle her.

She bats at me with her free hand uselessly, but I refuse to let go.

Gravity shifts and the two of us fall into the bed.

The weight of my body presses against her small frame. Loose strands of her dark chestnut hair spreads across the green covers, and my cock turns rock hard from the sudden proximity.

Her eyes widen and she stops struggling. But the look in her eyes isn't fear.

It's anger.

"If I release your mouth, promise me you won't scream."

Her eyes narrow in defiance, and my cock hardens at the sight.

Fine, I think savagely. *Have it your way.*

I release her mouth and she immediately shrieks at the top of her voice. "HELP!"

Wasting no time, I grab the handkerchief from my pocket, ball it up, and shove it into her mouth to gag her.

The irresistible scent of honeysuckle and brown sugar invades my nose again as she struggles.

I can't waste any more time here. I'm vulnerable if I'm attacked right now.

More importantly, I know there's no way I'm getting any answers in this apartment.

With a single swift motion, I flip her over. Panic seizes her and she starts flailing even harder. I undo my tie and quickly tie her hands behind her. In the process, my fingers brush against the soft curves of her ass—bouncing as she struggles—and I feel a familiar savage desire rushing through me. It's the same one that had set my blood aflame after I returned to the house and found her gone.

And now she's here, gagged and bound.

Her screams are muffled through the gag, and her feet flutter kick uselessly underneath me. She wrenches her head this way and that, but there's nowhere to go.

"I'm not the one you need to worry about!" I lean down and whisper savagely in her ear.

But is that true?

Who am I trying to convince? Her? Or myself?

There's no more time to waste.

I flip her back to face me, sling her over my shoulder— the same way a Viking might carry his newly conquered prize—and start making my way out of the apartment.

She kicks hard against my chest and I'm forced to tighten my grip around her soft milky thighs to keep her still. Her scent is overwhelming now, and I feel the tip of my cock growing wet as endless thoughts of what I *could* do to her right now—each imagined act filthier than the last— rush through my head.

Focus.

I slip on one of the stairs, bumping my shoulder roughly

on the wall. The peeling wallpaper shreds from the impact. Another door opens, a new face eyes me. I ignore them as I make my way through the front door and spring towards the car.

I yank the door open, and Sima glances up, doing a double take at the sight of Emily. "What the fuck is—"

I shove Emily into the back seat and bark at him in Russian. "Go! Now!"

I've barely closed my door when Sima slams on the gas, and sends us rocketing down the street.

Once the car is safely in motion and the doors are locked, I reach over to pull the gag out of Emily's mouth.

As soon as her mouth is free, she scrambles away from me, scrunching into the corner with her head against her window.

"Please," she pleads, her lips trembling. "Please let me go."

Her chest rises and falls as she stares at me with a wild expression in her sapphire-blue eyes.

Slowly, I reach over to brush away a strand of her hair. The tip of my finger grazes her skin and she gasps from the contact.

"I can't let you go, Kitty Cat." I tell her truthfully as I pull back. "Not after this."

15

EMILY

I THOUGHT STEPPING FOOT INTO MY DEAD SISTER'S APARTMENT and nearly getting killed by an unknown man was the most shocking thing that would happen to me today.

Turns out I was wrong.

So. Fucking. Wrong.

When Konstantin first showed up and saved me from certain death, my heart had swelled with gratitude.

When he wrenched the knife out of my hand and yanked me close to him, gratitude became doubt.

When he gagged me, flipped me on my stomach, and started tying my hands behind my back, doubt turned into fear.

When he slung me over his shoulder, his thick powerful fingers squeezing my thighs to keep me from kicking him in his muscular chest, fear transformed into something else.

Something primal and visceral.

Something that makes my thighs instinctively clamp together and squeeze.

Something that sends a searing throb between my legs.

Something that makes my toes curl and claw against the confines of my shoes.

And when he tells me that he can't let me go, all while his icy-blue eyes pierces me to my core, and the car continues to race towards some unknown destination ...

I can't help the needy whimper that escapes from my lips.

At the sound, Konstantin's gaze turns towards me, and I struggle against his silky tie that's still keeping my hands bound behind my back. He cocks his head to one side and then slowly reaches over.

There's nowhere for me to back up.

A maddening thought suddenly rushes through me. Panic and excitement suddenly wars in my mind.

Is he going to kiss me?

"Wait ..." I breathe.

He can't kiss me. Because if he does, I *know* I won't want him to stop.

Even though he'd just killed a man in front of me, even though he'd just *kidnapped* me, I can't help feel this dark attraction towards him.

Almost as if I *want* him to show me just how far he can go.

To show me how far *I* can go.

What the fuck is wrong with me?

But to my surprise and disappointment, he doesn't kiss me. Instead, he reaches behind me—the weight and heat of his body temptingly cruel against mine—and in one smooth, practiced motion, frees my hands from their restraints.

As soon as my hands are free, I glance at the locked door.

"Go ahead, try." He seems to be able to read my mind.

"At this speed, the air pressure will make it almost impossible to open that door far enough before I pull you back in."

And just like that, I know that there's no way out.

"Let me out of this car," I say quietly. My limbs suddenly feel heavy, and I know that it's the adrenaline leaving my body. "Now."

"I told you." He shakes his head. "I can't let you go anymore."

Here it comes, he's probably going to ask me again about what I'm doing in Olivia's apartment.

However, he surprises me with a different question instead.

"Why did you leave?"

"What?" I gasp.

"Italy," he says. "Why did you leave?"

Of all things he can ask me, he's asking me about why I didn't wait for him to come back?

I chew my lower lip. I have no good answers for him. Because as curious as he is about why I'm here, I'm equally curious about what *he's* doing here.

"I can't tell you that."

"Don't lie to me, Kitty Cat." His expression darkens, and I feel need throbbing between my legs again.

Yep, I'm officially fucked in the head now. That's the only explanation.

"It bothered you that I didn't stay," I say, my mouth working as fast as my brain. "Didn't it?"

He doesn't respond, and I have my answer.

"Why?" I ask.

"I'm the one asking questions here."

I look away, but I can still feel his gaze peeling back the layers of my mind, everywhere and nowhere. I know there's nothing and nowhere I can hide from him. I can *hear* him in my head even as the two of us sit here in silence.

"Where are we going?" I break the silence.

The car's tires crunch over gravel as we turn off the highway. Lifting his head, he motions out the windows.

I tear my gaze away from him just in time for the roar of a jet engine overhead to drown out all other sounds. And that's when I realize where we are.

The airport.

Oh God...

The tendril of dark excitement starts to snake around my core, wrapping its tentacle around my mind and squeezing until there's no other thought other than the same fantasy that refused to leave my mind since we danced the night away in the Amalfi Coast.

Konstantin laying me down to the floor and ripping my clothes away as his searing lips trace my body. His thick powerful fingers forcing my legs apart so that his tongue can explore me. The weight of his muscled body against mine, his cock filling me up until I can't take it anymore.

I clench my jaws and swallow as another warm drop of desire trickle between my legs.

That had been a reckless fantasy.

And now, it seems dangerously close to becoming reality.

THE CAR ROLLS TO A HALT. When it comes to a stop, the driver steps out and Konstantin follows. I try to stay back, but Konstantin yanks me out of the car.

The cacophony of the airport is overwhelming, and I

realize that I can scream as loud as I want out here, and no-one will hear me.

The driver mouths something that I can't catch, and then bounds up the stairs towards the jet.

"No! No! No!" I dig my heels into the asphalt. "You're not taking me on that!"

"Not afraid of flying, are you?" Konstantin asks as he tugs me behind him.

"I'm afraid of *you!*"

"That almost hurt my feelings, Kitty Cat."

Good. I think savagely. But I know better than to say it out loud at this point.

I have no idea where this man plans to take me, but I've ~~read~~ watched enough true crime documentaries to know that the moment your kidnapper takes you to a second location, your chance of survival drops to almost zero.

And I have a feeling that even in the best of circumstances, I'll have a hard time surviving being alone with Konstantin.

For a number of *very* different reasons.

I try to fight back with every step, but he still manages to force me inside the jet. The driver, with a scar on his face and narrow brown eyes, is waiting for us inside. Without asking, he hurries to close the door, sealing us in. He gives us one final look before vanishing into the cockpit.

Now that I can't escape, Konstantin finally releases my wrist. Rubbing my arm gingerly as I back away, I watch him warily like he might lunge for my throat.

And just like all of our interactions earlier today, the thought of his fingers wrapped around my throat sends another rush of excitement and want through me.

Dammit! What's wrong with me today?

"Are you finally going to tell me what the hell you're doing with me?" I finally force the words out of my mouth.

He doesn't answer.

"I'm done playing nice!" I snarl. "Answer me!"

"This is you being nice?" He points to the cut on his face, smirking.

That smirk. That stupid sexy lopsided smirk. Seeing that again makes it almost impossible for me to hate him.

Almost.

"Was I supposed to just politely let you *kidnap* me?"

"Stop using that word."

"Oh, I'm sorry, do you have a better word to describe what you just did?" I throw my hands up. "Because that's *exactly* what I'd call this whole experience. Also, why are you refusing to tell me one good reason why?"

With every word, I feel my anger slowly rising to the surface.

And then, I do something stupid.

I give him a hard shove.

To my own surprise, he doesn't react. Maybe the knowledge that I can't escape anymore is enough to restrain him.

Or, a tiny little voice whispers in the back of my head. *He's just thinking of new ways to punish you for this.*

"Well?" I ask. His silence and inaction make me bolder than I have any right to be. Crossing my arm and jutting out my chin, I stare into his inscrutable eyes. "You got me on your plane. Just what the hell are you going to do to me?"

He continues to stare at me, and I long to know just what kind of twisted thoughts are turning behind his handsome face. A hundred different thoughts race through my mind in a second, each one dirtier than the last.

Which is why his answer is all the more shocking.

Because it's the last thing I ever expected out of him.

"I'm going to marry you."

16

EMILY

"*Marry* you?" I work the word around in my mouth. It tastes nice, but the longer I let it linger on my tongue, the dirtier it sounds. "I'm not marrying you."

"You don't have any choice." Konstantin doesn't look surprised by my reaction. "Not anymore."

"Like hell I don't." The loud roar of the engines warming up makes my ears ache. The plane begins to roll over the tarmac, sending me rocking to one side. I lose my balance. Konstantin catches me, his hands supporting my shoulders.

"Buckle in, Kitty Cat," he says.

I pull away like he's burned me. Ignoring his advice, I reach for the cockpit door. "I'm telling the pilot to turn around."

"Door's locked," he says. "Not that it'll do you any good. He only listens to me."

"Then tell him to stop!"

Konstantin drops into one of the large, luxurious-looking seats by a window. The light coming through dances over his elegant face. His skin is perfect—except where I cut him.

"Sit. We need to discuss the terms of this marriage."

"Discuss? There's nothing to discuss here!" Scowling until my jaw hurts, I test the cockpit door again. It doesn't budge. "I'm not marrying you!"

"Sit down before you hurt yourself."

The jet scream grows louder. Gravity shifts, and I feel the cabin shudder as the plane lofts itself into the air. Konstantin gives me a pointed look. I hold my head high to show that my spirit isn't broken, and that I'm only listening because I don't want to snap my neck.

Still, I choose to sit as far from him as possible, which is proving very difficult given that there's only four seats in the entire jet.

"This marriage," Konstantin starts. "Only has to *seem* real."

My eyes pop wide. The bluntness of his answer hurts me more than I care to admit.

The jet lurches forward, sending my stomach into a dizzying spin that lasts a few minutes. We level out, and through the window, I watch in despair as the ground below turns into a patchwork of fields and farms.

Unless I find a parachute, I'm not getting away from him.

So much for parachuting into a hot stranger's bed.

"Tell me why," I demand. "Don't I deserve to know?"

He lifts a hand, rubbing the beauty mark by his eye, almost as if he's trying to figure out whether it's a good idea or not to tell me the truth.

"You're going to help me secure my inheritance from my grandmother," he says. "She won't release it to me until I'm married."

"And why do you need that inheritance?"

"Because my enemies have kidnapped my sister." He leans forward. "They tried to kill me so that the inheritance will pass to her upon my death. This is my way of breaking up their plans."

"Enemies ..." I breathe. "You talk like you're some kind of mob boss."

"Oh, Kitty Cat." The corner of his lips curls up in a smile, and my breath hitches in my throat. "You have no idea just how accurate you are."

Suddenly, everything about the past few days start making sense.

How could I be so blind?

Who else can just show up to a new place and immediately buy a Lamborghini on a whim?

Who else refuses to answer the question of what he does for work?

Who else can inspire fear from strangers in a club with a simple gesture?

The signs were all there, and I ignored them all.

Worse.

I went with him on my own accord.

I told him what I was doing in Italy.

I was one hundred percent ready to *fuck* him.

"But ... if you're a mob boss." I take a shaky breath. "Why do you need to be married to get your inheritance? Can't you just demand it from your grandmother?"

"There are so many things you don't understand about my world." He steeples his fingers together. "And things are rarely as simple as you think."

"This marriage." I swallow. "It just has to *seem* real?"

"That's exactly what I said."

He says it with such seriousness that I'm reminded of what he said to me just before we parted ways in Italy: *Don't misunderstand me. I will be back.*

Konstantin has the aura of a man who takes his

promises to the grave. *Or you're being naive and he's going to toss you into a shallow grave once he's had his fun.*

"And once you get what you want by having me pretend to be your wife, you'll let me go?" I ask. "You're not lying to me?"

"You have my word."

I close my eyes. I know what he's doing to me. It's no different than what almost every person in my life, other than Nadia and my sister, has done to me – from my parents to Phil to every failed relationship I've ever had.

Use me for their own selfish reasons, and caring about me only when I have any use for them.

"And what do I get out of this?" I finally find my voice and ask him softly.

"Whatever your heart desires," he replies.

"What do you mean whatever my heart desires?" I press. "Like you'll pay me?"

"If that's what you want, yes."

"I'm not a whore," I say before I can stop myself.

"And I have no intention of treating you like one, Kitty Cat," he replies, and his eyes flash as if he's insulted that I might think that. "By doing this, you'll be doing me a favor. I would be in your debt, and I'm a man who pays his debts with interest."

My hands clench and unclench. "But you'd still be using me."

"If that's the way you intend on seeing it, yes," he says.

I thought I had steeled myself for his answer. But no amount of mental preparation can stop my heart from splitting at hearing him say it so matter-of-factly, so bluntly, as if he's talking about the weather.

"I will make you a promise," he continues. "When this is

all over, you can have whatever you want. All you have to do is ask, and if it is within my power to grant, I will give it to you. Tell me, what is the one thing in the world that you want?"

The only thing I want in this world, I think sadly, *is to have my sister back. But you can't bring back the dead.*

"I don't know yet," I lie to him. "But I know it's not money. I'm not a whore."

"You don't have to tell me twice," he says. "And you don't have to tell me what you want just yet. We can discuss that at the end of this arrangement."

Arrangement ...

I want to scream at him. I want to shout that this isn't fair, that he doesn't get to just use me like this. I am a *person,* a human being with my own wants and feelings, not a tool that he can use and discard.

But I don't. Instead, all I hear is a tiny little voice in the back of my head. *At least he's upfront about it with you,* it says. *At least this way, you know what you're getting yourself into before he breaks your heart like every other man.*

I gulp down one breath after another until my heartbeat returns to something on the edge of a normal cadence. Konstantin just sits there, looking at me and waiting for me to say something.

"Why me?" I finally ask. "You could've asked anyone else. Why did it have to be me?"

He looks at me and his hand lifts form his armrest to scrub his jaw. The silence drags on for another heartbeat, and then he finally answers.

"Because I couldn't stop thinking about you."

Warmth balloons up in my chest and I close my eyes at his answer. I try to tell myself that he's lying, that he's just telling me what I want to hear. But I can't help believe—like a fool—that maybe, just maybe, he might actually give a damn about me.

———

As the plane levels out in the air, I feel my eyelids growing heavy. The past forty-eight hours have left me utterly exhausted. Unable to suppress my yawn, I try to get comfortable in my seat in an attempt to catch some sleep until we arrive at wherever the hell it is we're going.

When he sees me yawn, Konstantin rises from his seat. "You should rest before we arrive. It's a long flight."

"That's exactly what I'm doing."

He extends his hand at me again, and I can't help recall the moment when he first helped me up from the floor of the airport.

"Wouldn't you prefer something more comfortable?"

I want to tell him no, but I'm so tired that I place my hand in his. Instantly, the warmth that I felt during our first meeting returns, and I rise to follow him.

The jet didn't look big from the outside, so I'm surprised when he opens the door at the rear of the plane to expose a large suite with a bathroom in the rear.

And a single king-sized bed.

I have to squeeze by him to reach it. Our bodies brush just slightly, and a tremor of excitement rushes through me again. I force myself to hold my breath as his tantalizing scent of soap and aftershave wafts over.

I turn towards him, and in this confined space, I can't help but drink in every detail of his handsome face again. Slowly, his hand rises up and cups my cheek. I close my eyes, parting my lips, and feel his mouth gently press against mine.

Unlike our kisses in Italy, this one is gentle. For a brief dizzying moment, I allow myself to forget everything that had just taken place and what I just agreed to.

A soft moan pours forth from my nose as he deepens the kiss, and in the doorframe of the suite, my trembling fingers reach forward to feel his hard body. Almost as if I'm trying to beg him through touch to not break my heart when this is over.

Even though I know that he will.

They always do.

Slowly, my hands make their way down, until I feel the throbbing hard heat between his legs. The space between us is shrinking by the second, and I feel him slowly guiding my body effortlessly towards the bed until we're falling into it.

He drives apart my knees and I feel my pussy clenching in response to the closeness of his throbbing cock. My hands move up and down its length, and a shiver runs down my spine as I finally have a chance to feel just how big it is.

I mean, I've put my hands around my fair share of penises before, but this?

This is a *cock*.

Just the word itself sends a burst of wetness gushing to the entrance of my pussy. The swollen girth feels impossibly huge in my hands. It feels so big that I *know* I'll need both of my hands to handle it.

It feels so big that I shiver at the thought of it entering me.

A massive hand circles around my waist tracing up the curves of my body until it encloses around my ass. Konstantin squeezes, and all thoughts and doubts are chased away from my mind. A light gasp tumbles from my lips and he swallows it as his tongue sweeps into my mouth.

I grab at his pants, and just as I finally manage to take hold of his belt, I hear someone clearing his throat.

With a snarl of frustration, Konstantin breaks the kiss and withdraws his hand.

I almost beg him to come back.

"Sleep well, Kitty Cat." His deep voice rumbles just above my ear. "You're going to need your strength when we arrive."

I shiver.

He walks out to rejoin the driver who's waiting for him outside in the cabin, and closes the door behind him to leave me alone by my thoughts and unfulfilled frustration.

Stretching out on the bed, I cross my ankles, gazing at the low ceiling. But all I can think about is how massive his cock felt in my hand. How good it felt for him to squeeze my ass.

I wonder how hard he can make me scream.

I'm fucked. I am so fucked.

Feeling more alone by the second, I try to soothe my brain at the unknown waiting for me when we land. I fantasized about Konstantin ever since I walked away from that patio in the Amalfi Coast.

Now he has finally returned to my life.

And it's nothing like my fantasies.

It's *so* much more.

I don't know where he's taking me. I don't know when this will end.

But none of those thoughts remain within my head as I sink into the bed. Instead, all I can think about are the same questions running through my mind on that patio after he left.

Will he wake me with kisses? Will he keep calling me Kitty Cat when he fucks me?

Just then, a new question enters my mind, one that has been brewing under the surface ever since he shoved me inside of his car.

Will he ever let me go?

And how pathetic am I for knowing that I'll be disappointed if he does?

17

KONSTANTIN

"You're bleeding." Sima passes me a tissue when I close the door behind me.

He'd missed the entire conversation I had with Emily, and he's discreet enough to not say a single damn word about what he just saw.

I dab the tissue on my cheek, surprised to see the white paper come away with red smudges. "She got me better than I thought."

"Shallow cut for a knife."

"It was a key." At Sima's lifted brows, I crumple the tissue in my fist. "I found her in that apartment."

Sima nods. "Well, that answers *that* question."

"She was also on the Amalfi Coast when we were there."

I never mentioned my evening with Emily to Sima. There had been no reason to do so before. But after this?

I keep glancing at the door between us and Emily, almost as if I'm expecting her to appear. If she tries to eavesdrop, it won't work. The engines are too loud.

"Kostya, what are you going to do with her?"

"I told her that I'm going to marry her."

He freezes on the spot, his mouth dropping wide. "Did she give you a concussion alongside that cut?"

She's done plenty of things to my head, but not that.

"This is the cleanest way to handle the problem at hand," I explain. "Without access to the family inheritance—"

"You mean the signet ring?"

"Yes," I say. "Without that in my hand, both myself and the bratva will still be slave to Alla's wishes. You know as well as I do that there's a possibility that she *insists* I swallow my pride and allow Domenico to marry Alisa for the sake of peace." I shake my head angrily. "As if the Ferrata didn't just try to fucking kill me."

"And this is what you've decided to make your plan on? A desperate gamble to fool your grandmother?" Sima asks incredulously. "Even for you, Kostya. That's—"

"Bold?"

"Not the word I would've used."

"The marriage won't be real." I shake my head. "I've explained this to Emily that we just need to make it *look* real. At least, real enough to convince Alla to hand me that damn ring."

"Do you really believe it could work?" he snorts. "Old as she is, Alla Antonovna is still razor sharp. And there's just too many things that can go wrong in the meantime."

"There's no other choice," I insist. "I won't risk letting Domenico hold onto my sister."

"And what about you?"

I wrinkle my nose. "What about me?"

"Don't pretend that I didn't see what the two of you were doing before I interrupted." Sima tracks his eyes back to the closed door. "If this marriage is as fake as you say it is, how can you make sure that you won't *actually* fall in love with her?"

"I'd never." My laughter has a hollow edge. "She's just a means to an end. You know I'm incapable of love."

"That's not what I saw earlier."

"Careful, Sima." All the muscles in my neck tighten up, and my fists follow suit. "You may be my friend, but I am still your pakhan."

Sima leans backward in the chair in front of me, and folds his hands behind his head on the headrest. I don't know if he's smiling or frowning. I think he wants to say more.

He's never shied away from telling me things I'd rather not hear. It's why I trust him more than anyone else.

But this time, he doesn't.

The two of us watches as the plane continues rising until we emerge above the clouds into the endless blue all around us.

"What does she think of your plan?" Sima finally asks after a few more minutes of silence.

"I imagine the same as anyone who's been forced into a fake marriage to help a man secure his inheritance." I shrug. "She'll try to run the moment we arrive back home. Count on that."

"I'll keep an eye on her."

"Keep two." I open my hand, staring at the crushed ball of bloody tissue. "There's a reason she was at that apartment. And there must be a damn good reason someone tried to *kill* her there."

"Her?" Sima cocks an eyebrow. "What's so special about her?"

Everything, I think.

"That's what I intend to find out," I say instead. "Have you heard anything from Emilio Lanzzare?"

"Not when we left," Sima replies. "I'm sure he'll have some choice words for us once we land. You killed three men in his city, Kostya."

"Four." I correct him. "Don't forget the man that tried to kill Emily. And it's not just his city. There's not a single man who can claim all of New York."

"Anything else?" He reaches for his pocket.

"Don't play with your lighter up here," I remind him. "I don't need the jet blowing up before we arrive."

Chuckling, he reclines in his seat and puts his feet up in. There's only that single bedroom suite on the plane.

She's using it now.

I can't stop thinking about her in my bed.

Will she sleep with the covers wrapping her tight? What about her clothes? Are those staying on, or is she lying there in just her underwear?

The way she felt under me earlier returns to me like a half-remembered dream. Her soft body was intoxicating. I shift from side to side, trying to get comfortable, but my erection is distracting. Finally, I stand up.

"Let me know when we arrive."

"Do you want me to put in some earplugs?" Sima raises an eyebrow.

"Fuck you." I smirk. "I just need to go talk to her."

Giving one last stare out of the window, I walk over and open the door. Emily has turned away from the door, but I know she's not asleep. I slip into bed next to her, making sure to keep the thin blanket between us even as my cock hardens at her proximity to me.

She turns to me, and my breath catches in my throat when I gaze into her eyes. Sima is right to warn me.

Falling for her can be terrifyingly easy.

"You were right earlier, Kitty Cat, when you said that I'm using you." I tell her. "I won't deny that. You are a means to an end. But know this. Just because I'm using you, doesn't mean I won't burn the world down to keep you safe. You may not trust my intentions, but you need to believe that I'm a man of my word. And that I'll let you go when this is all over."

"Do you really expect me to believe anything you say after everything that's happened?"

She stares back at me with those dazzling eyes. And I see the *wildness* that I once detected churning under their sapphire-blue surface.

"I do." I nod. "Because both our future depends on it."

And then, I do something even more foolish. I hook my finger under her chin, and bring her close to my lips.

As I drown my senses in her scent—honeysuckle and brown sugar—and the feel of her soft luscious lips, I wonder ...

Can I really let her go when this is over?

Or am I just lying to her and to myself?

18

EMILY

THE PLANE JOSTLES ME AWAKE WHEN WE LAND, AND I WAKE UP more refreshed than I've ever been on a plane. I turn to my side, half expecting to find Konstantin in bed with me.

But to my disappointment, he's already gone.

Once the plane comes to a stop, the door to the suite opens. My disappointment balloons when the driver of the car pokes his head in.

He blinks, like he's surprised to see me. "We've landed," he says.

"I've noticed."

"Come." He inclines his head.

I don't budge. "What's your name?"

"Konstantin is waiting."

"Let him wait. I'm Emily. Who are you?"

He hesitates as he peers over his shoulder, back toward the main part of the jet.

I roll my eyes. "I know you understand me. And I'm not leaving until either you tell me your name, or Konstantin comes to get me himself."

"Call me Gerasim." He sighs. "Now will you come?"

"Gera—what?" I can't pronounce that. "Do you work for Konstantin?"

Sighing, he leans against the doorway. "Don't make me drag you down the aisle."

Very interesting choice of words. Now I'm thinking about this wedding again.

"Let me guess. Are you also part of this ridiculous plot forcing me to marry him?"

"Okay, you've been warned." He grabs my upper arm. His fingers are rough, textured by numerous scars. "Up!"

"I can walk," I snap, wrenching my arm out of his grip.

Straightening my wrinkled outfit, I follow him out of the bedroom and into the main cabin.

Konstantin is waiting by the exit. Sunlight glows through the rows of windows. Whether it's sunset or sunrise, I can't tell. But it doesn't matter. In the light, his tan skin looks ethereal. I want to hate him, but the combination of exhaustion and disorientation makes it impossible for me to ignore just how damn yummy he looks.

"Good morning, Kitty Cat."

Well, that answers that *question.*

"Where are we?" I ask.

"Come and see." He ducks through the door and down the steps.

Gerasim blocks my retreat—as if I *want* to stay on this plane. I hurry out of the jet, sucking in the fresh air as I go. The sunlight stabs at my eyes and I raise my hand to shield them from the brightness. On impulse, I reach for my phone to check the time and find nothing.

Konstantin must've taken that while I slept.

When my eyes adjust to my new surroundings, I look around and find that we're in the middle of an airstrip with just a single small control tower in the distance. The ground is painted with white lines. Not far away sits a pale green helicopter. The fringe of the field is shrubs and blue sky, nothing distinctive to tell me where I am.

"Where are we?"

"A few miles outside of Dubrovnik," Konstantin answers.

I dig through my mental maps with rapidly rising panic. "And where is *that?*"

"Croatia," he says. "You asked me where my real home is. Well, here we are."

Gripping the jet's stairs to keep my balance, I let this information sink in as I wrack my brain for an answer on just exactly where the hell either of those places are.

Dubrovnik. Croatia

They sound *vaguely* familiar, but for the life of me, I can't reason out why.

All I can focus is on the fact that he took me to another damn *country!*

"No one here will help you escape," he says. "I don't recommend that you try."

"Why would I try to escape?" I ask as indifferently as I can. "You said if I play my part, you'll let me go home with whatever I wanted. You promised."

"I did." Konstantin stares at me, and I swear he's trying to read my mind. I'm secretly relieved that he can't, because all I can think about is the kiss we shared just before I fell asleep. "Get in the helicopter. It will take us the rest of the way."

Gerasim joins us on the pavement. "Need me to go with you, Kostya?"

I blink. "Kostya? I thought your name was Konstantin?"

Gerasim tightens his jaw, acting like he's given something away he didn't mean to. I tuck this tidbit away for later.

"No." Konstantin raises his voice. "I need you to send

word to Alla Antonovna about my engagement." His hand circles my wrist, and my heart skips a beat at the contact. "Tell her that I've fulfilled all of the requirements for her to release the inheritance to me."

"Understood."

Engagement. The word hangs heavy in the air, and all of a sudden, I can feel the weight of our arrangement on my shoulders.

"Slow down!"

"Aren't you eager to change into some clean clothes and have some food after the flight?"

"You think you can win me over with a meal?"

"It worked in Italy." He smirks.

"Please, you didn't *win* anything."

"Is that why you didn't stay?"

I stop trying to pull away and nearly lose my footing. He's watching me over his shoulder with his dark eyebrows arched—checking my reaction. I can't hide my surprise before he sees it.

"It really bothered you that I left," I whisper. "Didn't it?"

He flips around, rips the helicopter door open, and brings us both inside. I topple into a cramped chair with a wince. He says something in a different language to the man in the pilot's seat. It sounds like the same language he used on the balcony just before we parted ways in Italy.

The big blades overhead begin to spin, and the noise drowns out any chance for conversation. I don't mind. Konstantin is all business right now. His attention is focused out towards the window, his fist clenched tight.

It actually upset him that I wasn't in his house when he came back. On the one hand, my heart is doing a little dance that I'm struggling to halt, because it means that on some level, he *did* care about me.

But on the other hand ...

Croatia ...

The name sounds vaguely Eastern European. That's all I can come up with. But it sounds so familiar.

I rack my brain for every morsel of information I can get but I'm coming up empty. The answer seems to hover on the tip of my tongue. Huffing, I decide to table that thought for later and choose to turn my attention outward towards the scenery.

The helicopter starts making its way from the airstrip and over a city. The red clay rooftops remind me so much of the Amalfi Coast. Just like that, I'm reminded of the texts that Nadia sent me. About how there was a shooting outside of Zebra Club and how it burned down.

I stare back at Konstantin's head. Is he connected to that somehow?

He must be, I tell myself. *He's a mob boss, remember?*

I turn my attention back to the rooftops. Is Nadia on her way back to America by now? Or is she still in the Amalfi Coast?

Does she even know that I've been taken?

The city below us passes by in a blur, and that's when I see something that looks familiar. An ancient castle rising up on a slope by the sea. And then that's when it hits me.

Dubrovnik! That's the city they filmed Game of Thrones *in!*

Funny, the castle looks so much smaller from up high. But the more important thing that pops into my mind is the tidbit that there's been a *lot* of tourism into Dubrovnik thanks to *Game of Thrones*.

Which means ...

A terrifyingly tantalizing thought enters into my mind. If I can just get to Dubrovnik and find an American tour group. Maybe I can ...

And then what? The same little voice that's been bugging me this entire time pipes up. *He'll just come find you again. You can't escape him.*

I start chewing my lip again.

"Something on your mind, Kitty Cat?"

Oh shit, have I been staring at him this entire time?

"Nothing," I reply. "Just getting used to being here."

Soon, the city disappears behind us as we crest over a massive mountain. I look out the windows and see what we're flying toward. Beyond a wide expanse of green hills, lying low in a valley, is a massive lake. Its placid surface has a lavender hue that mirrors the beautiful sky up above. Olive and cypress trees circle the water in man-made geometric shapes.

But what's really got my jaw dropping is the castle.

It sprawls out in the center of the lake like a dragon on a pile of treasure. The spires reach to the heavens—I count twelve of them along the stone base. It's hard to judge from up here, but I'm sure it's several acres wide.

We begin to dip toward it. My head has gone fuzzy from disbelief. "Is *that* where you live?"

"It is."

My eyes bulge at him. "Are you a prince as well as a mob boss?"

Throwing back his head, he begins to laugh with his full chest. He doesn't stop until the helicopter is beginning its final descent onto the flat roof of the castle.

"No, I'm not a prince."

"I've never met a mob boss with a castle before."

His sparkling smile fades and he considers me closely as the helicopter comes to a stop.

"Have you met many mob bosses in your life?"

"No." I'm forced to admit.

He pops the door open, ducking low as the still-spinning blades whip the wind overhead. I follow him, clutching my hands to my skull as visions of getting decapitated assault me. He doesn't slow down, and I have to take two steps for every one of his.

On one edge of the roof is a tower made from speckled stone. Built into the massive structure is a rounded wooden door.

Konstantin waits for me beside it, but he's in a hurry—he grabs my hand impatiently to pull me into the tower.

"Will you relax?" I argue. "I can't run away even if I want to!"

He says nothing, and continues to drag me down the flight of stairs. They circle downward in the darkened space, the hanging lamps giving enough visibility when the diamond-shaped windows don't. We go left, then right, and I'm struggling to keep track of my sense of direction.

Opening the door at the end of a wide hall, he throws me inside, shutting us in. I'm about to give him a piece of my mind when I see through a massive window over the lake I saw from the helicopter.

Holy shit.

From here, the view is even more awe-inspiring than from up in the air. Swans skirt over the water, leaving ripples in their wake. The olive trees on the rim cast long shadows that turn the blue water black.

"Beautiful, isn't it?" he asks.

"Yeah, I'll give you a five-star review on Airbnb when I leave." Shaking myself to my senses, I glare at him. "Amazing views, super scenic location. But the owner is a control freak who should be in jail."

"I don't remember you being this sarcastic."

"I wasn't pissed off at you in Italy!"

He sighs softly before leveling a hard look at me. "I'll do my best to keep you as comfortable as I can. As for food, I remember you said you weren't picky?"

I bristle and dig my nails into my palms. "I wish your ethics were as powerful as your memory."

He ignores my jab. "There are clean clothes in the wardrobe."

"Oh, you prepared for this kidnapping, then?"

His face darkens. "I told you to stop calling it that."

Boy, he really hates that word. I'll keep that in mind. "Just calling a spade a spade, *Kostya*."

If I thought his face darkened when I kept saying the word kidnapping, his expression is absolutely murderous at me calling him *that*. But I can't back down now.

And besides. What's he going to do? Kill me?

The knowledge that he's forcing me to marry him—no matter how twisted of a proposal it is—has given me the small assurance that he's not the one holding all the power.

He needs me more than he's willing to admit.

"Are you going to be this difficult for the entire wedding?"

"So what if I do?" I just my chin at him. "Are you going to drag me down to a torture chamber in this castle and string me up until I do what you want?"

"Only if that's what it takes, Kitty Cat." A shadow passes over his face, and a cruel smile twists on his lips before it disappears.

Tiny flutters creep up my ribs to play with my heart, and desire squeezes between my legs again at the images his words conjure up in my mind.

Oh my.

19

EMILY

I WONDER IF MAYBE HE *DOES* HAVE A TORTURE CHAMBER.

What would he even have in there? Chains? Whips? My knees buckle slightly, and I clench my teeth to stop my imagination from running wilder than they already have.

"Tell me more about the wedding."

When he doesn't respond, I press harder.

"I get that you're a mob boss and have secrets. But don't I deserve to know what I'll be getting into? At this rate, you might as well send me down the aisle in a literal blindfold."

"I told you." Konstantin squares his shoulders, and I prepare myself for more silence. It's a pleasant shock when he speaks. "It just needs to look real from start to finish. That means engagement photos, a wedding dress, and a ring."

"You seem to understand what goes into planning a wedding more than most people," I snort. "If I didn't know better, I'd think you've been planning your wedding for years, like Nadia."

"You've got the wrong idea about me."

"So." *I had the wrong idea about you from the start.* "Just how *real* do we have to be?" I taunt.

He doesn't answer me.

"You said that this is all about inheritance, right? Will they expect everything else that comes with a wedding?"

He stays silent.

"A happily ever after?"

He continues to walk in silence.

"*Babies?*"

Suddenly, he comes to a stop, and turns around so quickly that I take a step back.

There's an unreadable look on his face. His eyes are burning into me like embers. And then wordlessly, he turns back and exits the room.

I wanted to get under his skin. After all he's done to me, he deserves to be uncomfortable.

But his silence has told me *everything*.

Oh fuck ...

He should have laughed! But he didn't. He fucking didn't, and *that* scares me way more than anything else he's said or done this whole damn time.

Babies.

He *told* me that he was going to use me, and I was stupid enough to agree. Stupid enough to believe that there wouldn't be any consequences.

Babies ...

I'd call that some pretty fucking real consequences.

Suddenly, I can't suck in a full breath. The room starts spinning and I feel myself hyperventilating.

I'm having a panic attack.

Because of course I am.

He all but admitted that he's going to have *babies* with me.

I have to get away from this place.

Whipping my head from side to side, I search the room for a solution. It's *big,* and the view is great, but that's all it's got going for it. The paisley-patterned chair in the corner can't help me. And when I look in the drawers, there's nothing but some folded clothes.

My attention focuses on the window. A flock of tiny yellow birds explodes by the glass, fluttering away into the branches of a nearby cypress tree. The swans dip their heads, guzzling water. One by one they begin paddling across the lake toward the distant shore.

The thudding of my heart hastens until it becomes a hailstorm. *Fuck it. I'm swimming across the lake.* It's the only way to reach the other side. Once I'm there, I can bolt into the bushes and hide from Konstantin until I find the police.

I try to remember if there was a road that I might be able to flag down a car on the other side, but I can't. Everything was happening too fast on our way here.

There's only one way to find out.

Jutting out my chin, I study the lake again.

Growing up, there was a deep pond near my house. Olivia and I preferred to spend our time away from our parents. Since we were very broke, something free like swimming in a pond was a treasure for us.

She was always the better swimmer. For the first time in far too long, thinking of Olivia doesn't make me gloomy. The memory of her body powering through the water as we raced is inspiring.

Plus ... the sooner I get away from here, the sooner I can return to getting justice for her.

Cracking the door a few inches, I peer into the hallway. I haven't seen anyone else yet, but a place like this is too big to not have others living in it. *He's got to have cleaners and guards and whatever else. If they work for him, they can't be trusted. I'll make sure it's clear before ... aha!*

Two women in matching black pants and cinched tops with beaded hems stroll by my door. They're talking loudly to each other, but I can't make sense of what they're saying.

Holding my breath, I wait until I can't hear them anymore and nudge the door open to slip into the hall. I head in the opposite direction as them. *Where the hell is the exit?* The ceiling is high enough that I'd need a ladder to brush it with my fingertips, and you could practically drive a car through the corridor.

It's my first time in a real castle. I just wish I could enjoy it.

There! Around a corner I come across a circular room with colorful glass windows. A rectangular wooden door calls my name. Rushing at it, I tug it hard, terrified it will be locked.

I go dizzy with delight when it opens easily.

Olive-scented air tickles my nose. The birds from earlier flit around me, startled by my presence. There must be hundreds of them in the trees. But I only have eyes for the lake. Sprinting toward the water, I kick off my shoes. The bank is muddy. I stumble, falling in up to my waist, sputtering as I swallow a mouthful of water.

At least it's not freezing! I'll take every advantage I can get. Coughing, I throw my arms forward, wading eagerly into the lake. The ground falls away rapidly. I lose my footing before I'm six feet in. *It's deeper than I thought ... The shore is really far away, and I haven't eaten. Fuck.*

This was a terrible idea. But I have to escape.

If I don't, I know what's waiting for me.

Konstantin.

Wedding.

Babies.

Gritting my teeth, I begin to swim.

20

KONSTANTIN

A<small>FTER EVERYTHING</small> I'<small>VE BEEN DEALING WITH</small>, E<small>MILY MANAGED</small> to get under my skin with a single word.

Babies. I grit my teeth. *Why the hell did she have to bring babies up?*

I should've laughed. I should've dismissed it like the silly suggestion that it is.

But I didn't.

Maybe because a part of my mind drifted back to our night in Italy. And as soon as she asked that question, the only thing I can think of is her shapely legs wrapped around me, her neck exposed to me as she throws her head back in ecstasy.

Fuck.

But the part that's bothering me isn't the idea that I might *want* babies with Emily. It's the fact that if I want to make this marriage look *real* to my grandmother, then babies might actually be a part of the bargain.

And I know for a fact that Emily will *never* agree to that.

I pass a mirror in the hallway of my castle. I stop short to stare at myself. *I look like hell.* Leaning closer, I rub at the shadows under my eyes. And then I trace the light scratch that Emily gave me.

Once I get some food in her and she settles in, I can try a do-over. Torture isn't the only way to get what I want out of people. Manipulation can be softer ... sweeter, even.

Who knows what I'll gain if I try to be gentler with Emily.

But truthfully, I don't want gentle. The memory of kissing her and touching her invades my mind, and my pants strain again at the thought.

I can't seem to push out of my mind. She's somehow taken root deep inside.

And it's only a matter of time before those roots reach from my mind to somewhere else.

My phone buzzes in my pocket, and I yank it out before the first vibration finishes, eager for a distraction.

It's Sima.

"Emilio Lanzzare knows," He speaks as soon as the line connects. "And so does Augusto. Both of them seem equally pissed."

"And?"

"They want you to know that you broke protocol."

"That's the fucking point." I clench the phone in my hand. "Are the Ferratas calling for war?"

"As far as I can tell, yes." Sima answers. "But Emilio is sitting this one out. It seems that you made the right call in assuming he doesn't want to start something across the ocean. Not yet at least."

"Of course he doesn't, not with the East Coast Bratvas breathing down his neck as it is."

"There's more." Sima clears his throat. "Alla Antonovna wants to know if there's a date for the ceremony."

"Tell her that I will inform her in person."

"Understood."

I've barely lowered my phone when footsteps parade from the other end of the hall, rushing in my direction.

"Konstantin Yurevich! There you are!"

One of my gardeners, her thick overalls stained with grass and mud, halts in front of me. I think her name is Anna, but she looks so much like her cousin Polina, who also work for me, that I get them mixed up. Her cheeks are ruddy from the effort of sprinting.

"*Chto?*" I ask warily.

She points out the nearest window. "Your guest is trying to swim across the lake!"

I don't have to ask her any other questions to know that she's talking about Emily.

"Dammit, is she crazy?" I hiss under my breath, running down the corridor. Some of my staff gasp at the sight of me, dodging out of my way.

I open the first door I come across that takes me outside.

Well, I'll be goddamned.

Emily isn't quite halfway across the lake, and she's struggling in the water. I squint, and true to my initial suspicion, she's starting to flounder.

At the rate she's moving, she won't make it to the far shore before she drowns.

The lake is deceptive, with strong currents hidden under its placid surface from the rivers feeding into it.

Even on my best days, it's a challenge to swim this thing.

She's out of her mind if she thinks she can cross it right now.

Searching the shoreline, I spot what I need: a wooden boat—white as the swans that scatter when I jump into it and shaped like a diamond with the corners smoothed down.

She must've been so eager to escape that she didn't even see it.

Must be my answer to her question about babies, I muse as I start rowing.

My shoulders burn from how hard I twist the paddles. Emily doesn't see me approaching; she's singularly focused on her destination. When I draw closer, I notice just how much she's struggling—gasping for breath, kicking sluggishly, and barely sending up flecks of water with each slowing motion of her arms.

"You're exhausted," I say loudly.

"Fuck ... you ..." She inhales water, coughing. "Get ... away ... from me!"

I drop the paddles and lean over the side. She's within reach, but I don't grab her. "You'll never make it."

"Yes ... I ... will!"

"There's a quarter of a mile left to go, Kitty Cat."

Instead of responding, she summons another burst of energy and paddle her feet behind her with reckless abandon.

She was smart enough to remove her shoes, but her clothes are weighing her down.

"Your determination is admirable," I chuckle. "But you need to get in the boat before hurt yourself."

Emily narrows her eyes, pursing her lips together. They're not their normal, luscious red ... There's a sickly, pale blue to them.

She tries to lift her head higher, but all she manages to do is gulp down another mouthful of water. Her limbs part the water like she's making a snow angel, her next kicks becoming progressively slower. Bubbles break the surface before she gets her nose up.

But her chin stays under.

"Emily!" My heartbeat quickens.

She dips beneath the water again with her eyes scrunched tight. Another swing of her left arm, then her right ...

And then nothing.

She's drowning!

"EMILY!" I shout, reaching over to coil my hands in her shirt. The water has made her heavier. I wrench backwards, grunting, to pull her into the boat.

Her soaked body slams into mine. The boat rocks from the impact. But she's not moving.

"Emily!" I call to her.

Her lips were purple before, and now they're blue from lack of oxygen. Panic fills my heart. *No, no, no!* Laying her down on the boat, I start chest compressions.

"C'mon, c'mon, c'mon!" I beg to whoever might be listening as sweat pours down from my brows.

I tilt her head and press my lips to hers. Her lips are cold as ice.

No, please don't be dead. Please don't!

I offer up two quick breaths before I resume the chest compressions. Seconds pass by, and still, she doesn't respond.

"Emily! Wake up!" I scream as tears start to well in my eyes. "Wake up!"

I keep up the work, alternating between chest compressions and manual breathing. Suddenly, she coughs up a mouthful of water. Then another. And another. She takes a deep ragged breath, turning over, and I slump in the boat beside her, panting.

"You're alright," I whisper as I help pound her back to get the remaining lake water out of her lungs. "You're okay. You're okay."

Warm relief floods through my body, and I hold her close to me. She shivers and coughs, driving her tiny frame against me with each movement. Her body is enveloped in mine, and my clothes collect the water from hers until I'm just as wet as she is.

Groaning, Emily pushes herself back from my embrace. Long strands of her chestnut hair dangle and stick to her neck, and cheeks. She blinks at me with water droplets collecting on her eyelashes like diamonds on tree branches.

In the setting sun, she looks breathtaking.

Like a water nymph that has emerged from the lake.

And here she is, in my arms.

I forget what I was doing ... or why I'm in the boat.

Nothing exists but her.

My hand rises up to cup her face. The confusion in her expression morphs into something bitter, and she pushes me away, scooting as far as she can in the tiny space of the boat and curling into a tight ball.

She flips her middle finger at me and spits out another mouthful of water.

"I am *not* having your babies!"

It takes everything in me to not start laughing at her bravado. She barely survived a brush with death, and yet she's still willing to fight me at every turn.

This girl is beautiful. Unpredictable.

Irresistible. Wild.

She almost died trying to escape me.

"You saved me ..." she finally says as we near the shore.

"Of course I did," I reply.

"Because you need me to marry you?" Her voice is weak, but there's no hiding the strength of her anger towards me.

"No, Emily." I shake my head. "Because I made you a

promise that I'll keep you safe. And when I make a promise, I keep it."

I force myself to stop staring at her nearly transparent clothes. The only sound between us is the sound of the paddles scraping across the water and her labored breathing and occasional cough.

When the boat touches the shore, she turns to me again. "What's so funny?"

"What are you talking about?" I ask.

"You're smiling."

I respond with the only thing that comes to mind. "Because you're safe."

And that's the goddamn truth.

A NUMBER of people have gathered around the lake. They must have been transfixed by the spectacle of me rescuing Emily. Chatter rises up all at once as we near the shore, each person offering assistance and asking questions in a mix of Russian and Croatian.

Among the group I spot a short, older woman with soft curves and blonde braids worn in coils on her head.

"Ivica!" I call out. "Help me."

My head housekeeper hurries over to help me. But Emily wrenches away from both of us, her eyes narrowing in fierce slits.

"Easy now, dear," Ivica cautions.

"Get her cleaned up," I say gently. "Fresh clothes. Warm drinks. You know what to do."

Ivica nods emphatically.

Turning on my heel, I stride over the grass toward the castle, my socks squishing loudly in my shoes. I'm a goddamn mess, but the wind that strokes over my soaked clothes has no chill to it.

The warmth in me is firmly embedded in my veins.

Inside the castle, I pass by the mirror from earlier. This time, instead of my haggard face, I notice something else.

I'm still smiling.

Wiping the expression away, I smooth my damp hair off my forehead and sigh. Emily has a strong spirit. I'll have to stay on my toes around her. But as determined as she was to escape, I'm more determined to stop her.

This isn't the first time she's run from me.

But it will be the last.

21

EMILY

"That's it, dear. Lift up your arms."

I do as I'm told, but I'm moving on autopilot.

The woman, whom Konstantin referred to as Ivica, tosses my wet shirt into a basket.

"My goodness, you are soaked," she says. "Surprised there aren't fish in your ears."

She's been saying one folksy phrase after another ever since walking me back into the castle. I'm obeying because ... well. I'm just too damn tired to fight anyone at this point.

Physically and mentally.

"Pants next." She speaks like someone used to getting her way. Without lifting my eyes from my wrinkled toes, I peel my pants down my legs. She tosses those aside and passes me a fluffy brown towel. "Dry yourself before you catch a cold."

"That's a myth," I mumble.

She blinks. "What's that, dear?"

"You don't catch a cold *because* you're cold." Hugging the towel tighter, I sit on the end of the queen-sized bed.

Directly in front of me is the big window with its lovely view of the lake.

I turn to the left to stare at the wall instead.

Ivica sighs under her breath. "Well, my mother told me that a bad chill can make you weak to sickness, and she was never wrong about anything. Here, let me get you some dry clothes."

She swings her wide hips on her way to the wardrobe. The way she opens the drawers, gathering things, it's obvious she knows where everything is. She could retrieve them even if she was blind.

I push my damp hair from my face. "What are you, his maid?"

"Not since I was fourteen. I'm Konstantin Yurevich's head housekeeper, and I've earned that title through years of good service. Put this on, dear." She tosses me a pair of fleece pants and a loose, long-sleeved top. It would normally be too warm for the room's temp, but I'm shivering.

My failed escape has left me chilled to the bone.

I nearly died.

If Konstantin hadn't saved me, I'd be with my sister right now.

Clutching the shirt, I shove it over my head, and use it to rub away my tears. I'm not sad. I'm *angry*. It's too soon for me to die. I still have to find out who murdered Olivia and why.

When this is all over, you can have whatever you want. All you have to do is ask.

If I can't have my sister back ... then maybe I can use Konstantin to help avenge her death.

There's just one slight problem. A single word that sent me swimming across that lake in the first place.

Babies.

"Are you alright, dear?" Ivica asks.

"It's just lake water from my hair getting in my face." Wiping my cheeks, I slide on the pants, enjoying how soft they feel.

"It feels good to be dry, doesn't it?" she chuckles. "I've been in this castle for years, and I've never seen someone swim across that whole lake except for Konstantin Yurevich and Gerasim Petrovich. Those two love to race each other."

That gets my attention. "Do you know what the word *Kostya* means?"

"It's the diminutive for Konstantin," Ivica explains. When she sees the blank expression on my face, she adds, "An affectionate name, if you will."

"But why do you call him Konstantin Yurevich? I thought his last name was Siderov."

"Oh." Ivica musters a small laugh. "That's his patronymic."

"Patro-what?"

"You're not very familiar with Russian names, are you, dear?"

"I'm afraid not. Care to give me a crash course?"

"Gladly." Ivica smiles. "Every Russian person's name comes in three parts: the first name, the patronymic that tells us who their father is, and the family name. It is considered a show of deference and respect to call someone by their name and their patronymic."

"So," I start. "His full name is Konstantin Yurevich Siderov?"

"Precisely."

"But you wouldn't call him Kostya?"

"Never. Most of us here won't dare address him that way. It's too personal for someone in his position."

"Too personal even for his future wife?" I ask sourly.

"Well." Her cheeks redden before she turns away to pick up the basket of wet clothes. "That depends. My mother always told me that you can tell how close a husband is to his wife, by the name she calls him."

That driver ... Gerasim. He called Konstantin by his diminutive. They must be really close.

I jump up to block her from leaving. "Can you tell me what Gerasim's relationship is to Konstantin?"

Ivica's thin, almost invisibly blonde brows, furrow tight. "I'm afraid I can't do that."

I was starting to feel warm again, but all the ice returns to my blood at once. "Because he's a mob boss?"

At those words, the smile on Ivica's face falls.

"He is not a *mob boss*," she corrects me sharply. "He is a pakhan. For him, everyone in this castle is a member of his personal household, and we owe our lives and livelihood to him." Her expression softens again. "I'm sorry, dear. I shouldn't be cross with you. You are new here. But soon, you will learn. And please don't be angry with him. He's a good man who has his reasons for doing the things he does."

Like kidnapping random women and using them to secure an inheritance?

But I don't say that to Ivica. Instead, I just smile and thank her.

Satisfied, Ivica hunches her shoulder to make herself smaller, bows, and shuffles out of the room. I don't try and stop her from leaving this time. The door lock doesn't click into place, but it doesn't matter.

I'm not going anywhere.

Someone knocks lightly on my door. Before I can respond, the door is pushed open.

I'm preparing myself for Ivica or Konstantin, but it's neither.

A young woman, holding a plate loaded up with artisti-
cally peeled fruit, crusty sugar-laden bread rolls, and deli-
cately sliced roast beef, leans into my room.

"Hello," she says, voice thick with what I can only
assume is a Croatian accent. "Konstantin Yurevich wants
you to eat."

"Does he?" I muse. I want to act uninterested, but the
sight and smell of the food has my mouth watering.

She sets the plate on the table near the window, then
bows at her waist. "I'm also to tell you that your engagement
photo shoot will be tomorrow."

My appetite dissolves into rank mud. He's really in a
hurry. I shouldn't be surprised. "Sounds like Kostya sure is
impatient."

*Like hell I'm going to show him the "deference" he demands
from the staff.*

All the color drains from the woman's face. Covering her
mouth, she gawks at me like I just slathered myself in
pudding. She whispers to herself in another language.

"What?" I ask, blinking. "Can't I call my husband by his
diminutive?"

"Apologies, miss." Her head moves from side to side
slowly. "I've seldom heard him be addressed that way by
anyone else!"

*Well, tough luck, sister. Because if that's the easiest way for
me to get under his skin, then that's exactly what I'm going to do.*

The woman hurries from my room without looking
back. I don't spend any extra time thinking about her
though, because the food deserves my full attention.

Staring down at the food, I remember his comment
about me not being picky. Konstantin has a sharp memory.
Besides his power and influence here in his castle, he's using
every advantage available to make me do what he wants.

It's time for me to do the same.

With both hands, I shove fistfuls of fruit into my mouth. It's not about hunger. It's not even about how delicious the meal is. I barely taste anything with how fast I'm swallowing.

I need my strength if I'm going to make Konstantin regret picking me to be his wife.

22

EMILY

BREAKFAST IN BED IS ONE OF THOSE THINGS RESERVED FOR luxury hotels or Hallmark movies. Both are equally fictional to me, so I'm stunned when I wake up to find a different woman—yet another new face—delivering a silver tray heaped with food. She doesn't linger, doesn't bother to speak. Just a nod of her head before she rushes away.

Sitting up with the tray over my lap, propped on my overstuffed pillows, I marvel at my feast. I went to bed after eating to the brink of pain.

By all logic, I shouldn't be hungry, but my stomach is rumbling.

"It's because there are pancakes," I whisper to myself. "Who can resist those?"

The sunlight over the lake outside my window declares a beautiful day is waiting for me. Birdsong serenades me in a layer of music humans could never replicate. It's straight out of a fairy tale.

Konstantin said he isn't a prince, but he sure lives like one.

If it weren't for the tiny fact that he, you know, fucking *kidnapped me,* I'd be swooning.

Once I'm full of food—and a little extra to top it off—I dig through the closets for something to wear. I'm tempted to put on the ugliest outfit possible for this engagement shoot.

But before I can execute my plan, another girl—new face number four!—pops by to deliver a long gown in a protective sleeve.

I hang it up, unzipping the cover to reveal a calf-length dress that feels like butter under my palms. It's the same green as the lily pads outside my window. Stuck to it is a small note, and I recognize Konstantin's handwriting immediately.

Kitty Cat,

I've taken the liberty of choosing your outfit for today. Put this on. As a reminder, it's not built for swimming. Don't get any ideas. Meet me on the roof.

I yank the dress off the hanger as roughly as possible. If I could rip the threading, I'd be overjoyed, but the expensive material resists.

Sighing, I slip it on and finish getting ready.

Remember, he's just using you.

His biggest mistake is letting me know that.

Fueled by what must've been a pound of pancakes, I march from my room and head toward the stairs that lead to the roof.

He's waiting in front of the helicopter. The large, unmoving blades throw shadows over his face. His long legs stretch into the sunlight, one knee bent, his light brown oxfords gleaming. Not many men can pull off a pale green suit, especially a skinny fit, but Konstantin can.

I hate the fact that he's so absolutely fucking gorgeous.

"You look like you're ready to go on an Easter egg hunt," I call out.

His head snaps up; he spots me, running his eyes hungrily over my body. My insult doesn't even register. And now I'm flustered and hot in a way I really don't want to be.

"Good morning, Kitty Cat."

"Stop calling me that."

"Are you ready for the photo shoot? It's a beautiful day for it. We're very lucky."

"Oh yes, I feel *super lucky.*" Adjusting my dress, I take stiff steps toward the helicopter. His eyes stay on me the entire time; they're like fingers grazing over my naked shoulders. I can feel them in my hair, and I wish they were his actual hands.

The last time I saw him—huddled above me in the boat with concern in his eyes—keeps flitting into my mind. The way he stared at me was a mind-fuck.

It almost made me believe that he *cared.*

Almost enough to make me believe that he wants something *more* than just use me to get his stupid inheritance.

"How far away is this photo shoot?" I ask, frowning at the helicopter.

"It's not a long flight, but the location is easier to access from the air."

"Why? Is it in the clouds?" I snort.

Tugging at the bottom of his jacket, he opens the helicopter door for me. "You're not as far off as you think."

I stop in the middle of climbing into the helicopter to give him a glance.

He grins like a shark. "Don't you want to know?"

"No," I lie, hauling myself inside and into one of the cramped seats.

"Liar," he says, sitting across from me. Our legs nearly

touch in the small space, especially when he leans closer, his tone edged with pride. "This is the spot every Siderov has had their engagement photos taken."

His eyes gleam.

"In the clouds, you said?" I narrow my eyes slowly. "Sounds angelic."

"Exactly, Kitty Cat. This location is supposed to feel like heaven itself."

"I think it would be more fitting if it looked like hell."

Just before the pilot kicks the engine on, sending the blades whirring, I hear Konstantin growl. His hot breath brushes over the side of my face.

He's closed in to make sure I hear him over the noise.

"If this is a preview of how you're going to behave today, Kitty Cat, you're playing with fire."

"Sorry, *Kostya*," I drawl, feeling emboldened to speak a name I'm not allowed to use. *Two can play this game*. "I woke up on the wrong side of the bed, and I have an *awful* migraine."

My seat trembles from how hard he grabs it. "Then for your sake, I hope your *migraine* eases up before we land. Remember the terms of our agreement."

"Don't you worry," I say sweetly. "I can be *very* convincing."

The intensity of his glare sizzles on my skin. But I don't back down.

Konstantin works his jaw as the helicopter noise surrounds us, removing the opportunity for conversation. I mean, he *can* talk if he raised his voice, but that might feel like losing to him.

I haven't seen him yell yet, and he seems more of a quietly in control kind of guy.

But I wonder what he might do when he *loses* control.

I LOOK out the windows as the pilot guides us through the sky. The castle vanishes behind us, and the ground blurs into patches of green and yellow. The hills become chunks of rock that break apart occasionally to reveal big shining streams running through them. The blue makes curling shapes, like a child would scrawl with crayon.

We rise higher, traversing a series of cliffs until the ground fades away in chunks of mist.

In the clouds, I marvel.

I shoot a look at Konstantin and realize he's watching me. *He wants to see my reaction.* I'm amazed at the view, but I refuse to let him know that. Crinkling my nose, I cover my mouth and yawn.

He smirks, seeing through my ruse.

Dammit.

The mist clears away as we lower toward a section of flat gravel. At ground level I see the way the rocks create an arch, and through the big gap, partially hidden by wisps of white mist, is the sea.

When I was younger, Olivia and I would read under our covers with a flashlight. We had to be sneaky because if our parents caught us, they'd yell about how much it costs to replace the batteries.

One of our favorite books was about King Arthur. I adored fantasy, especially when there were stories of knights on horse-back. But what stuck with me the most was reading about the places they'd go. One of them was a mythical island swaddled in thick mists that hid fantastical fae and other magics.

"It looks just like Avalon," I whisper.

Konstantin sits up and blinks at me. I don't know if he

heard me; the helicopter blades are winding down, so it's possible. Blushing, I rise and hurry out of the helicopter. He's right behind me, following me onto solid ground.

"You made it! And right on time!" A young man with slicked-back, wheat-brown hair waves eagerly at us. In one hand he clutches a camera with a lens as big as a car head-light. In his rush to meet us, he loses traction on the gravel and stumbles. Immediately, he hugs the camera close to him, making sure it doesn't hit the ground.

"Are you alright?" I gasp, jogging over to his side to help him stand.

Flashing me a toothy grin, he brushes me off. "Don't worry, the camera is fine!"

I wasn't worried about the camera ... Though in hindsight, I wish it *had* smashed on the rocks. Then this photo shoot would be canceled.

He appraises me, backing away as he does it, like he needs distance to get a better look. "You're his bride-to-be, aren't you? Emily, is that right?"

I cringe. "That's right."

"I'm Josip, the lucky man who gets to take pictures of you. Though *clearly* Mr. Siderov is the lucky one." He brings his camera to his face and clicks the button. "*Bozhe moi,* you are beautiful!"

"I'm paying you to take pictures, Josip, not to ogle my fiancée." Konstantin has joined us. His face is inscrutable, but there's no mistaking the anger in his eyes. Almost as if he doesn't want Josip making such comments about me.

As I live and breathe.

Is he ... actually jealous?

Or is this just another part of this game we're playing today?

I link my hand with Konstantin's, and he twitches in surprise.

"Now, now, dear. No need to get jealous of Josip. He's just doing his job." I offer Josip my most sympathetic sigh. "Kostya *hates* when other men compliment me. He threw the last one out a window."

I glance at the nearby cliff with a drastic frown.

Josip turns white, and Konstantin sees red.

"My fiancée likes to tell jokes," he says tensely. "Let's get to the site while the lighting is good."

"Of course!" Josip babbles. There's sweat on his brow; my subtle warning hit home. He's reacting more than I thought he would though—as if he has a reason to believe Konstantin *would* hurt him.

I try to slip my hand out of Konstantin's, but he grips harder, preventing me.

"Let go," I hiss through my teeth.

"We should be holding hands. It's what couples do."

I turn my hip, bumping it against his as hard as I can.

He grunts, and I say lightly, "Smile, the camera is watching."

The irritation comes off Konstantin in waves, but to his credit, he plasters a smile on his face as we follow Josip down to the shoreline. He walks backward, his camera on us as he snaps photo after photo. He stumbles more than once, but it doesn't slow him down. The pictures don't stop.

Hand in hand like young lovers, we reach a valley of tall stones that create a frame with the sea in the background. Mist furls above and below, giving everything an ethereal tinge.

I can't say a single bad thing about this place. It truly is beautiful.

I glance up at Konstantin, and wonder if he'll look at me in surprise if I were to suddenly shove him over the edge.

"That was *perfect,*" Josip gushes.

I notice he's checking something in his camera's viewfinder. "What?"

"Your expression just now, your hand in his, the mists behind you ... It's the exact kind of energy we need for the rest of this shoot!"

Wonderful.

My fantasy of throwing Konstantin over the edge of the cliff is now somehow going to be forever memorialized as me *gushing* at him.

Bristling, I wrench my hand from Konstantin's. He's looking at me with a smug smirk that I want to wipe off with my fist. A smirk that says *I won.*

We'll see about that.

"Okay, now you two lean against that rock wall right there so I can catch the moment when the wave breaks over the shore!"

Konstantin follows the instruction, motioning for me to join him. Slipping on an indulgent smile, I begin to rest my body next to his—his arm lowers for my waist. At the last second, I jump away with a huff.

"No! I can't!"

Josip lowers his camera. "What's wrong?"

"Yes," Konstantin mutters. "What's *wrong,* Kitty Cat?"

"The rocks are too slimy and wet! My dress will get stained if I touch them!" I make a big show of fluffing my hem, checking it for dirt.

"Stop it," Konstantin says. "Don't be ridiculous."

I widen my eyes as big as possible. "But Kostya, dear, you *know* I hate to get dirty!"

"You jumped into the lake yesterday," he reminds me in a low tone. "Fully clothed, I might add."

"Excuse me." Batting my eyelashes, I shrug indifferently. "You know I slipped in. I'd never willingly jump into the lake with my clothes on. That's silly."

"Right, of course. I guess I forgot how *precious* my soon-to-be wife is." He runs his hand over his face as if he's trying to wipe away his scowl. It doesn't work.

Josip darts his eyes between us nervously. "Why don't we just try a shot with you standing in front of the rocks, not actually touching them?"

"Does that satisfy you?" Konstantin asks me darkly.

I tilt my head like I'm confused. "Why the tone? Did I do something wrong, Kostya?" Before he answers, I slide myself against his body. My fingers tug at his tie as I gaze up at him with a sugary smile. "Please don't be mad at me. I'm trying my best here, I swear."

His lips part as confusion steals his anger away. I like how he flares his nose when I rub my thigh against his leg.

"I'm not mad," he insists.

Oh yes you are. But you can't let Josip to see.

"Is there *anything* I can do to make you feel better?" I purr as my fingers dance along the length of his tie.

Konstantin's hands lower until they're on my waist. Tiny lightning bolts enter my skin where he touches, traveling down to my belly. "Just show him that we're in love so he gets good photos."

Oh, I can do more than that.

Turning around, I grind my ass against Konstantin. My head falls against his shoulder, one arm looping around his neck so I can stroke his jaw. "Like this?" I rub against him harder, peeking at Josip while I do it.

The camera can't hide how much he's blushing.

"Kitty Cat," Konstantin warns under his breath.

"What's wrong, Kostya?" My voice turns husky as my hand scrapes down, slow as tree sap, towards his inner thigh. "Isn't this what you wanted?"

All at once he catches my wrist, pinning my arm against my side. Into my ear he speaks in a low, burning voice that both satisfies my cruelty and wakes up the feral parts of me that want to jump his bones. "Stop it. Now."

"Or you'll do what?" I smirk.

"Oh, Kitty Cat." His voice purrs in my ear, low and dangerous, as he pushes his hips forward slightly. The pulsing heat rests against my ass—hard, insistent, and utterly irresistible. "Don't make me *punish* you later."

Heat sears my cheeks, and I find my hips backing into him as if they have a mind of their own. His throbbing cock is unmistakable against the small of my back, and my nipples stiffen in my bra. His grip around my wrists tightens ever-so-slightly, as if reminding me that if he wanted to, he can hold me down while I struggle and there's nothing I can do about it.

"What's wrong, Kitty Cat?" His other hand circles around my hips, pulling me closer against his erection to him as his warm breath kisses my ear. "No more bravado?"

Is he ... challenging me?

I grind my ass close to him, and draw out an appreciative exhale of air from his nostril in response.

You want to play? Oh, we can play.

"Do you think I should take out my nipple rings?" I ask loudly. "So they don't show up in the photos? Your camera looks pretty high-def." I tug at my neckline, eyeballing my cleavage with worry.

Josip staggers, nearly dropping his camera. Konstantin looks like his spirit is leaving his body.

"You don't have nipple rings," he growls softly in my ear.

"Are you sure about that?"

His eyes narrow drastically. "Last warning."

"Or what?" I whisper back.

"Fine. Have it your way."

Furrowing my brow, I start to ask what he means. The hand around my waist slowly snakes up, stroking across my belly until he curls it around to rest over my navel. With practiced expertise, he gives me a tug and I feel my weight shift upwards against him.

His cock is practically propped against my pussy. To my own frustration, my body betrays me, and I feel myself growing wet in anticipation again.

I swallow uncomfortably and hiss as he pulls me even closer. "Now who's being inappropriate?"

He pushes one leg forward to keep me from scooting away from his throbbing, inviting tip. "You haven't even *begun* to see what inappropriate looks like ..."

My heart thuds wildly in my ribs. I can't pull away. He's got me pinned in place.

And as much as I hate to admit it, I don't think I *want* him to pull away.

"I can *feel* how soaked you are, Kitty Cat." Konstantin presses his nose against my hair, inhales, and pushes his hips forward just enough so that the tip of his cock rubs against my dripping pussy.

My hips squirm, and pleasure spreads through my body at the motion.

He chuckles knowingly behind me as he releases my wrist. His finger trace along my jaw, leaving behind a blazing hot trail in its wake, until it hooks under my chin and turns me to look him in his eyes.

"Fuck you," I grumble. I don't have any other tricks in my arsenal.

Josip whistles sharply, startling us both—Konstantin jerks against me in surprise, and I resist a whimper as his hard-on just grinds deeper through my dress.

"Perfect!" Josip exclaims. "Just perfect!"

Konstantin releases me, dropping to one knee. I wait for him to tie his shoe, because why else would he get on the ground? His eyes travel up to mine. In his hand is a black velvet box. "It should fit," he assures me.

"What should ..." Trailing off, I stand frozen on the spot as he slips a platinum silver ring from the box. His hands are warm on mine, working the ring into place over the knuckle on my left hand.

The engagement ring. How could I forget?

The diamond in the center is as big as a pistachio. There are several smaller ones clustered around it. My heart is beating at such a furious pace, I'm worried not enough blood is getting to my brain. That has to be why I'm so dizzy.

Flashes of light bounce off the diamond as Josip, cataloging every moment of my amazement, snaps one photo after another.

Remember this is all fake!

"I could sell this and buy five Lamborghinis," I whisper coldly.

"Ten, actually." Konstantin starts to smile.

"Let's get a kiss on film!" Josip shouts.

And now I'm starting to panic. A kiss? Now? Konstantin's powerful hand takes me by the small of my back and pulls me close to him. I can *feel* his throbbing erection thudding against my belly. It practically juts against the bottom of my ribcage. Desire pours through my veins like lava.

Holy fucking shit.

If he kisses me now ...

There's no way I'll want him to stop with *just* a kiss.

"Remember, Kitty Cat." He grabs my chin, forcing me to stare into his eyes. "It needs to be believable."

I'm trying to think of a comeback, but my tongue is sticking to the roof of my mouth. Without warning, he crushes his lips to mine, closing the distance in a heartbeat. Pressure and warmth follow behind his lips, setting me ablaze in the heat of his powerful kiss.

My body melts into him effortlessly. His hand tightens on my chin, the other on my back, holding me close to him as my heart matches the pulsing rhythm of his cock throbbing against my belly. I wish Josip wasn't here, because all I want is for Konstantin to throw me down on the ground, hold me down as he rips this dress off me, and fuck me.

Instead, I'm forced to stay still, so close to his cock but yet so impossibly far as Josip captures every second of the ever-deepening kiss.

"All done!"

When did I close my eyes? I didn't even realize I had done it. Now they flutter open, staring into Konstantin's dilated pupils. His heat is *my* heat. Abruptly, he releases me, backs away, and adjusts his tie.

He's putting himself back together, just like me.

Both of us have somehow won and lost at the same time.

I clear my throat. "If we're done, I'll meet you at the helicopter."

He doesn't respond with words, only a simple nod. Then, he bends close to Josip, who is excitedly showing him the photos on his camera's screen.

Fists at my side, I power walk to the helicopter, head held high as I try and pretend that my panties aren't absolutely *soaked*.

The pilot nods to me when I climb into the helicopter. I buckle myself in, using the strap as a way to restrain my body. I have to do something, or I'm worried I'll grab Konstantin and beg him to fuck me right here and now.

Calm down, girl. Get yourself under control.

It's not my fault I'm attracted to him. He's the one with the stupid good looks and climb-on-top-of-me muscular chest.

My reaction is normal.

Super normal.

Konstantin steps up into the helicopter and my heart does a somersault. "Done already?" I ask. "Not going to dissect every photo he took to make sure they're all saccharine perfection, Kostya?"

He freezes, shooting me a long, hard look. Something turns behind his eyes. Facing the pilot, he taps his arm. "Get out."

I wait for the pilot to laugh. To my utter horror, he makes haste to get out of Konstantin's way.

"W-wait," I say anxiously. "Do you know how to fly this thing?"

Konstantin settles in the chair, putting on the headset and flicking some knobs. My stomach drops at the sight.

"I asked if you can fly this." My voice hits the top of my vocal range as all bravado dies in my throat. "Konstantin? Hello?"

The helicopter roars to life, lifting into the air faster than I remember it ever going. I look to the pilot for any sign that this is normal and okay.

He tightens his seat belt and shuts his eyes.

Fuck.

He banks the aircraft hard to the right, sending me

rocking in my seat. I'm not even sitting up straight before he flies us in the opposite direction.

"OH FUCK!" I shriek.

We level out, and I breathe a deep sigh of relief.

With quick, sure fingers, he flips more switches, shoves the stick forward, and sends us diving toward the earth. My heart circles down a drain into my guts.

"KONSTANTIN!"

The sea sweeps below us, waves rippling like monsters breaking the surface. I'm terrified. But when I lift my head, I spot Konstantin watching me from the front. He turns back around hastily, a ghost of a smirk playing at his lips.

And I realize ...

He's doing this on purpose!

Of course he knows how to fly—the pilot would never give him the controls otherwise. Konstantin is trying to scare me to death, but he wouldn't jeopardize his own life. The slow realization that I'm not in any danger turns my heart rate from a-hundred-fifty back to a more manageable eighty.

Still speedy, but reasonable.

With a clearer head, I gaze out the window at the scenery zipping by. It's like being on a roller coaster, the adrenaline making my skin tingle and my breath catch. I don't want to admit it, but ...

I'm enjoying this.

I've always had a taste for thrill rides. Roller coasters, especially the rickety wooden kind that get set up at local summer fairs back home. The ones that were made for kids too young to have a fear of death. Olivia and I would take turns daring each other to get on increasingly terrifying rides. The loser was whoever barfed up their cotton candy and popcorn.

She usually won ... But each of those hot summer nights

spent with her at my side left me feeling like the real winner.

The helicopter comes to a gentle stop on the roof of the castle. Konstantin shuts the engine down, the blades slowing to a gentle swirl. Popping off the headset, he hurries out the door. I follow, though less quickly, as my legs are wobbling.

"Need some help?" he asks me as I hesitate on the edge.

I turn up my nose. "Hardly."

"You look green."

"It matches your suit." I grip the edges of the door, preparing to hop to the ground. "I said I'm fine. Your flying skills suck, but they didn't bother me—ahh!"

The second my feet touch solid ground, my legs collapse. My mind might have come to terms with the thrilling flight, but my muscles are still recovering.

Konstantin loops his arms under my legs and sweep me into his arms before I can completely collapse.

"I told you to be careful." The concern in his voice is almost genuine.

I try to read his expression. My attempt fails and instead I'm consumed by something less logical. His lips, tight in a frown, tease me with the memory of our kiss. His body is strong, holding me up without any effort at all. His biceps are bunched over my arms as they flex to support me.

I want to be pissed at him for a hundred reasons. *Good* reasons. Yet here I am, gazing at his mouth.

And then, I do something reckless.

I grab hold of his face, and pull it down onto mine. This time, without an audience, the kiss feels *real*. The way my heart skips a beat in my chest as his tongue sweeps into my mouth feels real. The way Konstantin squeezes me closer to his chest feels real.

His lips and tongue are like fire, and sets my entire body ablaze.

It's everything I wanted.

And I know he knows it.

Because he suddenly breaks apart from me, sets me on my feet, and backs up just far enough to remove the possibility of this going any further.

Even though I can see his eyes are burning with desire.

I wait for him to say something—anything.

A remark to remind me that this is all fake. That this is all for show. That he's just using me.

But he says nothing, and that's when I know that we're in trouble.

23

KONSTANTIN

I CHECK MY TIE FOR THE FIFTH TIME. IT'S STRAIGHT AS A ruler, the knot symmetrical in all corners, and the black complementing my cream dress shirt. It doesn't need to be smoothed or fixed, but I keep doing it anyway.

Because Emily will be here any second.

In just two short days, Emily has managed to drive me insane in every sense of the word. I've never dealt with anyone like her before. She is determined to make this process be as difficult as she can. Her antics at the photo-shoot tested every bit of self-restraint I had.

I wouldn't trade it for anything else.

No, I wouldn't trade *her* for anyone else.

I tug my tie again until I start choking myself.

"Remember what this is for," I whisper. "She's just a means to an end."

It's become a common refrain to myself in the past two days. Yet each time I say it out loud, I find myself believing it less and less.

"Konstantin Yurevich," the tailor, Buric Kotka, comes in, interrupting my thoughts. "Welcome to my shop."

The man is short, and the measuring tape draped around his neck as yellow as his teeth. Yet his work is top of the line, which is the only reason I've opted to make an excursion from the castle grounds to his shop.

Under protection of dozens of guards all around, of course.

I'm not an idiot. Just last night, Sima informed me that there have been several reprisal hits in Taranto for the men I've killed in New York. Apparently, the corrupt cops on both Ferrata and Siderov payroll are having a hard time keeping things from boiling out to the surface.

If this keeps going, it could spell the end of both organizations.

Augusto should've thought about those consequences when he kidnapped Alisa.

My mood darkens again, and I feel the strong urge to break something.

"Let me go!"

Emily's voice breaks me out of my dark mood and I turn just in time to see her walk through the door, wrenching her arm from Sasha, the *boevik* tasked with bringing her here. She's wearing a simple green blouse and a knee-length lavender skirt. On any other woman, it wouldn't even warrant a second look from me.

But on her? It's positively entrancing.

Sasha bows to me when he sees me, but all I feel is anger when I spot Emily rubbing her arms where the man's hand has been.

I don't care that the man has been loyal to me since the day of his initiation.

He *dares* to manhandle Emily in front of me.

Nobody is allowed to touch her like that.

Nobody except *me*.

In three quick strides, I grab the cuff of his shirt in my fist.

"If I *ever* see you touch her like that again, Sasha," I snarl as I slam him against the doorframe so hard that the wood splinters. "I will kill you where you stand."

"P-please, Konstantin Yurevich!" he stammers. "I was just following your orders."

"My orders." I slam him into the doorframe again, and press my forearm against his throat, cutting off the flow of oxygen. "Were to *bring* her here! Not hurt her, *mudak!*"

Sasha tries to plead for mercy, but his face is rapidly turning red, then purple, and then blue. Anger rolls off me in waves, and I push my arm further into his neck, crushing his windpipe underneath.

Soft and gentle fingers touch my bicep, and I turn to see a pair of dazzling sapphire-blue eyes drilling into mine.

"Stop it!" Emily hisses. "He was just doing his job!"

With a roar, I release Sasha, and he slumps down the doorframe, gasping for air as his face starts returning to its usual color.

"Apologize," I say. "*Eto moi prikaz!*"

"I'm sorry, Konstantin Yurevich."

"Not to me, *mudak!*" I snap. "To *her!*"

"I'm sorry, Emily ..." Sasha immediately turns to her, but pauses when he realizes he doesn't know her patronymic.

I turn to Emily. "He needs to know your father's name to make a proper apology, my love."

My love?

The word had slipped out so easily, so instinctively. Judging by the way Emily's eyes widened, I know that she heard my slip-up.

"Sam," she says. "His name is Sam."

"I'm sorry, Emily Samovna," Sasha says.

"She saved your life, Sasha," I hiss. "You should kiss her feet for that mercy."

"That won't be necessary!" Emily interjects. "Please, stand up, Sasha. You were just doing your job. My fiancé can be just a tad overprotective. Can't you?" She pauses for a moment. "My love."

Those two words shouldn't hit me as hard as they do. Yet hearing them from her lips is like touching a lightning rod.

Sasha looks over at me and then back at Emily, unsure of what he should do.

"Do as she commands," I say. "And then get the fuck out."

Sasha scrambles to his feet, bows to both of us, and heads out, making sure to close the door behind him.

As soon as the door closes, Emily squares off with me. "You shouldn't have done that!"

"He hurt you." I point to her arm.

"That doesn't give you the right to hurt him!"

My eyes narrow in response to her stubborn belief in what's right and what's wrong. There's no fear in her eyes as she glares at me. *She probably thinks I'm a monster.*

She won't be wrong for thinking that. I've *killed* men for far less grievous offenses.

But even without knowing Sasha, Emily was so willing to forgive him, and willing to stand up for him to keep him safe from *me*. It tells me everything I suspected about who she is.

Someone good.

Someone far too good for a monster like me.

Buric clears his throat, drawing our attention back.

I nod at him. "*Dobriy den.*"

"Good morning, Konstantin Yurevich," Buric chooses to respond in English for Emily's benefit. "I am honored that you and your lovely fiancée have chosen to grace me with your patronage."

"Of course, Buric," I reply. "Your reputation precedes you, and I want nothing but the best for my Emily."

"Thank you, Konstantin Yurevich." Buric presses his hand to his chest and bows deeply. "I will endeavor to provide your bride to be with a dress that will far outshine all of my previous work."

With that, he claps his hands, and four women enter into the room. "Fetch the first options for the future Mrs. Siderov."

When the group is out of earshot, I bend close to Emily. "Don't try and have a repeat of yesterday."

Smiling at me, she smooths her hair over her shoulders, twisting the ends. "Give me some credit—I'm more original than that."

I watch her warily as she sways over to the racks of dresses the girls have rolled out. Each one is more elaborate than the rest. Pearls and gemstones are sewn into the gossamer material in impeccable lines. Not a single stitch is misplaced.

Buric is right. These are certain to outshine his previous work.

Emily runs her hands over the bodice of the closest dress, gasping when she touches the rows of diamonds. "It's incredible."

A breath of relief falls from my nose. So far, she's chosen to behave. "I'm glad you like it."

"Like it? I love it!" Running her hand over another dress, she lets out a dramatic sigh and turns to me, a devious look glinting in her eyes. "Kostya."

There it is again. The ease with which she uses my diminutive, as if she's known me and my secrets all of my life. I should rebuke her for this insolence, but I don't. From anyone else, it would've been a measure of disrespect.

But from her?

It's intoxicating.

Buric hooks his thumbs in his belt loops. "I'm happy to show you more options, Emily Samovna."

Emily sighs dreamily, and turns her head, eyes widening as more dresses are brought out. "Oh my gosh!" She scoops the heavy hem of a different dress into her arms. "I don't think I've ever seen anything as beautiful as this!"

Relaxing against the wall, I cross my arms with a pleased smile. The unease at her initial overdramatic reaction cautiously gives way to the possibility that this is *genuine*.

A thoughtful look appears on her face and her brows furrow slightly. "Although." Looking back and forth between the dresses, she continues to stroke their material lovingly. The motion of her fingers makes my pants strain again, and I feel my cock stirring to life at the thought of those fingers wrapped around *me*. "I can't choose."

"Take your time," I say.

"I have a request." She lights up and spins around toward Buric. "But I hope I'm not asking too much."

"Nothing is too much for you," he assures her. "My job is to please you and Konstantin Yurevich."

"In that case." Emily claps her hands together and presses them to her lips, as if she's in deep contemplation. "Can you combine the two?"

The seamstresses around us share a nervous look between them, and Buric's face falls. His hands start worrying over his measuring tape. "That ... would be a challenge. And expensive." He glances at me. Emily does the same, quietly waiting for my agreement.

There's that devious glint again.

I don't like where this is heading. But curiosity goads me on.

"She's the bride," I say calmly. "What she wants is what she'll get. Price is no objection."

"Very well, then." Buric inclines his head, and then snaps his fingers at the seamstresses, barking out instructions in Croatian.

Immediately, they carry the dresses to a long table, setting up their machines and tools to begin picking the stitches apart. Emily watches with her hands behind her back. She rocks on her heels, leaning close for a better look.

I stand behind her, and place a heavy hand on her shoulders. She turns her head to me in response, the scent of honeysuckle and brown sugar wafting towards me as she smiles gently, and I swallow back my own desires for her.

For a second there, I can believe that her smile is *real*.

"May I?" Buric asks as he takes the measuring tape from his neck. I nod, and he pulls Emily aside, quickly and efficiently getting her size. Once he's finished jotting down numbers, he hands them off to the seamstresses.

And true to his reputation, Buric has the new, combined dress ready to go in little under an hour.

It's not complete—that would be impossible—but the two dresses have been combined in a way that shows a glimpse of how the finished version might look.

"There!" he declares, gesturing proudly at the garment. "What do you think?"

Emily cranes her neck to study the dress. She circles it, and as her frown dips, so does my own mood.

"I don't like it."

"You don't?" I blurt simultaneously with Buric.

"No." Shaking her head, she turns her back on us and returns to eyeing the other dresses. "Honestly, I don't know what I was thinking. That dress will be too hot and heavy for the weather. I need something more appropriate, like ... this one." She pulls a floor-length gown.

The one she picks is completely different from the ostentatious one that she had just been cooing over. Thin straps hold it at the shoulder, and its surface has no jewels or pearls.

Buric gazes despondently at the cut-up pair of dresses. He won't say it out loud, but he's mourning the loss of several hundreds of thousands of Euros.

Her *harrumph* makes my hair stand on end. "Never mind, this one won't work either. Unless ..."

Gritting my teeth, I move quickly toward Emily.

She sees me coming and holds her ground. She doesn't cower. If anything, I spot a sly smirk.

"Is everything okay, *Kostya?* I was about to ask if they can alter this gown." Her fingers fly quickly to the neckline. "I *love* the purple here, but I would prefer something ..." She smiles sweetly.

I see what she's about to do before she does it.

"More like *this*."

Before either Buric or I can stop her, she gives it a sharp yank.

The sound of ripping fabric is joined by Buric's horrified cry as he watches Emily rip open the neckline of the dress.

My hands ball into fists. It takes every ounce of control I have to not lash out and say something and do something. It's been years since I've had to work this hard to control my emotions. The last time I failed, my life was turned upside down. I refuse to have another repeat of *anything* like that.

She's a tool, I remind myself. *Tools don't dictate their use.*

"Leave us." I glare at Emily as I command everyone else. "Now!"

Buric and the seamstresses scuttle past us, and when the door clicks shut to indicate that we're alone, that's when Emily's smile evaporates. Something shifts behind her sapphire-blue eyes. It's not quite fear. But it's also not defiance.

It's something else. Something I've seen before.

A *wildness* lurking just beneath the surface.

A wildness that demands to be tamed.

"Do you think this is a game?" I lean in and trap her between my arms.

"Isn't it?" she whispers. "You're the one that said I should be convincing, remember? What's more convincing than a bride who is so *exacting* about what she wants her dress to be that she's constantly making unreasonable demands?"

Her scent is overwhelming, and I feel my control slowly slipping. The tightness in my pants grows ever tighter, and my cock *aches* for release.

To remind her that she's just a tool for *me*.

That *I'm* still in control.

"You were told to choose a dress." Heat creeps up my neck as control continues to slip through my fingers like water. She's too good at getting under my skin. "Not ruin them."

"And I'll ruin a *lot* more until I find the exact one I want." She smiles defiantly. "Kostya."

"Careful, Kitty Cat." I smile dangerously. "I warned you yesterday that I would *punish* you later."

She stares at me defiantly for a heartbeat. The wildness in her eyes returns and my cock stirs to life in response.

"You wouldn't dare," she says. "Not here."

"Wouldn't I?"

I move even closer until my cock is throbbing against her belly through my pants. A surprised gasp escapes her soft lips. But her face also flushes in response, and my smile widens

Hooking my finger under her chin, I force her to look at me. The wildness in their sapphire-blue depths is unmistakable now.

She wants this as much as I do.

"Every dress you ruin." I lean in until I'm mere inches away from her lips, whispering. "Is another hole of yours that I'm going to *destroy*."

I can *feel* her pulse starting to race against my finger.

"And so far," I growl. "You've ruined *three*."

Clutching her jaw with one hand, I undo the buckle of my belt with my other. To her credit, she doesn't shy back from the sound of my pants unzipping, not that there's anywhere to go.

Instead, she tilts her head up a little bit more. Her jaw juts out in defiance, and her dazzling blue eyes betray no hint of fear as I reach down to grip my cock, rock hard and already slick from precum seeping from its angry throbbing head.

The tip of her pink tongue darts quickly between her soft full lips before she speaks.

"Do your fucking worst."

"Good girl." I smile darkly. "On your knees. We're going to start with hole number one."

24

EMILY

Holy fuck.

It's one thing to feel his cock through his pants. But nothing can prepare me to for just how *massive* it looks now that it's jutting up angrily in front of my face.

This is, without a doubt, the largest cock I've ever laid my eyes on. Konstantin's large hand is clenched around its length, and as he lowers me to the ground, he starts to stroke, smearing precum on the massive swollen tip until it glistens.

The smell of soap and aftershave, mixed with his own unique musk overwhelms me, and I shiver reflexively as I clamp my mouth shut.

"What's wrong, Kitty Cat?" His voice is voice silky and dangerous as he asks me the same question from the photo-shoot. "Having second thoughts?"

I want to tell him that I'm not scared. But that would be a fucking lie.

The only thing I can think of is a single thought flitting across my mind.

It won't fit ...

Suddenly, his words—that he'll destroy a different hole for every dress that I've ruined—sound a lot less like a threat, and more like a *promise.*

A promise that I have no hope of surviving.

I stare up at him, and I know that there's no chance in hell I can back out of this.

Because if I so much as dare to open my mouth to beg, he's going to shove that monstrosity deep into my mouth, deeper than anyone has ever reached.

So deep that he really *is* going to destroy me.

Once again, in my own fucked up mind, I feel wetness pooling between my legs. I'm wetter than I've ever been in my life.

Panic mixes with arousal until it's a heady concoction that wakes up every one of my senses and a different thought crosses my mind.

Good girl... he had said to me.

I'll be your good girl.

I shiver again.

Buric and the seamstresses are just outside the door. But I know they won't do a damn thing to stop him.

Not after they've already seen what he can do to one of his own men.

For a moment, I wonder: Is he really going to destroy all of my holes?

The answer comes as soon as the question: of course he is.

Slowly, inch by torturous inch, he pushes his hips forward until the tip of his cock—searing hot and slick with his precum—brushes against my lips. I keep my lips closed, swallowing as a whimper tumble from my nose.

The smile on his face darkens.

His large hand releases my jaw, and for a dizzying

moment, I think that he's changed his mind. The delusion *quickly* goes out the window when it moves behind my head and holds me in place.

There's nowhere for me to go.

"Open your mouth, Kitty Cat." A dark chuckle rumbles from his powerful chest.

I swallow one more time, trembling—but from what? Anticipation? Desire? I don't even know anymore. Slowly, I allow the engorged tip to push past my lips, and over my tongue.

"You've been *dreaming* about this, haven't you, Kitty Cat?" he grunts as he pushes himself deeper until the cock rests at the entrance of my throat and I'm struggling to breathe. "You've been *praying* for me to fuck your throat since Italy, haven't you?"

I try to swallow the moan fighting to punch its way out of my core, and all I manage to do is swallow him deeper.

Yes ...

His hand fists in my hair and gives it a hard yank, making me cry out against the cock and opening my mouth wider in the process. He surges forward until the angry head is throbbing *in* my throat. But he keeps pushing until my nose brushes against the rock-hard surface of his abs.

"Open your eyes, Kitty Cat." He commands me. "I want to look into those pretty blue eyes as I ruin your pretty little mouth."

I obey, looking up at him through a haze of tears that have welled up in my eyes from exertion.

And then finally, he starts to move. The massive cock pulls back in my throat for just long enough to make me think that he might pull it out completely before it rams forward again. I moan and shudder as his other hand wraps around my neck, tightening until he's practically jerking himself off using my throat.

My eyes roll back into my head. I shiver and sputter and choke against him as he face-fucks me without mercy.

Tears leak from the corner of my eyes, running down my cheeks to join the spit and precum leaking from the corner of my mouth. Together, they run down in rivulets down my chin, along my neck, and stain the front of my blouse.

Even if I want to scream at him to stop, I can't.

I won't.

And I know it would be useless because he won't stop.

Not now.

And I don't want him to.

Konstantin grunts with satisfaction, groaning with every thrust as he pounds at my throat without mercy. He buries himself to the hilt with each relentless thrust, forcing the tip of my nose to touch the rippling bands of muscles along his belly before pulling back himself completely back and buries himself again.

The sloppy sounds of my mouth slurping around his cock fills the air, and shamefully, I feel my pussy clenching in response. Slickness fills the space between my legs, running down my thighs and *coating* the back of my calves.

My vision starts to turn black from lack of oxygen. My feet start pitter-pattering underneath me as I beg him to pull back so that I might take a breath to avoid literally choking to death on his massive cock.

With a single roar, he pulls back and suddenly my mouth is free for me to take a long, ragged breath. Air rushes into my lungs, and the blackness at the edge of my vision fade away. But my reprieve is short as Konstantin grabs me by my hair and shoves his cock back in my mouth again.

This time, he leans forward, and I feel him pulling up the hem of my skirt to expose my ass.

His thrusts grow wilder and I *know* he can see just how *wet* I am for him.

"You haven't just been dreaming about this." He snarls above me as powerful fingers move down to my ass and under my panties. "You've been fucking *fantasizing* about this."

A temporary moment surge of panic is chased away by dark, dirty desire as his finger pushes past my cheeks. For a single insane moment, I think he'll push his thick fingers into my ass. When he doesn't, disappointment fills my mind.

"Having your mouth filled isn't enough, is it?" He snarls, drawing out another burst of wetness drips. "You greedy little cock slut."

Suddenly, he thrusts his fingers inside of my dripping wet hole the same time his cock punches deep into my throat. I cry out uselessly against the intrusions on both ends, and my pulse races from the fucked-up pleasure threatening to overwhelm me.

"Are you going to ruin any more dresses?" He demands in my ear as his finger starts to pump in sync with the cock in my throat.

Unable to answer, I do the only thing I can. I shake my head as clearly as I can, even as I gulp him down eagerly.

"Liar ..." he pumps me harder from both ends. "You *want* more. You *need* more. You *like* what I'm doing to you. You *love* it when I'm ruining you and using you. You won't do I damn thing to stop me until I'm leaking out of every one of your greedy little holes."

Yes! Yes! I feel my control slipping. *I want this. Use me. Ruin me. Break me.*

I can't hold myself back anymore ...

I'm going to ...

I'm ...

"That's it!" He hisses above me as his fingers and cock pump me relentlessly from above and below. "Fucking come!"

And I do.

Every muscle in my body tenses up. A scream tears itself out of my throat. The tidal wave of pleasure explodes from deep within my core to the tips of my fingers. Convulsions rock my body and chase away all thought from my mind.

I scream against his cock as my pussy squeezes around his finger, sending further bursts of pleasure stabbing through my body. Writhing against him on both ends, I'm carried higher and higher towards the impossible peak of my climax. A peak so far that I don't know when I'll ever reach it.

Konstantin's fist in my hair tightens and he shoves his cock deep into my throat until there's nowhere else to go. It grows harder for a split second, and then the floodgates open as he cums.

"Don't you dare spit out a single drop, my greedy little cum slut."

Yes! I scream silently. *I'm your greedy little cum slut.*

Obedient, I gulp down his cum as fast as I can, my raw and bruised throat working hard as one salty spurt after another surges down into my stomach. He holds me down in place while the aftershocks of my own orgasm reverberate through me. My eyes roll back as semen fills my convulsing throat, my bulging mouth, and threaten to spill beyond my lips wrapped tightly around his rock-hard length.

When he finally pulls his cock out of my mouth, I fall forward onto my hands, gasping.

"That's hole number one."

My heart races, and I stare up at him just in time as a drop of cum falls from the tip of his throbbing cock onto my face.

He can't be serious, can he? Is he about to fuck me in all of my holes right now? His cock is still rock hard, and I shiver again.

If he fucks me in my pussy and ass the way he fucked my face ...

His hand fists in my hair again and he yanks me to my feet. Pain turns to pleasure in my cum-addled brain as I stand on rubbery knees. He brings me over to the full-length mirror just a few steps away, grips my chin and turns my face towards it.

"Look at what you made me do to you, Kitty Cat."

I gasp when I see my reflection.

My cheeks are tinged red. Two long black streaks of mascara run from the corner of my eyes down my face until they join at the pointy end of my chin. The front of my blouse is completely *soaked* from the mixture of tears and sweat and spit. A single errant drop of cum hangs on the corner of my lips.

He's right.

He fucking *destroyed* me.

And he hasn't even fucked me yet.

Pulling me close against him until his cock rests above the small of my back, he plants a dark bite against the lobe of my ear—just hard enough to send another delicious burst of pain mixing with pleasure in my veins, but still gentle enough to leave no marks.

Holding me even closer, he reaches down and pushes a finger back inside of my dripping wet pussy, teasing another moan from me. Slowly, he starts to move his finger again.

My knees buckle in response, and I'm suddenly glad he's holding me up.

"You're not ready," he whispers.

I whimper as relief floods through me.

And following in its wake, disappointment.

My lip trembles and I almost start pleading that I *am* ready.

"Now, are you going to behave?" He asks.

"Yes ..." My voice rises almost an octave higher as I answer him breathily.

My toes curl as his thick fingers bring me so effortlessly towards the edge of another orgasm.

"You'll pick out a dress?"

"Yes..." I gasp. And then, as if to convince him, I add. "I'll be your good girl."

He stares at my reflection and chuckles darkly as he pushes a second finger into my pussy.

"Liar." His voice rumbles against my back, and his searing hot breath plays at my ear. "Good girls don't get this fucking wet for a monster like me."

25

EMILY
LATER

My whole body is still on fire by the time we return to the castle.

For the past three hours, I've lied in this bed, fanning myself hands over my face with the window open. But despite wearing nothing but my underwear with the cool evening breeze wafting over me, I can't find relief.

I try to convince myself that it's because the castle doesn't have central air.

But I know it's not true.

It's because Konstantin left me a hot fucking mess after the best damn orgasm of my life while his cock punished my throat.

Because he broke just about damn near every boundary I have.

But what's more fucked up is how much I want him to do it again.

I'm actually *disappointed* that he didn't follow up on his threat to destroy all of my holes for the three dresses that I ruined.

The worst part is ... I'm now *actively* thinking about ways to provoke him into doing exactly that.

Good girl... he said when he pushed me to my knees.

I'll be your good girl ... I told him as he made me look at the way he ruined me.

Now that I think about it, fucked-up doesn't even *start* to describe my current state of mind.

I wipe at my neck with both hands as I sink into the comfortable bed. But I don't dare close my eyes. If I do, all I'll see is Konstantin's massive cock in front of my face, and my own cock-drunk reflection staring back at me afterwards.

What did I expect? He'd been upfront with me since the moment he dragged me onto his plane.

I am using you. You are a means to an end.

One kiss that felt way more real than it should doesn't change that reality. One merciless face-fucking shouldn't have awoken my own dark cravings like this.

I can't even say that he hurt me. I mean, yes, my throat and jaw are aching from the punishment that his cock delivered.

But I'd be lying if I say that it wasn't what I wanted from him from the start.

And now, all I want is *more*.

The knock on my door makes me jump. My eyes fly open again and I stare down in shock at my hands between my parted thighs. I sigh as I briefly ponder just ignoring whoever is on the other side.

"I know you're in there, Kitty Cat." Konstantin says.

His voice sends a jolt through me and my pussy squeezes in response. Is he coming to make good on his threat to destroy my other holes? I bite my lip as my hands freeze between my spread thighs. Should I stay like this for him to find?

New heat surges through my blood, and I dip my finger into my pussy, letting out a moan—one loud enough for him to hear. But to my disappointment, the door doesn't open.

Ugh! My eyes fly open and I sit up in frustration.

"What do you want?" I yell, my voice still shaky with arousal.

"I have a gift for you," Konstantin replies.

Warmth sears my face at his words. *No, no, calm down. If he hasn't come in to fuck you, it's not happening tonight.*

"What kind of gift?" I snipe.

"Open the door, Kitty Cat, and see for yourself."

I stare briefly at the puddle of my clothes—ruined by what he did to me earlier today—in the corner and contemplate putting them back on. But when I reach out to pick up the skirt, I stop myself.

No, I think. I want him to see me like this.

Licking my lips, I open the door. If he's surprised by the state of my undress, he sure doesn't show it. He looks just as sexy and dangerous as he did at Buric's shop. The only thing that's changed since I saw him is that he's taken off his tie.

He walks inside and closes the door behind him. It *thuds* shut with a sense of finality.

A fresh burst of wetness pools between my legs. When he turns around, I notice the long box in his hand.

Is that my gift?

Suddenly, my mind goes crazy with speculation at the endless kinds of depravity that might be inside.

"If this is your attempt at provoking me, Kitty Cat." The dark familiar smile returns to his lips as he approaches me. "You're going to have to do better than that."

"What's in the box?" I breathe.

"Your gift," he replies. "I thought about giving this to you when our arrangement is over. But Buric insisted that I deliver it to you now."

Buric? I blink as I accept the box from Konstantin with trembling fingers.

"Go ahead," he says. "Open it."

I pull away the ribbon sealing it shut and holding my breath, crack the lid open.

I gasp when I realize what it is. "Oh!"

At first, I think I'm looking at the dress I wore for Nadia's bachelorette party. It's the same lavender color. But when I shake it out to its full length, I see it's a different dress.

The cap sleeves are shaped into flowers, the middle is fitted, and the neck scoops tastefully low. The back is entirely open from mid-thigh to the upper straps, the bodice is cinched with handmade boning that allows the long hem to drift like an opera curtain, and the slit runs all the way up the thigh. Small buttons—at least thirty of them—made from hand-carved pearl create the closures. The material feels like water in my hands.

"It's beautiful," I admit.

"It should fit you perfectly."

I squint at him suspiciously. "How do you know that?"

"Like I said, Buric insisted that I deliver this to you now. I had him use the same measurements he took earlier today."

That single word—*earlier*—sends a flush to my face again. Turning the dress from side to side, I marvel at the craftsmanship. "He made it so fast." Dragging my fingers over it, I stop fighting my smile. "Did you know this is the color Nadia picked for the bridal party?"

"I didn't pick it for her." He steps closer until he's

standing over me. "I picked it because I know you'd look gorgeous in it."

It takes every inch of concentration not to fall into him.

"Thank you."

"Turn around, Emily." He stares meaningfully at me, raking me with his eyes. "I want to see you in it."

Emily ... I'm so used to him calling me Kitty Cat by now, that hearing my name on his lips sends my stomach looping in excitement.

With trembling hands, I hand the dress to him and turn my back towards him, my heart hammering at my throat.

26

KONSTANTIN

"PUT YOUR ARMS ABOVE YOUR HEAD."

Her thick, wavy chestnut hair shifts in the gentle breeze billowing through the window as she complies with my request. Usually, it's straight as a pin, but sweat has given it some bounce and made it wilder.

Like Emily herself.

She's so close that I can count her freckles and trace the constellation they make over her skin. Her scent—that intoxicating light honeysuckle and brown sugar—beckons me closer. All I want right now is to take her into my arms. To plant my kisses along her neck, her shoulders, her body.

Wicked desire curls in my belly, exiting my lips with each laboring breath.

Keep your composure, I tell myself. *Before you fall so deep that you can't back out.*

"What are you waiting for?" she asks in a shaky voice.

Her delicate shoulders are so close.

I can bite them if I wanted to. Mark them.

Mine. Mine. Mine.

Her fingers curl and open at her hips, over and over. Her

breasts rise upward with every pull of air. Once again, I'm distracted and my cock hardens in my pants.

Pushing my urges aside, I drape the dress over her head. Emily gasps when my hand brings the rest of the dress down around her hips. She pushes her knees together and shifts, as if trying to shield herself from me.

It's not just her face that's red anymore. Her upper chest is flushed as well. And the freckles on her skin darken.

"Hold still," I breathe.

"I am."

She isn't. She keeps trembling, and her hips are swaying from side to side. My hands rest on them to steady her before I grab the button above her lower back, and feed it through its paired hole.

One by one, I work my way up her spine, closing her into the dress.

Emily's breathing quickens when I brush the closure of her bra. I can kiss her shoulder if I want to, and I fucking want to.

But I resist.

"Hmm," I hum.

"What?" She whispers.

"I don't remember you ever being this quiet."

Her shoulder blades pinch together. I can't see her face, and I wonder what she's thinking. If her body is telling the truth, she's spellbound by my touch. I stare at the back of her ear, recalling the light bite I left on it earlier today.

I want a repeat as much as she does.

That much is for certain.

But I can't. It's already hard enough for me to tear myself away from her. It's already hard enough to keep lying that I'm doing *more* than just using her.

I'm doing something *far* more dangerous.

Something that even I don't dare to give shape to, even in my thoughts.

Something that Sima warned me about the moment I brought Emily onto the plane.

Tucking the final button into place, my fingers trace over the soft material, marveling where it creates an upside-down heart on her back.

"Done."

She shivers down to her toes from my touch. "How do I look?"

Holding her hips, I turn her around. When she's final facing me, the world seems to fall away from around me.

She looks absolutely stunning.

The breeze rises again, and sends strands of her hair spiraling. Before I can help myself, I wind her hair in my fingers to brush it aside, exposing her naked shoulders and long neck.

"Well?" she asks.

The dress clings to her waist, enhancing her hips, giving them a rounder look. It covers her breasts but leaves a tanta-lizing gap of cleavage. The watery material clings to her curves, accentuating her beauty. My hands glide down her hourglass figure.

Her eyes widen as mine darken with lust.

"You are the most amazing thing I've ever seen." Slowly, I guide her over to the full-length mirror so that she can see us in there.

Chewing her lower lip, she stares at our reflection and rests her hands on my wrists to brace herself to me until we're locked together. "You have good taste."

I smile. "I chose you, after all."

She stiffens. Like butterflies in a storm, her hands flee mine and she walks away from my grasp, stroking her dress.

Her cheeks glow pink and she does everything she can to avoid my eyes.

And in that moment, both of us know.

This arrangement of ours.

This impending fake marriage.

All of it suddenly risks becoming *very* real.

27

EMILY

THE SMELL OF HAY PERMEATES THE AIR, ALONG WITH THE wild notes of soil and nature and sweat. Some people might find it unpleasant, but not me, because I know exactly what it is.

The fragrance of horses.

"Are these all yours?" I whisper, unable to mute my envy. The stable is massive, containing enough stalls to comfortably house the thirty horses I can count.

"Yes." Konstantin beams proudly at the animals. "My family has owned horses for as long as I can remember."

"They're beautiful."

His smile broadens. "I take it you like horses."

"They're okay." I shrug indifferently. *Fuck yeah, I like horses.*

"Do you have a favorite breed?"

"The Friesian." I say it automatically, proceeding to blush as I give myself away. "Okay, fine, I love horses."

Konstantin's glance is warm as fresh bread. "That breed is actually—" he stops for a moment, his smile widening. "My favorite as well."

We stare at the barn in a beat of awkward silence before I clear my throat. "Why are we here?"

"The wedding venue is best viewed on horseback."

My blood ripples like bubbles in a glass of champagne. "We're going to ride them?" *Yes! Yes! Yes!*

I haven't been on horseback since that one time in college when I went to the rodeo with Nadia.

"How far are we from the venue?"

"About a twenty-minute ride."

"There can't possibly be enough horses here for everyone—not unless you're only inviting a handful of people. How will others be getting to the venue?"

"Once you see it, you'll understand."

I push out my jaw. "Don't you ever get sick of being so cryptic?"

Konstantin shakes his head with a laugh and starts heading toward the stables. I follow behind him, my annoyance washing away as we draw closer to the animals. They poke their heads out of their stalls, their big, intelligent eyes studying us.

A gorgeous brown-and-white Arabian snorts in my direction. "Hey there, buddy," I coo.

"That's Hamlet."

"Hamlet, huh?" I offer my hand for the horse to sniff and he puffs out hot air onto my skin, flicking his ear. He nudges my palm, encouraging me to pet him across his muzzle.

I feel turn and see that Konstantin is staring at me intently.

"You're good with him," he notes.

"Thanks."

"Did you own horses back in Wisconsin?"

I continue to pet Hamlet. "Nope." *We could never dream of affording horses.*

His head tilts to one side. "Then how are you so experienced?"

"You're not the only one allowed to keep secrets," I say.

He doesn't press me for more info. Instead, he gathers up the saddles for the horses and opens up two stable doors. I try not to bounce on my heels as I watch him lead Hamlet out towards me, and expertly buckles the saddle on his back.

Konstantin does the same with an Akhal-Teke with a coat that shimmers like molten gold, and then hoists himself smoothly up.

"This is Midas," he says when he catches me staring. "My pride and joy."

Gripping Hamlet's saddle, I climb onto his muscular back. The animal grunts, flipping his head, but doesn't struggle. I squeeze my thighs to hold myself firmly in place. *It's funny how natural this feels,* I think.

"Ready?" he asks.

The reins slide through my grip. I give them a squeeze, checking how Hamlet reacts to that minor movement. He stamps his front hoof, inching forward—yes, he's wonderfully responsive.

"Ready."

Konstantin leads the way with Midas and I follow. The landscape curves up, like we're leaving a bowl. I glance back over my shoulder at the lake as it gets further away. Memories of falling below the surface, and of waking up to Konstantin's lips over mine.

"Keep up, Kitty Cat!" he shouts at me playfully, breaking me out of my reverie. "Don't fall behind."

He wants me to go faster, does he? Gritting my teeth, I dig my heels into Hamlet. The horse snorts, then trots faster until I come up beside Konstantin, smirking. "Is that better?"

"Does everything have to be a fight with you?"

"What fight?" I throw my hair back, enjoying the way his jaw clenches when he sees. "You said keep up. I'm keeping up."

"Your attitude drips off you, Kitty Cat."

That's not the only thing dripping, I think hotly. But I don't need to say it. Konstantin is choosing his words *very* deliberately.

"You're imagining things."

Facing forward, I smile while knowing he can't see it. Ahead of me are random groves of cypress trees dotting the horizon. Together, they fill the air with their menthol fragrance. I slow down, inhaling with a sigh.

Midas nickers when he pulls up beside me.

"These groves are hundreds of years old," Konstantin says. He waves an arm at the thick, conifer-like branches. "I spent hours here when I was younger."

"Here?" I laugh dubiously. "Hard to imagine *you* running around in the woods."

"I didn't come here by choice. It was meant as a punishment."

"I don't understand."

Konstantin stares up at the trees, but his gaze is far away, seeing something else. "Cypress oil is supposed to calm your soul. It relaxes you when you're angry."

"Sending you off to the trees ... That's one hell of a way to have a timeout."

His tone shifts, taking on a crisper edge. "My grandmother had her methods."

"Is this the grandmother that we need to convince?"

"The very same," he nods. "Come."

Staring at his tense shoulders as he rides in front of me away from the trees, I ponder what I learned. But once we crest over a hill and the trees disappear from view, I stop thinking about his childhood.

"Holy crap," I gush.

We look down towards a deep valley. The rim of a massive trench is poised before me, the grass waving where it dangles into the air. Below us is a field of verdant green dotted by flowers in such a variety of colors I swear there are ones I'm seeing for the first time.

The sea licks at the outer edge of the valley, where it curves like a crescent around a flat section of stone. It's a natural dais surrounded by curved rows of rock slabs that create benches for sitting. You can fit several hundred people here, and when I visualize marching down the aisle in front of them all, my stomach drops away.

Last night, when Konstantin put that dress on me, I know he felt the same thing I did.

That this fake marriage doesn't feel as fake anymore.

I want to make myself not think about it. But it's hard not too when I'm staring at the venue.

"There," he says, pointing at a few areas where the grass has been leveled. "See the helicopter pads? The rest of the attendees who don't come on horseback will arrive that way."

"Not too many people can afford personal helicopters," I sigh.

He arches a dense eyebrow. "You've seen where I live. Do you think my guests aren't as wealthy?"

My stomach is back to wringing itself out.

Mom and Dad would go nuts for him if they ever find out about this.

"Great. Just ... great."

"Let's get a closer look." He taps Midas with his heels and clicks his tongue, heading over a slope that acts as a path into the valley. Hamlet follows behind, tugging at the reins in my hands as I try to make him stay at the rear.

WHEN WE REACH the deepest section of the valley, Hamlet grunts, trotting in front of Konstantin. I laugh in surprise, enjoying how the horse canters in the flower patches.

Maybe it's the way that riding has chafed my thighs. Or how the bouncing motion shifts my hips. But suddenly, I'm seized by a dangerously tempting idea.

A way to provoke Konstantin.

The idea springs into existence so suddenly my mind is one step behind my body. Digging my heels into Hamlet's sides, I lean over the saddle, my face in his thick mane, and we take off.

"Emily!"

Ignoring his shout, I bend tighter against the horse's body. *Go! Go! Go!* Wind rushes through my hair, making my eyes water, but I don't shut them. I need to see where I'm going.

More importantly, I need to be able to go *fast* so that Konstantin will chase.

Hamlet snorts, his breathing loud and heavy as I push him to his limit. He shakes beneath me like I'm hugging an earthquake. Riding is the closest to flying I'll ever get.

I've never felt so alive.

The steep rocks that let us into the valley click under the horse's hooves as he climbs upward. A few bits of rocks break free, bouncing up to scratch my face. I ignore the pain. Nothing can touch me, and nothing matters except going *faster.*

Midas shrieks when he suddenly appears in my path, blocking Hamlet from galloping further. My horse balks, rearing up and retreating back into the grass-covered valley.

"Hamlet!" Konstantin's voice rings out. "Stay."

When Konstantin speaks, he obeys. Panting, the animal turns in place, trotting anxiously.

"C'mon!" I beg, flapping the reins with increasing desperation. "C'mon!"

Hamlet stomps the ground but stays where he is.

Of course he listens to Konstantin ... It's *his* horse.

Konstantin dashes at me on Midas and grabs Hamlet's bridle, murder in his eyes.

"Did you think I wouldn't catch you, Kitty Cat?"

"Actually." I smile at him. "I was counting on it."

Dropping the reins, I throw myself over the saddle, and land hard on the grass. My knees are scraped, but the pain is muted by my adrenaline. Every vein is pounding along with my heart as I sprint through the valley.

Vaulting over the stone benches, I weave through more fields of flowers. Red petals scatter as I shove my way past the stems, bees zooming into the sky, startled by my presence.

Thudding hooves sound behind me, and suddenly I feel myself hoisted off the ground and thrown across the front of Konstantin's saddle.

"Oof!" I grunt.

"Gotcha," Konstantin snarls triumphantly.

I'm struggling on the saddle and he captures my wrist in one of his big hands. Pressing my arms against my back, he bends down and whispers in my ear.

"I know what you're doing, Kitty Cat," he says. "And as much as I love a good chase, you'll have to do better than that."

Writhing under him until my muscles grow sore, I let out a frustrated growl.

His hips shift, rolling against the side of my body. But he keeps my hands immobile, so that even though I can feel the heat between his powerful legs, there's *nothing* more that I can do.

Then, as if to complete my humiliation, Konstantin grabs hold of my legs with his powerful hands and push them apart so that he can spins me onto the saddle until I'm seated upright again.

And completely covered in his embrace.

His legs are pressed tightly against the backs of my thighs, and his groin pushes into my ass.

I gasp as his cock starts hardening behind me.

Reaching around me, he takes my hands and puts them around the reins. The motion pushes his hard chest along my spine, enveloping me in his scent and searing me with his breath.

"If you want me to stop, Kitty Cat," he whispers in my ear as he starts to nibble. "Just say so."

I bite down my lips, and I can *feel* the smile curling on his lips.

His body rubs against mine more firmly and I swallow, fighting down an intense wave of lust that makes my thighs quake. In this position, I'm completely at his mercy. He can do whatever he wants to, and there's nothing I can do to stop him.

I close my eyes and lean back into his muscular body.

As we ride through the grass, the bouncing motion

forces me to sway in the saddle. My ass rubs the front of Konstantin's pants and I can feel him growing harder.

Oh ... I clench my jaw as he presses a searing kiss at the base of my neck.

His arms close in on me, his biceps rubbing lightly over my shoulders, but inevitably, they drift towards my breasts. It's subtle at first, the kind of movement that I might almost mistake for unintentional. But the way he licks up and down the side of my neck, the way his heavy breathing tickles my sensitive skin, and the way his cock is poking so insistently at the small of my back reminds me that he's doing all of this on purpose.

My nipples grow sensitive as we continue. Heat blossoms, slipping through my body until it's pools in my lower belly. Every time the horse rocks, my pussy rubs the saddle. Between this and Konstantin's arms on my breasts, I'm growing slick between my legs.

"I can smell how *wet* you are, Kitty Cat."

I sit up straighter, but this just makes my breasts rub harder against his arms. A whimper escapes me. "You're imagining things."

"Am I?" he asks softly. His hands holding the reins dip lower and he releases one, setting it on my right thigh. I gasp as his fingers dance their way along my inner thigh. "Are you calling me a liar, my greedy little cock slut?"

My pussy clenches in response.

"Let's find out who's telling the truth."

He slides his hand right over the front of the thin material of my riding pants. The heat of his hand is overwhelming. When he presses his hand against my soaked pussy, I can *hear* my arousal squishing from his touch.

Heat flushes on my face, and my clit throbs.

But I want him to do more than touch.

Suddenly, he pulls away, and I gasp angrily.

I blush harder at how desperate I sound.

"Liar." He chuckles darkly.

Eager to take control back, I edge my ass backward, and press myself against his erection. He hisses appreciatively in my ear as his other hand rises up to squeeze my breast, leaving me the only person holding and steering the horse. My pussy thrums wildly from the reaction I'm getting out of him.

"Is this what you want me to do?" His fingers glide over my pussy through my pants, pressing deliciously against my clit and drawing lazy circles that makes my thighs squeeze against the saddle. He traces my swollen lips, pushing the material inside, lightly at first, then harder.

"Konstantin," I moan. "This is ... this is dangerous ... I can't ..."

"Can't what, Kitty Cat?" He nips at my neck. "Keep us in a straight line?"

"Yes ..." I admit.

All at once his fingers abandon my pussy. I groan through clenched teeth in anguish as my hips begin rocking against him again.

"Don't worry." He returns, but this time, he slips his entire hand down the front of my pants. "I won't let you fall from here."

I know he's telling me the truth.

Pleasure that's been building in me for some time continues to coil tighter. I'm trembling against his chest as he toys with my clit through my soaked panties.

"Oh ..." I close my eyes as pleasure threatens to over-whelm me completely. "Oh fuck ..."

He doesn't reply. Brushing my panties aside, he slides a single thick finger inside of me. I squeal in response and reflexively grind against his hand. The sensation of being filled is glorious.

It leaves me disoriented and fuzzy. But all I want is his thick punishing cock splitting me in two, and I start to lose myself from the pleasure he's drawing from me.

All I care about is release from the wet heat in my lower belly.

He's going to make me explode.

"That's it, Kitty Cat."

His cock spears into my back. His hand slips under my shirt, and squeezes my breast so hard that it drives all breath out of me. He holds me against him like an instrument, and he the master musician who teases one long wailing note from me after another.

"You *wanted* me to chase you," he purrs. "That's why you started running, isn't it?"

Yes ...

Wet heat overtakes me as he clamps his mouth around the crook where my neck joins my collarbone and sucks greedily against the skin. Pain and pleasure mixes into a whirlwind inside of me as his finger starts pumping my pussy without mercy.

My hands tighten around the reins, holding onto the hard leather for purchase even as my hips begin to buck wildly against Konstantin's.

"Did you think I was going to do something different when I caught you?"

I nod, another whimper escaping my lips as I do so.

"Tell me what you wanted me to do when I caught you." A second finger joins the first, and I can't hold back my moans anymore. "And be specific."

"I ..." It's getting hard to talk now. "I wanted you to hold me down."

"Mmm." His hand slips under my bra and pinches at the sensitive bud of my nipple. My pussy quivers and drips in response to his thick fingers buried inside. "And then?"

"I wanted you to rip my clothes off."

His powerful hand releases my nipple and pushes up until it encloses around my throat. My pulse thunders in my throat as he gives it a gentle squeeze, as if to remind me just how powerless I am in this position with my body pressed against his.

His to play with.

His to use to his heart's content.

"And what happens after I rip your clothes off?" The hand between my legs overwhelms my swollen clit with its searing heat.

"Hold me down." I tremble, closing my eyes to savor the way he's setting my body on fire. "Until there's nowhere for me to go."

"Like this?"

"Yes, just like this," I tell him. "And then ..." I gasp as the hand around his neck moves back down to resume the attack on my other breast aching to be touched.

"And then what?" He presses his searing lips against my ears as both his hands begin moving faster, chasing away all sanity from my mind until I become exactly what he says I am—his slut. A slave to his cock and desires.

"Force my legs apart ..."

"They're already forced apart, Kitty Cat."

My eyes fly open and I turn to stare into his darkening blue eyes. His lips are so close yet so far. All I want is to press mine against them.

I know what I'm about to say, but I'm afraid of saying it out loud.

Because if I do ...

"Say it, Kitty Cat." A third finger enters my pussy, and inhibition flies away like dusts on the wind. "What happens after I force your legs apart?"

"You'll fuck me."

"Be *specific*." His fingers move even faster between my legs. "Be *honest*. And tell me *exactly* what you want me to do."

I've never felt so powerless than this moment, unable to do anything other than to receive the endless pleasures of his hands, his tongue, and his mouth.

I've never felt so *reckless*.

I've never felt so *good*.

And with every passing second, with every racing heart-beat, the words swirling around my cock-hungry brain—the words that he *demands* slowly start to make their way to my lips. His tongue rasps the delicate skin along my neck while his fingers hook inside of me, as if he plans to drag my orgasms out of me.

But not until I confess.

The proximity to the edge of my own pleasure gives me that one final push I needed to say the truth ...

"I want you to fuck me with that huge cock of yours." I confess, whimpering. "I want you to stretch out my tiny slutty hole." His fingers curl, and control starts to crack.

"I want you to make me scream." A tiny flutter starts out deep inside of me. He pulls out a single finger and starts rubbing against my clit.

"I want you to make me beg and lose control while you do whatever you want to me." I whisper on the edge of my sanity. *I'm close ... I'm so close ...* "And don't you dare stop until you've *ruined* me."

"Good girl." He plants a searing kiss against my neck.

Oh God ...

That's when I shatter against him.

"FUCK!" I shriek, throwing my head against his shoulder. My pussy squeezes his fingers, my inner walls rippling as my toes clench and flex in my shoes.

I shudder with the wind blowing through my air and the scent of grass hanging in my nose. The searing heat of Konstantin's breath lathers my skin.

His hand stays in my pants for a few more minutes as we ride through the top of my orgasm. And finally, when I'm done trembling against his hard body, he withdraws and shoves his soaked fingers into my mouth.

"Taste yourself," he nibbles at my ear again. "Taste how fucking sweet your honesty is."

I close my lips against his fingers and suck. The scent of my own arousal floods my mouth. My face is blazing hot, I can't open my eyes even if I want to. A bead of sweat rolls down my face.

Although I'm still riding the aftershocks of my orgasm, I feel unsatisfied.

Unfilled.

OUR LITTLE ESCAPADE apparently took us in the wrong direction, and it takes another half hour of riding before we get back on track. As we ride, I notice Hamlet is snorting, his head low as he walks unevenly.

"Hamlet is limping." I point. "He's bleeding!"

"There are stables at the venue." Konstantin grips the

reins with both hands to slow Midas down. "We can keep going."

"When we get to the stable, he'll need to have the wound washed and disinfected. Otherwise, it could fester. I'd also suggest cold therapy ... An ice pack under his bandages to control inflammation."

I can't see his face because of how we're sitting, but I feel him staring at me. "How do you know so much about horses?"

It would be easy to lie. Which is why I'm baffled when I decide not to.

"I went to vet school."

"You're a veterinarian?"

"Well, that was the plan. Not anymore."

"Why did you stop?"

Searching for the right words, I run my fingers through Midas's mane. "I didn't have a choice."

"Why not?"

"I—" I clench my jaw, hoping he won't keep prying. I don't want to have to tell him about what happened. About the expulsion. About Phil. If I do, it'll make it so much harder to walk away from him.

Because it's damn near hard enough to walk away as is.

"It's personal. Let's just leave it at that."

To my relief, Konstantin doesn't press further as we crest over the horizon. As we arrive at the stables at the venue, I notice that there are a few figures standing nearby.

"Who are they?"

Konstantin tenses up like every joint has become ice. A large, muscular man in a spotless black tailored suit approaches and lowers his head when he sees Konstantin.

"Konstantin Yurevich, Alla Antonovna is here to see you."

My gaze follows Konstantin's as he looks at someone standing behind a wall of men in suits, and right away, I know what they are.

Bodyguards.

I know exactly who's waiting for us.

"Is that?" I ask.

"Yes." His jaw works as if he's chewing something terrible. "My grandmother."

28

EMILY

I'VE NEVER SEEN A WOMAN AS TALL AS HER.

If it weren't for the faint lines all over her face, I wouldn't have guessed she was a day older than forty from the way she carries herself like a haughty queen.

One look and I know she's definitely related to Konstantin. They share the same strong jaw and grim-set eyes, though her left one is cloudy from a cataract.

She adjusts her flowing, beaded tunic-style shirt over her wide-legged pants. The outfit makes her look bigger and more imposing than she already is.

I have a feeling that even if I were taller than her, she'd still find a way to look down on me.

"*Dobriy den*, Alla Antonovna," Konstantin says. He stands like a steel rod has been shoved into his spine. "I didn't think you'd come so soon."

She flips her long, elaborate gray braid over her shoulder. "You knew I'd be here the second I heard from Gerasim Petrovich what you were up to. Leave." She turns her eyes towards me. "I want to speak to this one alone."

"Alla—"

"Don't make me repeat myself."

I'm stunned at the way Konstantin purses his lips and dips his head like everyone else does to him. He gives me a look that swims with concern, and my heart rattles faster.

Remember, I tell myself. *This has to look real.*

She's the one both of us need to convince.

I do my best to straighten out my hair and make sure that I don't have any signs of what Konstantin and I just did earlier. Is my face still flushed? Can she see just how much of a mess I was earlier?

Alla's eyes zero in on me. The ferocity of her gaze nearly sends me stumbling backward. Konstantin is no more than a few yards away, but I feel like I'm alone on an island with this woman.

I clear my throat. "Nice to meet you, Alla. I'm—"

"Your name isn't important to me," she says coldly. "I'll forget it by nightfall."

I wither under her tone. "Are you angry at me?"

"Does a dog feel anger at its fleas? No, my anger is reserved for my stupid grandson." Her stabbing attention darts briefly to him before returning to me. "And this *ridiculous* idea of his."

Heat makes the back of my neck sizzle. "Ridiculous?"

"Do you take me for a fool?" she smiles, but the smile never reaches her eyes. They continue to glare at me, as if I'm nothing more than a speck of dirt on her shoe. "I know my grandson's worth. And it is *far* too valuable to be wasted on the likes of you."

My jaw drops. I hadn't counted on her words to hurt as much as they do. From the way Konstantin looked at her from the distance, I knew that this was going to be a tough battle to convince her that this fake marriage is real.

But not like this ...

"I ..." I take a deep breath. *This is it, Emily.* Make it convincing. "I love your grandson."

Alla's eyes become thin slits. She leans closer to me, her slim hands running over her defined jaw. "Liar."

"What?" Panic rises in my throat.

"You don't love him," she says. "Trash like you love things about him, but never him."

Trash. That word sends me spiraling. Alla is talking to me the same way my parents would talk to Olivia. Even the judgment in her eyes is the same. I'm frozen on the spot.

She doesn't believe me.

Which means all of this is already starting to fall apart.

"You're only marrying him for the money." Alla scoffs dismissively. "I can see it in your eyes. I can practically *smell* it on you." she studies my face more intently, a nasty smile twisting onto her face. "How much is he paying you for this, little whore?"

Whore ...

It would've hurt less if she slapped me in the face.

"N-nothing ..." I say hoarsely.

"A cheap whore, then."

"I'm not a whore," I say, feeling panic and indignation squeezing around my heart as Alla sneers at me. "I love him! It's the truth!"

Is it? Do I?

"Don't lie to me again, whore." The smile disappears and she closes the distance between us, her aura suffocating and chilling my bones.

Suddenly, I have the awful premonition of her strangling me.

I try to back away, and that's when she suddenly seizes my forearm, holding me in place with remarkable strength as her talon-like fingernails dig into my flesh.

I bite back the cry of pain that nearly escapes my throat.

She's just looking for a reaction, and I can't give her one.

I can't give her more reasons to doubt this marriage. I can't give her more reasons to hate me than she already does.

"You're either very brave." She chuckles, the sound slippery as oil. "Or very stupid to agree to his scheme. Either way, you can't fool me. I know what my Kostya is doing. He thinks this will convince me into giving *him* control of the Bratva."

Control? I thought he said this was about an inheritance? Curiosity now overrides my fear, and despite her painful grip on my arm tightening, I don't try to escape her anymore.

Is ... is his inheritance the bratva itself?

"Oh." Alla's cruel smile widens. "You had no idea, did you, *devushka*? You had no idea and you still agreed?" She scoffs. "Not only a cheap whore, but a dumb one too."

"I'm marrying your grandson because I love him." I try my best to sound convincing as I repeat myself. "And he loves me."

Does he?

"No, he doesn't." Alla snaps. "He doesn't care about you. Nobody here cares about you. When this is all over and he gets what he wants, he'll cast you aside and forget your name like the gold-digging whore that you are. But I won't." She leans in closer and whispers venomously in my ear. "I'll remember the mockery you helped him make of this family. And I will make you *hurt*. In ways you cannot possibly begin to imagine. *Ponimayesh?*"

My hands and feet have gone numb. All the blood has fled to my brain, working to keep me from passing out.

Above all that is something more painful—a spiky knot

in my guts that works upward, pressing at the backs of my eyes, threatening to become tears.

She's lying, Emily. Don't let her get to you.

But is she?

After all, it's what Konstantin told me from the start, right? He's just using me until he gets what he wants.

Maybe ... the only person to tell me the truth this whole damn time is standing in front of me.

Am I really so stupid that I started believing otherwise?

Suddenly, my nose stings, and I can't stop the tears from welling up in my eyes.

"Save your tears, little whore," Alla says curtly. "You'll need them by the time this is over." And then, releasing me, she calls out. "Kostya! *Idi suda!*"

Grateful to be excused, I step away from Alla, rubbing my forearm where five half-moon shapes are turning an angry shade of red. I want to get as far away from her as I can.

I want to get as far away from this place as I can.

I want to tell myself to ignore her insults because she's a stranger—that nothing she says matters.

But I can't help believe that maybe she's right.

Konstantin doesn't care about me. He'll forget me when this is all over.

Konstantin strides quickly towards Alla, and when our paths cross, he stops me with a gentle touch.

I make the mistake of looking up and our eyes meet.

His widen when he sees the tears in mine. I turn to hide my forearm from his gaze, but one darting glance and I know he's seen the marks.

Slowly, he reaches up and wipes away my tears, his touch impossibly gentle.

And just like that, I am foolish enough to believe that Alla is wrong.

That he cares about me.

That he won't forget me when this is over.

"Kitty Cat," he says, whispering.

"Don't ..." My lower lip trembles as I wrench my face away from his finger. "Please don't ..."

Please don't break my heart.

29

KONSTANTIN

She's crying.

I clench my hands until my forearms cramp.

She's fucking crying.

I'm starting to turn to follow Emily, my instinct guiding my body, when Alla claps her hands together like a thunderbolt and calls out to me in Russian.

"Don't you fucking dare!" she bellows. "Come here at once!"

Knotting up my shoulders, I face my grandmother with extreme patience. Every cell in my body is shaking and I fight the urge to chase Emily down and comfort her. *Why is she crying?* I'm not the type to be softened by someone else's emotions.

But it's happening now.

"What did you say to her?" I ask in Russian.

"Nothing she didn't already know."

"She looked upset."

"She should be." Alla glares at me. "Don't treat me like I'm a fool, Kostya. You've already insulted me enough with your little stunt in Italy." She sighs, shaking her head so slowly her braid doesn't shift. "What the fuck were you thinking?"

"I was thinking about saving my sister," I say curtly. "Who's still just a few weeks over eighteen, in case you've forgotten!"

Alla's slap is whip-quick. My cheek burns but I don't break my gaze. Her eyes flare with rage as she looks at me.

"You were sixteen when you sat in the chair that belonged to my son, you impudent little rat," she says.

I remain silent, and resist the urge to rub my face where the sting lingers.

"Do you think you're the only one who cares about Aliska?" she asks, using my sister's diminutive because it's the only other way she knows how to hurt me. "You think you're the only one who still mourns my Yuri? Never forget that I gave birth to him, that I felt him kick in my womb for months, nursed him at my breast, and held his little hands until he became the man that he was." She stabs at me with her finger. "The man that *your* actions killed."

"Yet you would allow Aliska to be wedded to the very family that *ordered* father's death?"

"I would." She nods. "If that's what it takes to end this pointless war."

"Did you know they tried to kill me?" I ask her. "That's what my so-called little stunt in Italy was. Do you imagine that the future of the Bratva would've been secure if I died that day and allowed it to pass to Alisa?"

"And *this* is your solution?" She casts a furious glance towards Emily before returning her anger towards me. "To marry an American whore?"

My fists shake by my hips. "Don't fucking call her that." I warn her.

"What else would you have me call her?"

"She is to be my wife!" I roar.

"If you wanted to be married so badly." Alla jabs another finger at my chest. "I could've arranged for a union with the Bratva royalties of Moscow, or Kiev. Instead, you went behind my back and brought a *whore* into the house where I birthed your father."

"I am the pakhan, grandmother," I remind her, seething. "Not you."

"A pakhan in name." She dismisses me with a flick of her hand. "Otherwise, why try and fool me with this farce of a wedding?"

"I'm about to satisfy the demands you yourself have set out for me."

"Is the future of the bratva secure?" She cocks her head to the side. "Is the whore pregnant? Can I expect an heir from you by spring?"

Will they expect everything else that comes with a wedding? Emily's questions from the day she arrived at the castle suddenly echoes in my head. *A happily ever after?*

Babies?

And then I remember what she said to me when I pulled her out of the water.

I am not *having your babies.*

Fuck.

"Have you even fucked her?"

Heat rises along my neck. "What I do with my fiancée is none of your concern."

"Your response has told me everything I need to know, Kostya." Alla scoffs. "You tell me that you're the pakhan, but a pakhan must be ruthless. A pakhan must do everything in his power to secure a future for his bratva. If you want to marry this American whore so badly, I can't stop you."

"I'm warning you, grandmother ..."

"But if you want me to hand the signet ring—and by extension the bratva—to you," Alla ignores me as she continues talking. "Then you'll show me that our future is secure. And you'll do that by putting a baby in that whore's belly, whether she wants one or not."

My nails dig into my palm. I can't clench my fists any tighter. I know what Alla is demanding from me. What she's ordering me to do.

"I will not rape her to satisfy your conditions!"

"Then you will *never* get the signet ring from me, Konstantin Yurevich!" Alla flicks her wrist. "If you want to take total control of the bratva, then you will do what the bratva demands. Put a baby in that whore's belly, and I'll give the ring to you. Do you understand?"

I want to yell at her. I want to tell her that what she's asking me to do is unconscionable.

It's wrong.

But I know that the demands of the bratva is rigid and unyielding. No man, neither *boevik* nor a *pakhan*, can reject its demands.

The bratva must always come first, no matter what.

"I understand, Alla Antonovna, but I don't agree with it."

"You don't need to agree with it," she hisses. "You only need to do what's necessary when the time comes. Once you've performed your duty, then and only then will I hand you full control of the bratva."

She lifts her chin and whistles sharply. The pair of guards who accompanied her now rush to flank her as she walks to the ferry.

Once she's far enough, I glance towards the stable. Emily is pressing herself against Hamlet where he leans out of the stall. Next to the huge horse, she seems smaller than ever. Her face rests on his muzzle, her hands petting his neck.

Slowly, I make my way over to her. "Emily ..."

She jumps like I touched her to a live wire. Walking my way, her attention moves from me to just past my shoulder. I know she's eyeing Alla.

She was crying.

I take her hand in mine, shielding her from Alla with my body so that no-one behind me can see her. Emily's fingers squeeze tightly against mine.

"Your grandmother," she whispers. "She doesn't believe that this is real."

No, it's so much worse ...

But I can't bring myself to tell her.

I frown and lay my other hand over top of hers. "She's just overprotective of the family."

"She hates me."

"She hates everyone," I admit. "But she'll allow this marriage to go forth."

Emily blinks rapidly at me. "She will?"

Am I imagining things or does Emily look ... relieved? *Will she still look this way when I tell her what needs to happen next?*

And if I do ... will she hate me for it? Will I lose her forever?

I wrap my fingers more firmly around hers, pull her close, and press my lips to hers.

It's the only way I can stop those endless questions in my mind.

I'VE NEVER WORN A DRESS SO BEAUTIFUL AS THIS ONE.

"You look unbelievable, Emily Samovna!"

I pucker my mouth at how they're addressing me. My desire for more information about this castle and its people has dwindled as the wedding approaches. Now, with the ceremony only an hour away, I'm expending all my energy on not fainting.

The young woman who called me beautiful moves around to view me from every angle. Her dark hair is cut short, enhancing her soft features.

"Yes," she says. "I think he will be delighted."

_He._ She means Konstantin. The group of women—six in total—have been giggling all day as they get me ready for my wedding. They speak almost entirely in either Russian or Croatian, but I can always pick out his name.

They practically swoon every time they say _Konstantin Yurevich._

And every time I hear the adoration in their voice, I get annoyed.

Annoyed? Or jealous?

Exhaling, I study myself in the large, circular mirror. The dress fits me like I was born to wear it. I turn from side to side, eyeing the way it dips along my back in an inverted heart. It really is perfect.

I trace the thin shoulder straps, remembering the way he stood behind me that other night, his skin caressing mine, his cock digging into my thigh. But right now, I have another memory ... one where I allowed him to hear my dark confessions.

"Are you alright, Emily Samovna?" One of the girls frowns. "You're all red."

"I'm fine," I insist, flapping my hands to fan my face.

The door to the bridal suite—a sunroom in another part of the castle—swings open.

"We have to get to the stables," Ivica says urgently at the girls. "*Toropit'sya! Toropit'sya!*"

The group of girls attending me leaps to life, rushing around to grab flowers, extra makeup, and a few last sips from their glasses of champagne. I haven't touched a drop. I'm worried that if I start, I'll be tempted to polish off the bottle.

With me in the middle of the line, they usher me from the room and out of the castle. It's a sunny day, easily the most picturesque weather a bride could pray for. I stare at the clouds and wish they'd turn black as ink.

But I doubt even a thunderstorm would dare delay Konstantin.

Hiking up my dress as we cross the grass to the stables, I catch a whiff of hay. The scent relaxes my rapidly pounding heart. The sight of a familiar horse helps even more.

I rub Hamlet's muzzle. He snorts, tail flicking. "Well, look at that," I say softly. The bandages around his rear leg are clean and crisp. "You're healing nicely."

"Emily Samovna?" A young woman, one of my entourage, hovers by my elbow. "Your ride is this way."

Giving Hamlet a final loving pat, I lift my dress hem and hurry after the girl. When I see the massive white stallion with flowers woven in his hair, I let out a silent gasp. He's *stunning*—no two ways about it. His clean hooves, large enough to crush a pumpkin, are draped in long white fur. Someone has wrapped silver circlets around all four ankles.

The other women stare at me uneasily. One of them clears her throat. "Is it alright?"

"Is what alright?" I ask.

Each of them shares a look. "Can you sit on such a big horse?"

Their wary faces draw a giggle out of me. "I'll be fine."

Gripping the pommel of the elaborate saddle with filigree curling over the edges, I haul myself up onto the horse. The stallion whinnies quietly, holding steady as I adjust.

"Sitting on a horse in a wedding dress is ... a little complicated," I announce.

A woman rushes over, helping to bustle the gown in a way that leaves my legs free without exposing my upper thigh. Another girl drapes some layers of chiffon over my lap, adding to my modesty.

"Take these too." Someone holds up a bouquet of white and yellow roses. I accept it with some resistance. They match the flowers woven into the horse's mane and tail. "Are you ready?"

Cradling the bouquet between my legs, I grip the reins tight.

"Let's go get married," I say with a grin, trying to ease the tension in the air. Except the tension is *inside* of me there's not a single joke in the world that can reach it.

We ride in a group through the cypress trees. *He said these were supposed to be calming.* I suck in a big gulp of air.

It does nothing for my nerves.

When we reach the top of the hill overlooking the venue, I nearly fall off my horse. *What the hell? How many people are down there?* Multiple helicopters and boats—no, yachts—are parked like giant bugs in the distance. There have to be at least three hundred people in the valley. One of the girls with me claps. The others copy her. It's meant to draw attention—and it succeeds.

A wave of heads turn until everyone is staring at me.

I'm going to black out. If I do, will they cancel the wedding?

"It's time," someone whispers at my elbow.

Sitting up as tall as I can manage, I tap the stallion with my heels. Music serenades the valley as my horse begins the descent. I can't help but remember the last time I was here —how Konstantin chased me down, hoisting me onto his horse.

The way he made me come apart ...

Clenching my thighs around the burst of wet heat, I can feel the emotions warring inside of me as I look at the sea of faces. Some are smiling happily, while others judge me in their cups.

Alla, sitting at the front of the row of benches, doesn't bother hiding her disdain for me.

Don't be intimidated by her. Just get this over with. Jutting out my jaw, I do my best to look as regal as I think someone marrying a man like Konstantin should look.

It's funny, I think, as I trot over the layer of yellow flower petals someone has laid out. *All these people ... and I don't know a single one of them.*

I wish Nadia is here.

Nadia ...

I'm overcome with shame as I think about how *I'm* getting married before her.

What kind of friend pulls a stunt like this?

Nothing about this wedding has anything to do with me. I remind myself. *It's all so that Konstantin can get what he wants.*

Even if he kisses me like he cares, even if he touches me like he cares, and even if he wipes my tears away gently. I can't forget that fact.

But sometimes, I dare to imagine otherwise.

My heart thuds against my chest at the thought and I shake my head sharply.

I just have to smile and play my part.

Look convincing.

Make them all believe it's real.

After all, I'm already starting to believe it is.

I lift my eyes and sees Konstantin standing at the end of the natural path that forms the aisle, and I feel my hands tighten against the reins. My horse snorts, retreating and starting to rear.

"Easy, easy," I soothe him.

The sight of Konstantin left me dazzled.

I don't think that will ever change.

Even after our paths inevitably part.

He's dressed in a black suit that hugs him like it's his own shadow. It hugs his legs, his tapered waist, and makes his broad shoulders look even wider. His ice-blue eyes seem lighter thanks to the rich material. That's the only way to explain the glimmer in the stare that's fixated on me.

He almost looks happy.

Suddenly I'm struggling to breathe. I forget to guide my

horse, but people gather near me, halting it in place, and helping me off its back.

Seconds ago, I was surrounded. Now, I stand poised at the end of the aisle, entirely alone.

Go on, Emily ... walk.

My heel skids forward, crushing flower petals behind me as I go. Konstantin never once takes his eyes off me as I approach him. Gerasim is beside him, and though they wear similar outfits, they look nothing alike.

He's watches me almost in the same way that Alla does.

Nobody here cares about you. Alla's voice echoes in my head.

Nobody but Konstantin ... I tell myself.

But even then, I'm not sure if that's the truth.

I didn't ask for this! I want to scream, but I can't. It's too late now.

You can do this. Just get to the end of that aisle and get this over with. Alla has already allowed this marriage to move forward, which means it's almost over.

Right?

Maybe before we go our separate ways, Konstantin will hold up the promise he made me in Buric's shop. My cheeks redden at the thought.

Leave me something to remember him by as I return to my normal life.

My miserable, fractured life, where I have no future, no sister.

And no Konstantin.

The music changes tune when I'm standing in front of him. It becomes slower, sweeter, until it fades with the final note extending out over the sea. Silence hangs like a fruit desperate to be picked before it falls to the ground. In that moment, Konstantin takes a breath.

I *hear* it more than I see it.

Is he nervous too?

No. He can't be.

Someone like him can't be nervous.

I just *want* him to be because it would make him more human.

Because it might be proof that he cares about me.

"Emily Samovna," someone whispers and reaches to take my bouquet. I hand it to her quickly before focusing on the priest in his heavy robes.

Feet shuffle behind us, and Konstantin moves until he stands beside me. Something glints overhead. I steal a glance upwards and see a pair of dazzling crowns being held over both our heads.

The priest begins, his voice carrying words that I can't understand naturally over the valley as he drones on in Russian. The only words I recognize are our names.

Konstantin Yurevich Siderov.

Emily Samovna Sullivan.

Samovna, I think bitterly. *That's not even my name.*

Have I made a terrible mistake agreeing to this? Was I really so foolish as to believe that he won't break my heart? That just because he told me up front that he was going to use me, that this is all somehow okay?

Before I know it, the priest motions to Konstantin to speak, and asks something in Russian. I don't need to understand to know what he's asked.

Do you take this woman to be your lawfully wedded wife?

To cherish and protect.

To love and hold.

Until death do you part?

"*Da*," he says seriously, like he needs everyone listening to believe this ruse.

In that moment, *I* almost believe him.

The priest turns to me, and repeats the same phrase.

When he finishes, I glance at the sea. It's bad luck to imagine drowning on your own wedding day, but I can't resist.

"I—" I clear my throat as the word come out crunchy and soft. Konstantin takes my hand in his, and gives it a reassuring squeeze as if to comfort me. I stare into his icy-blue eyes, and for the first time, it feels like he sees me.

Like really sees me.

"I do," I say.

The priest says something else, and motions his hand.

The crowns are lowered upon our heads, and their weight feels impossibly heavy on my neck.

Konstantin turns toward Gerasim, who reaches into his jacket pocket. He brings out a pair of small, thick rings on the flat of his palm. Konstantin takes both, and hands me one of them.

I drop it.

Someone in the crowd makes a noise of disapproval.

"Sorry!" I gasp, crouching on the ground, brushing aside flower petals as I frantically search for the ring. My face burns like fireside coals when I jump back up with the piece of metal pinched in my fingers.

Konstantin stares down at me, but unlike the angry energy rolling off Alla, he's *smiling*. He catches himself, smoothing the smile over, but the mirth still lives in his eyes as he looks at me.

"Careful, Kitty Cat," he whispers under his breath. "That ring is extremely important."

The priest bobs his head pointedly at me. I take my cue, and reach for Konstantin's hand. I'm trembling violently and there's no way to hide it. The ring with its ash-gray swirl glides into place over his long finger until it passes his knuckle.

He flexes his hand, his fingertips brushing mine. My stomach does a twirl.

"My turn," he says, holding my wrist. He steadies my hand in his firm grip, pressing the wedding ring down my finger until it grazes the engagement ring. The jewelry on my hand is worth more than I could earn in five lifetimes.

But that's not what I'm thinking about.

I wish it was.

Instead, all I keep thinking is a single thought.

Why does this feel so real?

My heart is dancing in my throat, and a blanket of heat hangs off my shoulders. The wedding dress isn't heavy, but I feel it clinging to my skin. In the distance, the horses whinny louder than the crashing waves. I could never picture a wedding as lavish as this for myself.

Yet, if I'd thought it was possible, this is exactly the kind I'd have fantasized about.

The priest announces something to the crowd, and then motions at us once again.

My world shrinks as Konstantin takes my hands in his again. Gone is the wide blue water and the rows upon rows of attendees with their probing stares. His lips part and my knees begin to wobble.

Remember, it has to look real.

His mouth closes on mine, warm and tender unlike his hard kisses before. His hand rises to caress my back, tracing my skin through the materials of my wedding dress. My heart races as his tongue sweeps into my mouth just like it did in Italy.

My hand rises to grip him by his immaculate shirt,

clinging to him desperately as if I'm begging him to never stop kissing me.

This is all supposed to be fake, I remind myself as my lips trap his, nudging harder, deeper, until I can't tell where he ends and where I begin.

I desperately want this to be fake.

Because as long as this marriage is fake, it won't break my heart when the terms of our arrangement is finally over and we go our separate ways. It won't break my heart when I have to confront the reality that this was never going to be something that lasts.

As long as this marriage is fake, I can keep my heart protected and whole.

But as Konstantin pulls me closer, and swallow the moans pouring forth from the bottom of my soul to deepen the kiss, I know—even as my heart starts to splinter and crack—that this is the most real kiss I've ever had.

31

KONSTANTIN

Every time I lift my arm to stare at the ring, my shoulder aches, as if the damn thing weighs a ton.

How can a simple ring feel so heavy?

"Have you eaten?" Sima asks, coming up to me in the corner of the huge white tent. The valley wasn't ideal for the reception, so I had three massive tents constructed on the upper grassy fields. My team assembled them while the ceremony went on, working quickly enough that when I finished kissing Emily, the caterers were already passing out trays of champagne to each attendee as they walked up the slope.

That fucking kiss. Emily's lips were sweet as honey and soft as cream. I refused to drink any champagne afterward to make sure her taste isn't washed away.

"Kostya." Sima nudges me. "I asked if you'd eaten yet."

"No," I admit.

"Then get some before it's gone, even if there's enough food to last all summer. You really went all out."

"Cutting corners at this stage would be foolish."

"All in the name of appearances, huh?" Sima asks.

I look out at the crowd. "Is she surviving out there?" I ask Sima, trying to change the subject.

She's going to hate me when I tell her that the terms of this agreement have just changed.

"For now." Chuckling, he snatches a shot glass off a passing tray. "I'd save her from herself if I were you." Draining it in a single draw, he lets out a laugh that ricochets around the valley. "*Yebats*, never mind the food—this vodka is the good stuff!"

Save her from herself? I move through the tent, acknowledging all who call my name, pausing where I must to spare a word. So far, this wedding is going exactly according to plan.

It's what needs to happen *after* that I'm worried about.

Babies ...

I catch sight of my grandmother. She's difficult to ignore. The bright pink-and-green beaded dress makes her look like a parrot. The circle of men in black and gray suits around her make her stand out even more.

As I pass, her eyes drift up. The single good one spots me, the dark center black as night. She doesn't stop speaking or smiling to her companions. But I can practically hear her voice in my head.

Put a baby in her belly. Whether she wants one or not.

I feel my fists clenching again.

I turn away from her, eyes searching for my new wife.

There!

Emily is surrounded by a crowd. A mixture of acquaintances and bootlickers, they're crowding her as they speak. As I approach, I can hear Emily's voice rising in the evening air as she faces everyone with a tense smile.

"I'm from Wisconsin, actually," she replies to someone.

"How did Konstantin Yurevich meet you in the States?" a woman gapes, covering her mouth like it's a huge scandal.

Emily shrugs. "He didn't—it was in Italy."

"Ah," a man with a thick mustache says knowingly. "That makes more sense."

"There you are, my love," I interrupt. Everyone stares at me, but my attention is reserved for Emily alone. "It's time for our first dance."

She takes my offered hand without hesitation, mouthing 'thank you' silently to me. I pull her away from the crowd. Something hard rubs under my thumb.

The wedding ring.

I let go of Emily when we make it to the glossy platform situated on the grass. The tent still shields us, but we're on the outer edge, the fresh air is a welcome respite. She steps back, eyeballing me with a mild frown as she mutters something I can't hear.

"What?" I ask.

"Forget it." She smooths her hands over her chestnut hair. It's pinned up in an elaborate French twist that leaves her milky neck exposed. It makes her look vulnerable ... and makes me want to scoop her up so I can keep every inch of her safe from the world.

When she walked down the aisle in her gown, all I could think about was how much I want to run my hand over her naked skin.

I swallow down the flash of raw desire. "Are you ready, Kitty Cat?"

Those dazzling sapphire-blue eyes are swimming in emotion. "It has to look real, right?"

I feel my heart breaking at those words. "Right."

Nodding, I take her hands in mine and pull her close.

Just like that night in Italy.

The music starts, and the familiar riff of bachata fills the air. Emily gasps. "Is that?"

"The same band from the Amalfi Coast? Yes."

A sad smile breaks across her face, and all I want to do is kiss it away. "Why?"

"Because this has to look real, remember? And what's more real than the first song we ever danced to?" Crushing the unease as deep in my gut as I can, I sweep her into my arms. "I hope you remember the moves."

"A little," she replies. "But I don't think I've gotten any nimbler on my feet since then."

"Don't worry, Kitty Cat." My lips move to her ear. "Just follow my lead and you'll be fine."

Emily tenses up, her body stiff and heavy as we start. She stumbles through the first couple of steps. People gather to watch us. A few clap along to the tempo, and I hear a loud whistle from Sima. But my attention is only on Emily.

I've wanted this moment since I saw her again.

"Easy on the grip," she whispers.

Loosening my hold on her, I spin her to my right, and catch her around her middle. "Move your hips, remember?"

"I remember," she mutters.

"Good." I tuck a strand of hair behind her ear, smiling. "Like riding a horse."

God, her blush is delicious. Emily narrows her eyes, determined not to fall behind me as the steps get quicker. Others join us on the dance floor. But I don't care about them.

The only thing that matters is Emily in my arms.

Our bodies sync up as she gets into the rhythm. Despite what she said, she's gotten far better than last time.

"You seem pretty nimble to me," I say.

"Maybe because I don't want you to show me up at our wedding."

"Our wedding?" I repeat, lifting an eyebrow.

She darts her eyes to the floor. Suddenly she catches my hands, interlocking our fingers. With a fierce glare that makes her blue eyes shimmer, she quickens her steps. Her legs weave, knees bending, and I'm hypnotized.

She's giving this her all, because she's trying to imprint this memory in her head.

How will she react when I tell her that this *isn't* the end?

Will she hate me for it? Will she call me unfair?

My heart swells the longer we dance. *She's the most stubborn girl I've ever met. Everything is a game to her, and she always wants to win.* Determined ... argumentative ... challenging ... and ready to frustrate me at every turn.

I'm intrigued. Hopelessly drawn to her.

Enamored, even.

Strong people are the only ones who can lead. No one else has the courage to make the choices that matter. Hard choices ... Fuck, no. Impossible ones.

Emily can do it.

She understands what it means to lead the bratva, even if she doesn't realize it yet.

She's exactly who I want for my future.

The music becomes ear-splitting, hundreds of *pops,* like someone is slapping the shaker. Somewhere, a glass shatters.

Only when someone screams do I realize that it's no longer the beat of the music.

It's gunfire.

"What's happening?" Emily yells.

Whipping around with her still wrapped in my arms, I spot multiple figures rushing toward the tents. Some stop, crouching, before aiming their guns and firing again. With the sun falling low behind the sea, the flashes from the muzzles are bright as shooting stars.

"It's the fucking Ferrata!" Sima roars, leaping to my side.

He already has his pistol drawn. He's been carrying it since we got dressed in our suits for the wedding. Taking aim, he fires off a few quick shots.

"Get out of here, Kostya! We'll hold them off!"

Emily shakes in my arms. "What's happening?"

Tucking Emily tightly against me, I check for the nearest way out. The attendees are in a panic, fleeing in every direction and knocking over tables of expensive glassware.

"Kostya!" My grandmother's shriek draws my attention for a brief second. "Help me!"

She's cowering behind a table. Two of her guards are already dead, and the rest are exchanging gunfire. A bullet cracks overhead and I duck, pushing Emily lower and shielding her with my body.

Suddenly, I realize that fate is compelling me to choose.

Emily, or the bratva.

I know exactly which one I will choose.

"Stay low, we need to move!" I tell Emily as I cover her body under mine, and start dragging her towards the nearest exit.

Multiple men are hurrying toward me with their guns drawn. Emily starts to scream, but I hug her to reassure her.

"They're my *boeviki*. We'll be alright."

The first reaches me, his face grim as he waits on my every word.

"Cover us!" I order.

"Yes, pakhan!" they roar unanimously as they take aim at the attackers and let out a stream of bullets from their chattering rifles.

The gunfire is constant now, and I half-drag, half-carry Emily towards safety.

"Don't leave me," she whimpers into my chest.

"I won't." Cradling the back of her head, I glance back over my shoulder.

Sima stands atop of a table with a bottle held in his hand, a flaming napkin stuffed into its neck. He hurls the makeshift Molotov cocktail at the nearest group of Ferrata soldiers. They try to scatter, but not before the bottle explodes in a plume of fire and smoke.

"I told you, Kostya! That vodka is the good stuff!" Sima laughs maniacally, orange glow tracing over his outline as he pulls out his gun. "Now come, you Ferrata dogs! Come and die!"

As much as I want to join him, I need to get Emily out to safety. Holding her closely in my arms, I weave through the chaotic scene. People bump into me as they run away. I trip over bloody bodies dressed in expensive suits and dresses that will never be worn again.

How the fuck did the Ferrata Mafia get here already?

I expected them to react, but not this quickly.

Beneath my buzzing adrenaline comes a flicker of satisfaction. The only reason they would dare break protocol like this to attack a wedding is because I fucked up their plans.

Bullets rip apart the fabric of the tent, and moonlight streams in. A support beam snaps with an ear-splitting *clank.*

"Are we going to die?" Emily whispers.

"Not while I'm around, Kitty Cat." Sprinting out the back of the tent, I look from side to side. *There!* Midas is tied to a post, his eyes rolling with fear from the noise. "Up you go," I place Emily in the saddle, and climb up behind her.

Driven by a fresh desire to protect this woman who doesn't belong in the middle of my bloody war, I take the reins as hard as I can. Midas snorts before he thunders over the grass, snorting with the staccato bursts of gunfire behind us.

By the time the gunfire fades, I spare a look back.

Alla won't forgive me for choosing Emily over her.

But I don't care.

The beautiful venue is ablaze. Whether it's Sima's doing or not doesn't matter. Everything is will turn to blackened charcoal. By sunrise, there will only be a smoldering wreck. No evidence of my wedding night will remain in this place.

But I'm alive.

Emily is alive.

And that's all that matters.

Tightening my embrace around her trembling body, I urge Midas forward towards safety.

32

EMILY

THE HORSES IN THE STABLE SNORT AS WE APPROACH. THEY sense our panic, and how can they not? It's coming off me in sticky waves.

We almost died back there!

Konstantin slows Midas to a trot and then hops off to guide him into the stable. I follow him to the ground. The second Midas is safely encased inside a stall, I grab Konstantin's shoulders from behind and force him to face me.

"What just happened?"

He pulls out his phone, and reads something on the screen. "I didn't think the Ferrata could move this fast."

"The Ferrata?" I ask, recalling our conversation when I first guessed that he was a mob boss. "Are they the ones who took your sister?"

"Yes." He should be looking down in shame, but instead, he holds my gaze as he shoves his phone away and leans against the stable wall.

"No more secrets, Konstantin," I tell him. "Tell me the

whole truth. Everything, from the moment we met until this point. You owe me that much."

He looks at me, his icy-blue eyes shifting as if he's annoyed that he has to explain everything. But to my surprise, he sighs and starts talking.

"Like I told you when we met in Italy, I was there for work," he says, and before I can interrupt, he holds up his hand. "Augusto, the Don of the Ferrata Mafia, invited me to the Zebra Club to discuss terms of peace after fifteen years of war."

My jaw drops. "Is that why you said you happen to know the owner of almost every establishment in the Amalfi Coast?"

"Yes." He nods. "The entirety of southwestern Italy, from Naples down to the Amalfi Coast, is Ferrata Mafia territory."

Hackles rise up on my neck, and my heart starts racing as I slowly start connecting the dots. "Was I in danger when I met you there?"

"That night?" He closes his eyes and shakes his head. "No. You were safe. It wasn't until morning that everything went to shit."

"The shoot-out."

"That was when Augusto tried to kill me." He nods.

"And when you said you had to leave ..." I start. "It was because you found out about your sister, wasn't it?"

"Yes." He nods again. "My little sister Alisa was kidnapped in New York, about a week before the meeting took place in Italy."

A week before the meeting took place in Italy.

Suddenly, I recall what Mom told me as I waited for Konstantin alone on the balcony under the brightening sky.

That junkie is dead. She killed herself a week ago.

Could the two events be related? I fight to keep myself from shivering.

I don't see why not.

After all, someone tried to kill *me* as well, and all I did was be in Olivia's apartment.

"So when we met again in New York," I force myself to speak. "In that apartment ..."

"That was the last place that Alisa was taken to before her trail disappeared entirely."

I gasp, not because of what he says about his sister, but because of the thought that suddenly appears in my head about mine.

Oh Olivia ... Dread coils around my heart and begins to squeeze. *How did you get yourself involved in this?*

"Imagine my surprise when I found *you* in that apartment." He pushes off the stable wall and takes a step towards me, hay crunching beneath his feet. "The girl who allegedly grabbed my bag by accident, almost charmed her way into my bed, and then left without so much as a good-bye."

"That's why you took me with you ..." I say slowly. "It wasn't because you couldn't get me out of your mind like you told me on the plane. It's because you wanted *answers* from me!"

Somehow, despite the fact that the two of us nearly died, despite the fact that I *knew* he was using me from the beginning, the realization that he was only ever interested in me because of his own *curiosity* cuts me deeper than any words from Alla ever could.

He doesn't care about me.

"No, Kitty Cat," he corrects me. "I told you the truth. I *couldn't* get you out of my mind. As much as I wanted answers, I wanted so badly to return that morning to find you back in my bed."

"This inheritance," I start, almost afraid to hear his answer. "What is it? Because when I spoke with your grandmother, she didn't make it seem like it's money."

Finally, he looks away, and I feel my heart slowly cracking in fear of what I might hear.

"It's the family signet ring," he answers. "Whoever holds that ring holds the fate of the bratva in their hands."

"But, why does did she have it?"

He turns and looks at me sharply, and I know that I've just asked a question that I have no right to ask.

No, I think. *I nearly died just now. The least he can do is answer my question.*

And to my surprise, he starts talking again.

"When I was sixteen, I got into a fight with Augusto's son, Domenico." He looks away, his jaw working. "And when it was over, I broke both his legs. My father Yuri commended me for not backing down."

I keep silent, watching as he rubs his face with his hand as an ocean of turmoil play out across his handsome features.

"But my grandmother didn't share my father's views," he says. "She told me that I was reckless, that I was a fool, and more importantly, that I did something that no boss would ever forgive."

He closes his eyes and sighs. When he opens them again, his ice-blue pupils are shimmering. He blinks rapidly as he takes a deep breath to calm himself.

"She was right," he says. "Augusto's retribution came quickly. And it was only by luck that Alla convinced my father to give the signet ring to her for safekeeping on the same night Augusto had him and my mother murdered. For fifteen years, she's held onto it. Even though she allowed me to sit in the chair my father once sat, it's her who still holds the bratva in her hands."

My jaw drops, but Konstantin isn't finished.

"For fifteen years," he says. "She told me that the only way she'll allow me to have that signet ring is if I present her a bride. Without it, I may wear the title of pakhan, but I can't muster the full might of the bratva to save my sister."

"So that's why you needed to marry me," I say quietly.

"Yes." He steps even closer, and the smell of soap and aftershave mixes with the scent of hay and horses. "I should've told you the truth earlier."

"I don't know what I expected." I close my eyes, scoffing softly. "You *told* me that you were going to use me. And yet here I am, feeling sorry for myself when I *knew* what I was getting myself into." I open my eyes and glance up at him. "Since we're both here to tell each other the truths, I might as well tell you mine."

Alarm flits across his beautiful face, and his icy-blue eyes narrow ever so slightly. The beauty mark by his eye shifts. I expect him to say something. But he doesn't.

He's waiting for me.

"That apartment you found me in?" I start. "It belonged to *my* sister Olivia."

Now, it's Konstantin's turn to drop his jaw. He steps closer to me, and his large hand takes hold of my arm even though he stays silent, urging me to say more.

"The reason I left that day in Italy was because I learned that my sister died a week ago." I confess. "The police said it was a suicide by overdose. My parents believed that. But they didn't bother to check, and asked *me* to follow up instead."

His brows furrow, and confusion fills his gorgeous eyes. "Why?"

"Because they didn't care about her," I answer, not wanting to mention Mom asking about Olivia's life insurance. "Because she was always a failure in their minds."

Junkie. Junkie. Junkie.

"But the moment I stepped inside of her apartment ..." I hang my head lower as I speak. "I felt in my heart that Olivia didn't commit suicide. And when that man tried to kill me, I knew that she had to have been murdered. And now ... after everything you've told me. I'm surer than ever that my sister's death and your sister's kidnapping are connected. I don't know *how* they're connected, but they are. There are too many coincidences for them not to be."

He tips my chin up so that he's the only thing I can see. He looks at me with a deep sadness that makes me tremble.

I've never seen him look so vulnerable before.

And there's one more truth left to tell him.

"Do you remember what you said to me on the plane?" I ask softly.

My nose is stinging again, and I know it'll only be a matter of time before the tears come. But I don't care anymore.

I need to say it out loud.

"You promised me that when this is all over, I can have whatever I want." I place my hand on his chest and feel the steady drumming of his heart speeding up. "And what I want more than anything in the world is to have my sister back. But I know that's impossible. So I want the next best thing."

I blink, and the world turns hazy with tears that start running down my cheeks. Konstantin reaches up gently and wipes them away, but each one he wipes away is followed by another.

"If I can't have her back." I sniffle. "Then I want to *avenge* her death."

"Emily ..."

"I know." I turn away from him. "I agreed to this marriage because I wanted to use you the same way you're using me. But somewhere along the way, I did something stupid." Keeping my hand against my chest, I lean toward him. "I started to believe that you actually *wanted* me here with you."

"Emily." The corners of his nose wrinkle, and he bends forward to take my hand in his, pouring his warmth into me as he speaks in a gruff baritone. "I *do* want you here with me."

I gasp at his words. Not because it shocks me, but because I know there's no lie there. Because I know he's serious about what he just said.

I smooth my tongue over my bottom lip as tears well up in my eyes.

"That's why I'm making you a new deal," he continues.

"Which is?"

"Stay here with me," he says. "Be my wife. My *real* wife. Help me take control of this bratva. Help me get my sister back, and I *will* avenge your sister's death."

The moonlight is glowing through the windows of the stable now, casting light along his strong jaw. In the moonlight, he looks like a fierce angel of vengeance.

He told me that he was a monster.

But he's much more than that.

He's *my* monster.

Slowly, I nod my head as my heart starts beating faster than it ever has in my whole life.

"Do you promise?" I ask.

"I do."

Then he wraps his fingers deep in my hair and kisses me.

33

KONSTANTIN

I'M NOT ONE FOR IMPULSE. I LIKE TO PLOT MY ACTIONS OUT, review them, rewrite them, then review them all over again. But sometimes my desire trumps all logic.

It's what led me to Emily, and now, it's responsible for *this*.

I've kissed her countless times before now. Each time has been different but amazing.

This is beyond any of them.

She whimpers down my throat. Her soft hands grab at my shoulders, forcing me closer, demanding more of me. I'm eager to give her everything I can. I bury my fingers deeper into her hair until I've undone her French twist. The long pins holding it together topple to the floor, forever lost among the stable hay.

She fumbles for my black jacket, pushing it down my arms. I help her get it off and toss it carelessly to the floor. Emily ends our kiss long enough to gulp some air before diving in with new energy. With feverish excitement I explore the length of her neck, and then my mouth moves to her shoulders, one after the other, kissing them lightly.

She moans each time, and my cock stirs to life, throbbing in anticipation.

Shifting until I'm behind her, I begin to undo each clasp. It's agonizingly slow work. Every sliver of her skin I reveal makes my cock harder and harder.

Slowly, the dress loses its rigid shape like a cocoon coming undone. Emily breathes heavily, her shoulders shaking as she endures my touch.

"What's taking so long?" she asks.

"I'm giving you the reverence you deserve," I reply breathily. "After all, it is our wedding night."

She shoots a look at me. Her chestnut hair covers most of her face as the wild look returns in her dazzling sapphire eyes.

"What happens if *you* destroy this dress?"

Catching her chin, I force her to look at me. "Then you can do whatever you want to me."

Her pink lips twist into a million shapes before she presses her lips feverishly against mine. Her soft fingers start tugging at my pants, stroking the length of my rock-hard cock.

Clutching her dress in turn, I pull it down over her hips to free her from it. Underneath, she wears a simple pair of white lace panties and a matching demi-bra. Freckles dot her chest and ribs. They make a path down to the dimples in her hip, like a galaxy full of stars.

"You're beautiful, Kitty Cat."

"Stop it," she says bashfully.

"Never." Taking her wrists, I kiss the insides of them before I tug apart my own tie.

Emily's hands soon join the work, attacking my buttons with less control than I did with her dress. When she exposes my collarbone, she tears the shirt from my chest

"Oh!"

She gasps at my exposed chest, dotted with the tattoos that tell the story of my criminal life. Everything from the stars above my chest to the skulls and crosses beneath them.

But her eyes aren't focused on those.

I know what she's *really* staring at.

Taking her right hand, I place it on my left pec. "Knife scars," I explain.

"From Domenico?"

I answer her with a nod and nothing more. I have no intention of reliving that memory and its awful consequences. Not now, not when those consequences have nearly taken her away from me.

To her credit, she doesn't press any further. Instead, she closes the distance between us and kisses me with a renewed urgency.

My tongue traces the roof of her mouth, and she moans deliciously in response.

Holding her by her middle, I push her against the nearest wooden beam. Her cry of surprise makes the horses shuffle uneasily. "Konstantin, what are you doing?"

"I want to get a good look at the ass you've been teasing me with for days."

"Yes, please." she whispers under her breath. But she puts her chest against the post, presenting her ass to me without any argument.

My cock surges painfully in my pants. Her panties strains over her pussy, the fabric already soaked. But my attention is reserved for her curvy ass—smooth and perfectly shaped. Her petite form fits perfect in my large hands as if she was tailor made for me. Placing my palms on her ass, I lean forward to bite her gently on the shoulder.

"I seem to recall you still owe me two holes for the dresses."

"I do," she moans. She gazes over her shoulder wantonly. Her whole face is beet red, and her eyes are positively *wild*. "Come and take them," she breathes. "I'm your greedy little cock slut, remember?"

My heart thunders in my cock. "Careful what you wish for, Kitty Cat."

I give her right cheek a slap, and she yelps playfully. This time, she doesn't shy away. Instead, she pushes her ass out further, inviting me to spank her again.

And I do.

She whimpers as I leave another red handprint on her delicate pale skin. My own groan of anticipation is loud enough to overpower hers.

I can shove my cock inside of her right here and now, but I won't.

Not until she's begging me for it.

"How badly do you want me to fuck you, Kitty Cat?" I bend down and unclasp her bra, freeing her breasts. I hook my fingers under her panties to peel them away, and marvel at the thin gossamer wetness that follows like silk from her dripping wet pussy.

Placing my hand against her, I give that pussy a single stroke with my finger, teasing out a long moan of pleasure from her throat before I lean in closer to her ear.

"To hold you down until there's nowhere to go," I repeat her own words back to her.

She shudders.

My hands move to grip her creamy thighs, and part them with an effortless push. "To force your legs apart."

"Yes ..."

"To fuck you without mercy." I dip a single finger in her

inviting pussy. She bucks under my touch. "To use your greedy little holes." Her back arches, and her delectable ass rises higher in the moonlight. "To make you scream." I start kneading her breast and tugging on her nipples with my other hand. "Make you come." I kiss my way down her spine, periodically breaking the line of kisses with a tiny little bite that draws out tiny little mewing sounds from her quivering lips.

"Make you beg." My finger pumps faster, and her wetness starts to soak my hand. "And lose control."

"But not yet." I tell her as I flip her around to face me.

"Please, Konstantin!" She bites her lips as she begs. "PLEASE!"

"You're not ready yet, Kitty Cat." I drape my fingers over her inner thighs, spreading her legs wider.

"I am ready ..." she protests. "I swear I am!"

"Not. Yet."

Slowly, I start kissing my way down. Past her long neck, her delicious breasts, her perky little pink nipples that are quivering in the moonlight. Past her flat pale belly dotted with her freckles, until my mouth settles at the space between her legs.

My tongue rides over her lower lips, savoring her pink sweetness. Emily gasps sharply, her thighs squeezing around my head. Her hands wind in my hair, tugging like she wants to stop me, but it's a waste of time.

"Oh!" she whimpers. "Oh fuck! That feels amazing!"

I grin around her clit, letting my tongue make lazy circles around the sensitive nub. My fingers push into her tight walls and spread her wider, stretching her with each inch of my knuckles so that I can drink down her sweet nectar. I can feel her burning up in my hands. I can feel her control slipping against my mouth.

The more insistently I lick, the tighter she squeezes.

Her pussy pulses around my fingers at the same pace as her breathing. I watch her breasts rise, bouncing as she rides the wave of her impending orgasm higher and higher.

Her inner muscles start quivering.

That's it. Come for me, Kitty Cat. I can feel how close you are.

With a ragged moan, she throws her head back, arching into my face. Her orgasm makes her shake down to her ankles. Her sharp heels slide on the hay and I push her against the wooden beam as I support her weight on my face, lapping at her pussy, and making sure I don't waste a single drop.

Her clit twitches against my lips and she shrieks again and again.

She's still trying to catch her breath when I pull away. Her wild blue eyes, drunken with a haze of lust, shimmers with the starlight as she gazes down at me.

Running my thumb along my tongue, I chuckle as I savor her sweet taste. "Now you're ready, Kitty Cat."

34

EMILY

I SHIVER IN ANTICIPATION WHEN HE STEPS BACK, UNZIPS HIS pants, and lets his massive cock tumble out. My pussy squeezes at the sight of it, and the momentary panic that it won't fit flits across my mind briefly.

I'm in over my head.

But I don't care anymore.

Konstantin is the perfect mix of sexy good looks and domineering energy. Men like him don't move with such confidence unless they can back it up.

Temptation like this is as good as surrendering all control.

And I'm more than ready to surrender all control over to him.

He makes me feel good ... Better than anyone has ever made me feel.

The orgasm incinerates the last remnants of sense from my mind.

He grabs a fistful of my hair and tilts my head up before he crushes his lips against mine. I taste my own tangy sweetness, my clit thrumming eagerly at the filthiness of it all.

His muscular body presses up against mine and I reach forward to grab hold of his thick cock—so thick that I can barely wrap my fingers around it.

It twitches appreciatively as silky precum coats my fingers, and my thighs squeeze together at the thought of Konstantin pushing me against the wooden beam and fucking me mercilessly until I break.

He kicks my legs further apart as I quicken my pace.

"Beg me, Kitty Cat." He whispers darkly in my ear, groaning as I rub my thumb along the underside of the swollen tip. "You know what you want me to do."

Say it ...

My eyes flutter open, and the musky scent of our mutual arousal fills the air between us.

"You know the words."

I take a trembling breath. It was one thing to say it when he held me in the saddle against him. But now ... with his cock throbbing in my hands. The monstrous size of it so real and present.

Will I even survive?

Yes ... the little voice that had goaded me forward since day one returns.

I breathe, but my voice dies in my throat.

Konstantin takes hold of both my hands in his, and pins them under my body. Slowly, he pushes the tip of his massive cock past my dripping entrance, but no further. The heat is overwhelming and I feel my every nerve being set on fire.

If I say it now ... If I tell him to do that ...

There would be no going back.

But that's exactly what I want.

I whimper and grind my hips forward to him, trying to

accommodate his large size. But he, like the master torturer that he is, pulls back just enough to keep himself at my entrance. The same empty unfilled feeling from atop the saddle returns.

"Say it, my greedy little slut." He growls in my ear.

I take one more shuddering breath. It's the only way for me to get what I want.

"Please ..." I whimper, and he rewards me by pushing his cock another inch forward, and heat rushes through my veins.

"You like begging me, don't you, Kitty Cat?"

"Yes ..." I whimper.

"You *want* me to ruin you, don't you? To break you?"

"Yes."

He edges himself even deeper until the head of his cock is completely inside. My pussy squeezes in response, trying desperately to pull him in deeper. But he holds himself in check. His massive hands reach underneath my thighs, giving each side a hard squeeze.

He raises one of my thighs and I feel myself stretching to my limit as I start sinking down on to his cock. *Oh my god ...* I realize. He's not even halfway inside yet.

"You can't *wait* for me to destroy this greedy little hole, can you?"

As soon as he says those words, I shudder as another burst of wetness coats his cock. But I know it won't matter. No amount of wetness can save me from what's coming.

No amount of begging can make him stop once he starts.

And I don't care.

"Don't ..." I moan against his lips, and I almost panic when he stops moving. "Don't make me wait anymore. Please. Please. Please!"

He lifts up my other leg until he's the only thing holding me up. Inch by inch, he starts lowering me onto his cock until it's almost impossible for me to breath.

I'm no stranger to sex, but this ... this is different.

This is what it must feel like to be claimed.

To be *owned.*

"Please, what?" he asks with infinite patience even as he continues to spear me slowly. "Be specific, Kitty Cat."

Jesus, fuck, why is that hot too? I work my tongue in my mouth. It feels swollen and sticky. Staring into his icy-blue eyes, my pussy tingles. *Just tell him. Tell him so he can give you what you want.*

It's not like I'm lying.

And it's not like he doesn't know.

My arms are still pinned behind my back as he drains the air from my lungs with a single powerful kiss. Our chests sandwich together. His hard muscles rake over my sensitive nipples. My clit swells and throbs, making me writhe with passion as he impales me—helpless and completely at his mercy—on his cock.

I can't take any more of this.

I can't wait any longer.

"Please fuck me, Konstantin!" I scream. "I want you to ruin me! I want you to destroy me! I want you to make me your dirty little cum slut"

"Good girl." He growls.

It's the only warning I have before my world drops away completely and he yanks me down to the hilt. His cock rocks upwards inside of my ravenous pussy until it feels like it's punched its way past my stomach and into my throat. I squeal, heels kicking helplessly in the air as my body is overtaken by the thrill of it all. Before I have a chance to recover, he raises me up along his impossible length before impaling me again.

The second stroke comes quick and hard, and pushes all air from my lungs as I shriek in pleasure.

By the third stroke, I'm seeing stars.

After that, I lose all sense of who and what I am.

He rocks his hips against mine as he balances me on his forearms. His huge hands grab hold of my ass to control the rhythm and pull me even closer to him with every following thrust. His movements become faster and faster until my blood is singing in my veins.

The motions remind me of the dance in Italy, the dance at the wedding. His cock forces one cry of pleasure after another until my throat is raw from screaming.

I've never felt so simultaneously connected to another body while I'm torn so far from my own. Every small thing he does, I can feel. The tiny hairs on my arms and the nape of my neck stand on end when he scrapes his teeth against my shoulder.

He bites, and I feel my hips start moving as if they are possessed.

I never want this moment to stop.

"Oh fuck! Oh fuck!" I shriek, quivering as the rush of heat starts tingling in my legs. I curl my toes in my heels, grinding against him as I chase the edge of my orgasm.

I'm so close. So fucking close.

"Whose pussy is this?" He asks as his thrusts grows faster and faster as he ruts against me, as he claims me.

"Yours!" I scream as my hands fly out from behind me and wrap around his neck, holding on for dear life.

He pounds mercilessly into me and snarls. "Who do you belong to?"

"You!"

Coming is all I care about. His cock has left my brain empty of all other thoughts.

All except one single, dangerous thought.

My eyes flutter open and for a moment, conflicting thoughts war in my mind.

Because I know what my cock-drunk brain wants right now.

And it's the exact opposite from what I told him three days ago after he pulled me out of the lake.

Should I? Can he?

The massive cock shoves mercilessly to the hilt again, its engorged head pressing at the entrance of my womb. The sensation drives all logical thought from my mind.

His lips meet mine again, and this time, I eagerly open my mouth and send my tongue forward to meet his. My legs wrap around him, urging him to go deeper, harder, faster, until I lose myself to every merciless thrust.

Until we're all that exists in this world.

Until he's the only thing that's real.

Sweat glistens on his muscles in the moonlight, and I can feel his cock growing harder inside of me.

My muscles ache from my need to orgasm. He breaks the kiss and lowers his lips to my breasts, teeth grazing my left nipple, while his tongue lashes the sensitive surface. Sparks explode behind my eyes. I'm dizzy from heat and want.

And that's when it happens.

"Oh God!" I scream, arching my back, forcing my nipple deeper into his mouth. My pleasure rises, crests, and crashes like a tidal wave tearing through a helpless beach-town, leaving me boneless as I writhe and twitch all over his cock.

My pussy clenches in unison with my racing heart, and I relish in the sensation of being filled.

Of being complete.

He's pushed me beyond my limit and I never want it to end.

And before I can stop myself, I scream. "Cum inside of me! Make me yours!"

His shaft swells and thickens beyond what I thought possible. The girth pressing against my quaking walls nearly makes me climax again. A guttural roar punches out from his throat.

That's all the warning that I receive.

His large hands grip my ass and pull me close, holding me in place as thick spurts of warm wet cum surge deep inside of me. The searing hot wave flows past my dripping hole until it floods my womb. He continues to thrust as he cums, as if he's not willing to accept that we're finished.

I wince when he finally withdraws, breath shuddering as he pulls back.

The ache of being empty is a different kind of pain.

When he releases me, I slide down the wooden beam, panting. Resting on his elbows above me, he stares into my eyes as his semen oozing out of me, puddling on the hay beneath us.

He did it ... I think through the haze of pleasure as the aftershocks of our mutual orgasm tremors through my body. *He came inside of me like I asked him to ... and I loved it.*

"Emily ..."

I love it when he calls me by my name, and I push away the tiny hint of doubt nibbling at the edge of my mind.

Kissing his pensive frown, I run my nails through his hair. "Do you think every couple gets a wedding night like that?" I ask breathily.

"Only the wild ones." His eyes turn up at the corners as he smiles.

He hooks his finger under my chin and pulls me in for another kiss. A gentle kiss that's the perfect ending to the insanity of what we just did.

Then, he whispers, "That's hole number two."

35

KONSTANTIN

ONE WEEK LATER

MY FIST TIGHTENS IN HER DARK CHESTNUT HAIR, AND I GIVE IT a hard yank so that our eyes lock in the mirror.

"Look at yourself while I fuck you."

Emily's teeth clench around the pillow, barely muffling her cries as I spear into her from behind. She bucks like a wild horse in response as she stares at our reflections.

When she catches my gaze in the mirror, her body arches instinctively against mine and she pushes her perfect ass against my hips, pussy squeezing my cock with wanton abandon over the edge until I empty myself inside of her.

I collapse into her, panting as my lips brush along her spine to draw a steady line to the small of her back. My cock twitches one final time against her inviting wet warmth before I pull out to marvel at the way my cum oozes from her quivering slit.

We've been inseparable every night and morning since our wedding. One night, I found myself shivering awake with her mouth wrapped around my cock under the sheets until she sucked me dry. I repaid the favor a few hours later in the morning, burying my face between her legs until she woke up screaming as she soaked my chin and the sheets.

Our bodies are dotted with marks that we've left on each other. Her nails run long tracks along my back, and my teeth imprint on her neck, her shoulders, and her hips.

A new understanding seems to have arisen between us since she agreed to be my real wife. Rather than shying back, Emily has embraced it with enthusiasm.

But her enthusiasm only increases my guilt.

I still haven't told her about how my grandmother changed the conditions for giving me the signet ring.

To Emily's credit, she hasn't asked about it.

Because I don't know how I might be able to explain it to her if she does.

I'm afraid that if I tell her, she'll want to leave.

And that's the last thing I want.

"Good morning to you, too." She flips over, her perky breasts glistening with sweat as she pulls the thin sheet over herself.

Before I can respond, a knock comes at my door. I'm tempted to shout at them to leave, but the knock comes again.

"Kostya! It's me!" Sima barks behind the door in Russian.

"Go," Emily says. "We'll pick this up later."

Smiling, I press my mouth around her soft lips before I reluctantly get out of bed and slip on a pair of slacks from the chair nearby. Emily lies back still in the faint glow of the morning outside my window.

Opening my door, I slip into the hallway. Sima stands there, a grim expression on his face. He also looks like he hasn't slept this entire week.

But for less happy reasons.

"Glad to see you're still willing to take the time for the rest of us." He picks at the inside of his palm, toying with an old burn scar.

I wipe my hand over my mouth. "What do you need?"

"It's best if we discuss all this in private."

I cast a glance at the door behind me, knowing that Emily is waiting for me to return. Well, she's going to have to wait. I've wasted enough time already.

Without another word, I follow Sima as he leads me towards my office.

———

"WE NEED to talk about the aftermath of your wedding," he says as soon as the door closes behind us. "And funeral arrangements for the dead."

And in an instant, my good mood is chased away and replaced with guilt. For a whole week, I'd been so enamored by Emily, so obsessed with her, that I've been neglecting both my duties as pakhan.

"What's the final body count?"

"With or without the guests?"

"Without."

"Nine of ours, and thirty of theirs."

"And with?"

"Thirty."

One for one. I hiss. "Not exactly the trade I'd been hoping for."

"The good news is that none of our friends have seen fit to turn their backs on us yet," Sima says quickly. "But the longer we wait ..."

"In that case, send them my condolences," I tell him. "Pay out any widows in accordance to the years of service their husbands gave us, and offer to take care of any children who are now fatherless, motherless, or both."

Sima nods. "That should suffice for now."

"Is that all you wanted to talk about?"

"No." He sighs. "There's more. I have both good news and bad news. Which one do you want to hear first?"

"Let's start with the bad news."

"Fair enough." He unlocks his phone, scrolls until he finds what he's looking for, and hands me the phone. "You're going to want to see this."

Huffing, I sit and accept the phone from him and my heart stops when I see what's on screen.

I'm looking at the building in East Flatbush, the same one that I found Emily at. The same one where Alisa's trail ended.

"What is this?"

"While you've been busy with your new wife, I've been digging around based on the information she provided you," he explains. "I haven't found anything that might help us locate Alisa Yurevna, but I did find this. It's the security camera footage from the building across the street. And the only one that hasn't been scrubbed."

I look down at the video and hit play.

The grainy video is clear enough for me to make out the details. I glance at the timestamp.

Three weeks ago. This must've been right when Alisa was kidnapped.

A man with long hair approaches near the front door of the walk-up at midday. My heart thuds quicker when I recognize him.

It's the same person I killed inside of that apartment.

And he's dragging Alisa behind him.

The video ends.

"Is that it?" I look up. "We know she was there."

"There's more." Sima's face darkens. "Keep going."

I do, and play the second video.

I check the timestamp. A full twelve hours has passed between the first video and this.

It's night time in the video, and the door to the walk-up opens. The hitman I killed walks forward. Behind him, someone else enters into the frame.

I can recognize his tell-tale limp from anywhere.

Domenico.

He lights a cigarette and takes a long drag, the glowing tip throwing the lines of his face into clarity.

"What does this prove, Sima?" I pause the video turn to him. "We know that the Ferratas are responsible for the kidnapping."

"Keep watching." He says quietly. "And look closely."

And then I see it.

There *is* someone else there.

A woman stands behind Domenico around the corner of the entrance, almost completely tucked out of sight. Something about her looks familiar. Domenico takes one final drag on his cigarette, and tosses it on the ground.

And I see the telltale dark chestnut hair.

Emily?

No ... it's not her. This must be her sister, Olivia.

They look nearly identical.

"That's Emily's sister, Olivia." I sigh. "Emily told me that it was *her* apartment where the trail ended."

"Keep watching, Kostya."

Domenico starts to limp towards the steps heading down, but he suddenly stops. Turning around, he walks over towards Olivia. My breath goes still as I watch.

He raises his hand up and beckons her towards him. She

does. And then he does something unexpected. He caresses her cheek, as if they're old lovers, and leans in close to her. At first, I think he's kissing her on the cheek, but when she nods, I realize that he said something to her.

There's a tenderness in the way they're acting, and I feel like a voyeur spying on an intimate moment I'm not supposed to be witnessing.

"There's more."

The video changes. I look at the timestamp. It's a week after Alisa first arrived at the apartment, and a full week before I showed up.

The door to the building opens, and Alisa is the first person to walk out. Her arms are wrapped around herself, and there's no mistaking that she's crying.

My hand balls into a fist around the phone, but I force myself to keep watching.

A man places a blindfold around Alisa's eyes and marches her forward.

Squinting, I press the phone closer and press play again, doing my best to ignore Alisa's fear as she is shoved into a waiting car.

A few moments later, Domenico walks out, flanked with several men.

This time, I don't see Olivia.

"There was no chance that Alisa Yurevna was ever there by the time we arrived," Sima says.

"Is that supposed to be the bad news?"

"No," Sima answers. "The bad news is *who* gave me this footage."

Unease creeps into my chest, and I clear my throat before I ask. "Who?"

"Alexander Vorobyov," Sima says. "One of Gennady Starukhin's brigadiers."

Fuck!

"Did he say anything else?" I start. "Does the rest of the East Coast Bratvas know about this?"

"We can only assume that they do." Sima sighs. "This is starting to get out of hand. I told you it was a bad idea to go to New York."

"I hope the good news you have outweighs this."

"It doesn't, but it's still good news." Sima nods. "Augusto is dead."

The news hits me like a clap of thunder, and glee pours through my body. But at the same time, I feel disappointment running through me at the thought that I won't have the satisfaction of killing him myself.

I glance back at the still image on his phone, and feel any remaining elation evaporate. Sima's right. It doesn't outweigh the bad news so far.

"How?" I ask.

"Heart attack if you can believe it," Sima says. "I asked Zampa if it's true, and he doesn't seem to think so. He's under the impression that father and son might've had a little disagreement. One thing led to another, and here we are."

"He thinks Domenico murdered his own father?"

"That's the theory so far." Sima starts playing with the lighter again. "He wouldn't share any details with me beyond that. Most likely because he doesn't know the specifics."

I rub my face. "Did Zampa say anything else?"

"Nothing more other than the fact that Augusto's untimely death is shaking things up in New York," Sima replies. "Zampa says there's a lot of commotion right now. Tempers are running high, and everyone's jockeying for favors for the transition period."

"That doesn't help us find Alisa," I say.

"No, it doesn't. But it does mean that whatever Domenico and Augusto planned will have been delayed."

"You mean the wedding."

"Exactly. This buys us time, Kostya. More importantly, it leaves the Ferrata Mafia in a temporary weakened state. We might be able to exploit this."

"Anything we do short of a killing blow won't change the overall balance of power." I rub my temples. "Nor does it solve the problem of Alla going behind my back to give her blessings for any potential marriage."

Augusto's death lessened that possibility of that, but it certainly hasn't eliminated it completely.

"I don't understand." Sima blinks. "How can Alla Antonova go behind your back on this anymore? Didn't she give you the signet ring now that you've fulfilled the conditions she set out?"

"No, she didn't." I look at him and shake my head. "She saw right through the whole thing, and she's clarified the conditions upon which she'll hand me total control."

"Which is?"

I sigh as I remember what Alla told me after she met Emily and made her cry. The memories of Emily's tears cause my hands to ball into fists. My nails dig into my palm.

"Kostya ..." Sima insists, urging me to tell him. "What did she say the condition is?"

As much as I hate saying the words out loud, I know I have to.

"The only way my grandmother will release my inheritance," I say as each word breaks off another piece of my heart. "Is after I put a baby in Emily's belly."

36

EMILY

After Konstantin had left from our bed to talk with Gerasim, I got up on wobbly legs, slipped on a robe, and ventured out—driven by hunger and thirst—just in time to catch the two of them walk away with their heads bent low and whispering.

Whatever it is they're talking about, it seemed important.

Against my better instincts, I followed just out of sight behind them to a different wing of the castle.

And now, I wish I hadn't.

With my ear pressed against the door, I can only hear some muffled voices as Konstantin speaks with Gerasim.

Whatever it is, both men sound agitated.

But nothing can prepare me for the next set of muffled words coming from behind the door.

"The only way my grandmother will release my inheritance is after I put a baby in Emily's belly."

I clap my hand to my mouth to stop myself from gasping as soon as I hear them.

A cold trickle of sweat rolls down my ribcage, and I back away from the door.

What did he mean by that? I ask myself. *He can't be serious ...*

I turn, head looking down on the floor as I walk. I'm so wrapped up in my thought that I don't even notice the massive man standing in my way until I crash against him and fall to the floor.

I look up and see that he's not alone.

There's an entire *wall* of men in suits.

Then, they part, and my heart drops away when I see Alla staring at me. Both her eyes, the good one and the one cloudy from cataract, drill into mine, and I fight the urge to shrink back from her.

"Up," she says coldly.

It's not a request. It's a command. I scramble to my feet, and instinctively, my hands clutch around my arms as her withering gaze follows my motion.

"Come."

Heart-rate spiking, I spare one final look at the door, hoping desperately that Konstantin might emerge. If he does, I'll confess that I was listening. He'll be mad, but he'll understand.

But the door remains closed. Konstantin must still be talking with Gerasim.

"Don't make me ask again, *devushka,*" Alla says as she continues to walk.

A man moves behind me gives me a hard shove forward, and I follow after her.

ALLA LEADS me to what seems to be a sun-filled library. As soon as I enter, the guard behind me closes the door with a *thud* of finality, trapping me inside with her. He then stands with his arms folded in front of him and stares forward at nothing in particular.

There's nowhere for me to go.

"Sit." Alla gestures to one of the armchairs by the window as she takes a seat in the one opposite it.

Reluctantly, I obey. Although the chair is in direct sunlight, I feel impossibly cold. My stomach turns uncomfortably. Partly from hunger, but mostly from the fact that I'm trapped in this room with Alla and her guards.

To say that I'm scared is the understatement of the century.

"Something to drink, *devushka?*" she asks, her voice hard as iron. "Tea? Coffee?"

"No, thank you," I look down answer shakily. "I'm not thirsty."

"Liar." A steaming cup of tea on a dish is shoved before me and I look up to see one of her guards towering over me. "It's rude to reject a host's offer."

Realizing that all she's offering me is the illusion of choice, I accept the tea with trembling hand and take a small sip before setting it down on the table nearby. It does nothing to warm me.

The man who handed me the tea takes a step back, but hovers nearby, ready to spring into action at a moment's notice.

"Why were you outside my grandson's office?" she asks. "No lies this time."

"I ..." I chew my lip. Can I even risk telling her the truth? She hates me enough already. What will she do if I tell her that I was spying on him from outside?

Her mouth purses into a line and she inclines her head, demanding that I answer.

I take a deep breath.

There's no way out other than the truth.

"I was listening." I confess.

"I'm aware." She nods. "Why?"

Because I wanted to know just what it is that's so important that he left our bed.

"Talk!" she barks when I take too long to find an answer.

"Because I was curious," I stammer. "I wanted to know what he and Gerasim were talking about."

"What do you think gives you the right to do that?" She scowls.

"I'm his wife," I answer. "I have a right to know what he's doing."

"Do you?" she cocks her head to her side for a second.

Her eye suddenly darts to the man standing behind my chair and she barks a command in Russian.

Immediately, rough hands haul me up to my feet.

Before I can protest, my robe is yanked away, exposing my body for everyone in the room to see.

I yelp in surprise and try to cover myself up, but several tattooed hands wrench mine away, pinning them at my side and holding me still until I'm exposed before Alla.

Her one good eye rakes my naked body, going over every inch in methodical detail like I'm a horse on sale.

For a moment, I have the absurd notion that she'll even ask me to open my mouth so that she can count my teeth.

She says something else in Russian, and I'm turned around for her to examine.

A few seconds later, I find myself flipped around to face her again. The robe is draped haphazardly over my shoulder and I quickly wrap it around myself.

What the *fuck* just happened?

My lower lips start to tremble, but I know better than to show her any sign of weakness.

Pushing my fears deep down to somewhere I can't reach, I stand up just a little bit taller as I meet her hateful gaze.

"Do you imagine that just because of the ring on your finger?" she says softly, venom dripping with every word. "It makes you one of us?"

My heart pounds. "Doesn't it?" I ask back.

"No." Alla shakes her head. "Your ink-less skin is proof that you are not. You are an outsider." She leans forward, and exposes her shoulder to reveal the tattoo of a five-pointed star. "And your marriage is as *worthless* as you are, you gold-digging whore."

Worthless ...

Whore ...

Her word stabs at me like needles, and all I can think of is memories of Olivia as she stood before our parents as they berated her in the same tone. *Useless. Ungrateful. Worthless.*

"I'm not a gold-digging whore." I whisper. "I am *not* worthless. This marriage is real! Konstantin told me so himself."

But even as I say those words, they feel hollow.

The only way my grandmother will release my inheritance is after I put a baby in Emily's belly.

Was *that* why he asked me to be his real wife?

I asked him about babies from the moment I arrived in this castle.

I should've known that his silence *was* an answer!

I've been reckless with him in bed since the wedding, having sex without any protection.

Stupid! Stupid! Stupid!

Alla smirks as if she can read my mind. "What did you hear through that door, little whore?"

The room spins around me, growing colder by the second.

My mouth opens, but no sound comes out.

"Answer me." The smirk on Alla's face twists into a cruel smile as she spares a glance at a guard standing by her side. "Or I'll have Styopa beat it out of you!"

The man cracks his neck menacingly, and I gulp down my fear.

"H-He said ..."

"Speak up!" Alla barks. "And speak clearly!"

My hands ball into fists and I take a trembling breath to steady myself before speaking. "He said that you'll only release the inheritance if he ..."

The words die on my lips.

"If he what, little whore?"

My breaths start coming rapidly, and I have the sudden urge to vomit. But Alla's vicious gaze roots me in place, demanding an answer.

"... If he puts a baby in my belly."

The smile on her face turns sickly sweet as it widens, and her piercing gaze travels down my body until it rests on my belly.

"Has he?"

"I don't know. It's only been a week."

Alla stands up and I snap my mouth shut as she approaches me. She reaches out with those talon-like fingers and grip my arm again.

"Then in that case," she whispers as her fingers dig at my flesh. "You will march yourself back into his bed, spread your legs like the good little whore that you are, and take every drop of his seed until you *are* pregnant."

I wince from pain but I don't dare pull back.

"And if I find out you dare to spill even a single drop anywhere else," she snarls. "I will have you *begging* on your knees for me to end your pathetic little life."

She releases her grip and gives me a slight shove.

"Now get the fuck out so I can have my tea in peace."

37

EMILY

I CINCH THE ROBE TIGHTER AROUND MYSELF AS I WALK IN A daze. I'm not sure of where I'm walking to, or when I plan to stop, but all I know is that I don't want to be anywhere near her.

I should've stayed in bed. My fingers tighten around the robe and I pull it tighter still even though it's as tight as it can be. *I should've just waited for Konstantin to come back.*

The stinging sensation returns to my nose and my lip trembles.

I've never felt so humiliated in my entire life.

"Emily Samovna?" Ivica's warm voice snaps me out of my reverie. When she sees me, a worried expression dawns on her face and she immediately rushes over. "What happened, dear?"

I look at her, and even though there's no malice in her eyes, I don't know that I can trust her.

I don't know if I can trust anyone anymore.

Blinking away my tears, I put on a weak smile, as if I hadn't just been stripped and interrogated by the devil herself.

"Nothing, Ivica," I lie. "I'm just looking for something to eat, that's all."

"Oh," she says, but her worried gaze doesn't change. "Sit, please. I'll bring you a plate from the kitchen." She reaches out and takes her hand in mine. "*Bozhe moi*, your hands are freezing. Do you want a hot drink? Some tea, perhaps?"

I shiver at the offer. I don't want any more tea. I just want to disappear.

I just want to go somewhere where Alla will *never* be able to find me.

Where Konstantin will never be able to find me.

Ivica continues to look at me as she waits for my answer. Widening my smile, I tell her. "No, thank you, Ivica. But I would love some pancakes."

She nods as she guides me to a nearby chair. "Okay, sit for a while. I'll be right back, dear."

Only after she is safely out of sight do I dare to let the tears start falling. Once they start, I can't make them stop even if I want to.

"Kitty Cat?"

I raise my head in alarm when I hear Konstantin's voice, and turn to find him walking towards me with concern in his eyes. *Oh no ...*

I knew I shouldn't have started crying. Now, he's going to ask me why I'm crying.

The fabric of the robe scrunches under my fingers as he closes the distance and kneels down in front of me. He takes my hand in his, chasing the cold that's wrapped itself around my heart away.

"What's wrong?"

"I ..." The words die on my lips.

I can't tell him the truth.

Not after I heard what *he* said he was going to do to me.

Not after what Alla promised to do to me.

"What is it?" he asks as he cradles my face.

I wrack my brain for an answer, for something—anything—that I can tell him so that he might go away. Or convincing enough so that he won't make me reveal the awful truth that I learned.

"I was just thinking about Nadia," I lie.

It shocks me how easy it is to lie. As much as I hate doing it, I justify to myself that this is the only way I can keep myself safe.

From him. From his grandmother. From everyone here.

"About what?"

"About ..." I start haltingly. "She hasn't heard from me since the bachelorette party." I settle on a topic I know he'd believe. "And the last time we spoke with each other, she had just dropped me off at the airport so that I could go to New York to deal with my sister's death. She must be worried sick. I just ... I just wish I can talk to her. Let her know that I'm okay."

Konstantin looks at me for a while, and then something shifts inside of his eyes. Without releasing my hand, he stands up.

"Wait here," he tells me, and then he walks away.

A few minutes later, he returns and hands my phone back to me.

"I kept this charged for you," he explains. "I was planning on giving it back to you after the wedding. But since you're staying a little longer ..." He smiles. "Here."

I look at the phone in his hand.

Staying a little longer ...

Stop lying to me. I know what you're really after. You're just like your grandmother.

He places it in my palm, closing my other hand around

it with a smile. "I know you won't do anything that would upset me."

Konstantin may be speaking, but all I can hear are Alla's venomous words.

You will march yourself back into his bed, spread your legs like the good little whore that you are, and take every drop of his seed until you are *pregnant.*

Just then, Ivica arrives with a plate of pancakes. She yelps when she sees Konstantin and immediately bows.

"Konstantin Yurevich! I didn't see you there. I was bringing some food for Emily Samovna. Had I known that you would be here as well, I—"

"That's alright, Ivica." I interrupt her with a smile, one more genuine than before. "I didn't tell you. You can leave the pancakes here, thank you."

"Of course." She does as I command. After giving both of us a short bow, turns and walks away.

"Go ahead," Konstantin turns his attention back to me. "Take the time you need. The castle is wired with an international data line, so it'll be as if you never even left the States. When you're ready, I'll be in my office."

His office ... I'm not sure that I'm ready to find him there after everything that's happened this morning.

"Okay." It's all I can manage to say.

Konstantin walks away, and I wait until he's out of view before turning my phone on. Just like he says, it's fully charged. As soon as I turn it on, a stream of missed messages starts rolling in. Every one of them is from my parents asking if I've made any progress on finding out anything else about Olivia's life insurance policy.

But as I scroll towards the recent ones, Nadia's texts start taking over.

Every one of them is asking if I'm doing okay and if there's anything she can do to help me.

My heart sinks the longer I scroll. She must be worried sick that I haven't responded. A few of them must have been sent when she was drinking. But it's the most recent ones that stab at my heart.

> NADIA: Emily, what's going on? Talk to me, please!

> NADIA: Are you okay? Please talk to me. I'm worried about you!

> NADIA: Please call me back. If I don't hear back from you soon, I'm going to NYPD.

"Oh no".

What had started as a lie to stop Konstantin from finding out about what his grandmother did to me turned out to be the awful truth.

I have to call her.

I scroll to her contact info and press the call button. *Please answer. Please, please, answer!* The line rings, and my anxiety crawls ever higher.

"Emily? Is that you?"

"Nadia! Yes, oh my God, I'm so sorry!"

"Oh my god!" she says on the other end. "Thank goodness. I thought you might've, I don't know, gotten kidnapped or murdered or something. Because when I went over to your sister's apartment, there was police tape everywhere. Apparently some guy got murdered there the other day, and you weren't answering and so I thought ... I thought that you ..."

Oh, Nadia ... Guilt washes over me again.

"Nadia it's okay." I muster up a weak laugh. "I'm fine. I'm alive. I'm talking to you right now, aren't I?"

"Yeah, you are." She breathes a sigh of relief. But then, her voice gets sharper. "What's going on? Wait ... where the hell are you? I haven't heard a damn thing from you since Italy!"

"I know, I know, I'm sorry. I'm so sorry."

"Tell me what's going on."

Panicking on the spot, I drill my brain for options. If I tell her I'm in Croatia, she'll have a hundred more questions. And I have a feeling that if I were to start telling her about Konstantin, about the deal we made, and about the truth of why he's keeping me here ...

I can't tell her. I can't make her worry about me when she can't do anything to help.

So, despite my own reservations, I lie again. "I'm staying at another friend's place in Brooklyn. But I must've caught something on the way back from Italy because I'm as sick as a dog right now."

"For almost two weeks?" Her voice lilts higher at the end. "Jesus, are you okay?"

"Yeah ... I'm starting to turn around. It's been pretty hard."

"Well, which neighborhood in Brooklyn are you in? Do you need me to come bring you anything?"

"N-No!" I stammer. "No, you don't have to. I'm getting better. It's just ... I don't want to get you sick. Y'know, in case I might still be infectious."

God, I hope she believes me.

"Okay ..." she says slowly. "Well, I'm just glad you're okay. You could have at least texted me back this whole time."

"I know. But I didn't want you to worry."

Somehow, I thought lying would be hard. But the words are coming out quick and easy, as if I've known how to do this my entire life.

"Not texting me back made me even more worried."

"Yeah, I shouldn't have done that," I say sadly.

Nadia goes quiet. I check to make sure the line is still connected.

"Emily, I know you're not sick, and you don't have to keep lying to me."

My heart shoots into my throat. "What do you mean."

"Look, I know you and your sister were close. And I know it can't have been easy to fly back on such short notice to deal with her death. You needed the space, and I totally respect that. I just ...." She pauses, as if she's searching for the right word. "I just wish you would've let me help you. You don't have to bear the weight of the world yourself."

Her voice is soft, and all it does is compound my guilt.

"Thanks, Nadia," I tell her. "That means a lot."

"I love you, okay?"

"I love you too," I insist.

She laughs sheepishly. I hear bedsprings, like she's rolling around. "Wanna get dinner soon? There's this new Greek restaurant that opened up in Astoria that I've been *dying* to go to. But Lawrence isn't interested. He tells me that it might set unrealistic expectations for our home meals together after the wedding."

I can't help laugh at that suggestion. "As if you ever plan on cooking."

"I know, right?" She exclaims. "So, what do you say? Wanna go tonight?"

Tonight ...

"I ..."

"It's totally cool if you can't. It's super short notice, I

know, and we probably can't even get a table since they're going to be slammed with reservations. But I really want to see you. I've missed you. And I've just been so worried that maybe ... I don't know, that something might've happened to you. It's good to hear from you."

"I've missed you too," I admit. *I wish I can tell you every-thing that's happened in the last ten days.* "Tell you what. Text me the place and I'll let you know if maybe we can—I don't know—go check it out sometime soon?"

What are you doing, Emily? You know you can't possibly keep that promise!

"I can do that!" Nadia's enthusiasm only makes me feel even worse about digging myself deeper in a hole. "I'll shoot that text over in a bit." Then, she adds softly. "I'm glad you're okay, Em. It's good to hear from you."

Except I'm not.

I'm anything but okay.

I have to get out of here.

38

KONSTANTIN

I LOOK UP WHEN THE DOORS OPEN, AND MY HEART SKIPS A beat when I catch sight of Emily. She's still wearing her robe. And although it's cinched tightly at her waist, I can see the ghosts of her nipples poking through the material to know that she's naked underneath.

"I need to talk to you." She says as her one and only greeting.

"Of course." I nod. "Anything."

"I have to go back to the States," she says. "I need to be there for Nadia."

Of all things that she can ask for, she asks for the *one* impossible thing.

"I can't, Kitty Cat," I explain. "By protocol, New York is off-limits to me, especially now. I've caused too much of a stir among the other bosses in New York the last time I went. And now they're all paying attention to see if I dare show up again."

Her face falls, but it's more than disappointment that swims in her dazzling sapphire-blue eyes.

"But ... *You* don't have to go!" she protests. "I can go

myself! You promised that when this is over ... You'd let me go and—"

"A pakhan cannot allow his wife to travel without him by her side," I tell her. "You agreed to be my real wife, remember? The bratva will never permit you to go to New York alone. These are rules that even I cannot break within the bratva."

Her face falls further, and her lip starts trembling. "So that's it? You're keeping me here? Forever? Because of the bratva?"

"Not forever," I correct her. "Just ... a little while longer."

"Until when?"

"I don't know. But soon," I finally say. "I promise."

"Promise ..." she mutters.

A prickle of guilt makes me clench my hands. I stand up from my desk, close the distance between us and pull her close by her waist. The light scent of our lovemaking from this morning still clings to her skin, and her freckles appear more prominent in the dim light of my office.

She doesn't press her shoulders deeper into my hands as I expect.

One of my knuckles tucks her loose hair behind her ears. She trembles as she catches her breath. My pulse quickens, and I debate kissing her. The thought of taking her right here on my desk is tempting, but I can't just keep thinking with my dick when I'm around her.

"I have an idea for how you can make it up to her. Even if you can't go back."

She narrows her eyes. "How?"

I smile and plant a light kiss on her lips. "I'll show you."

SUNLIGHT GLITTERS across the smooth vines, turning them from green to gold. Clusters of grapes ranging from bruise-purple to enchanting emerald hang heavily, their weight pulling the vines to the churned earth.

Azure butterflies soar unevenly between the thick bushes. They float more than fly from the array of wild-flowers sprinkling the land around the grapes.

There are more than I remember, I think, turning to catch sight of a cloud of them as they chase each other.

Emily would've asked for details the entire car ride along the coast, but she stays silent the entire ride this time.

No plaintive requests for info, and no attempts at pushing my buttons.

The wildness that I've come to expect from her seems to have been extinguished after this morning.

Something is bothering her. Something *other* than her guilt.

A few buildings with metal sides frame the end of the road, the main structure painted the same salt-water-scrubbed-yellow it has been for years.

"Where are we?" Emily finally asks when we come to a stop.

"It's my family's vineyard."

She scrunches her nose at me. "I see."

Frowning, I wander down the path created by heavy wagons. "Nadia will appreciate it."

"You want to send her wine?" she asks flatly.

I pause in the middle of a thicket of vines. The leaves would brush my ankles if the vineyard weren't tended to with precision to keep the paths clear. Nothing taller than my knee stretches for miles around, allowing a gorgeous view of the blue waters of the Adriatic Sea.

"Pick a vintage from the barrels in that building down

there, any one you like, and I'll ship it to Nadia as an apology on your behalf."

She rubs her upper arms like she's cold in spite of the warm sun. "I ..."

Crouching, I cradle a handful of the plump grapes. "I can help you choose. I'll narrow it down for you. You don't have to be worried about picking a wine she won't like."

"I don't want to pick a wine!"

"Are you afraid it's too much, Kitty Cat?" Her eyes dart away at my question. "To me, this seems like exactly the sort of gift that'll paper over your absence."

"No it isn't," she says tersely.

What is the matter with her? "I thought you wanted to apologize to her."

"I do!" She winds her arms around herself ever tighter. "But sending Nadia a barrel of wine seems ... inappropriate."

I stand quickly, my back muscles twitching from a flare of annoyance. "I don't understand."

"You think you can solve everything with money?" Emily lifts her hands.

Now it's my turn to be annoyed. Her reaction baffles me. It's like she's insulting me on purpose. "What's the matter with you?" I ask harshly.

It feels like I've swallowed a mouthful of butterflies. The fluttering sensation moves in my guts, settling in my veins until it feeds right into my heart. I touch my chest to make sure I'm not imagining how hard it's rattling.

Her shoulders bunch upward in a shrug. "Nothing ..."

The ground crunches under my shoes. I stand over her, searching her eyes for a hint of ... anything. Anything other than this stoic attitude.

"Emily, talk to me." I whisper. "What's wrong?"

She turns away, her gaze focusing on nothing in particular. There's nothing to see except the grapevines and clouds. There aren't even any workers around now that evening is fast approaching. Soon, the sun will be dipping behind the horizon.

Finally, she turns around. "Am I *your* wife? Or am I the pakhan's wife?"

I take her chin and tilt her gaze back to me. "Why do you ask?"

She flinches, and suspicion overtakes me.

"Forget it," she says.

A draft from the nearby sea tugs at my shirt. It claws at her dress next, making me jealous with the way it openly caresses her chest. The current of air teases the fabric open, exposing more of her throat. The hem flutters until her right thigh is in the sun. I've seen her naked, yet the sight of her clothed is driving me mad. It leaves me aching for more.

"Don't hide things from me, Kitty Cat."

At those words, Emily flinches again, and her hand drifts to her forearm. It's the same one that Alla grabbed after we rode to the wedding venue.

Anger and suspicion surges through me.

"Emily."

She turns her chin upward, bringing her face an inch closer to mine at the sound of her name.

"Did my grandmother say something to you?"

She turns her face away from me again. But there's no mistaking the tears in her eyes.

"Emily, tell me the truth." I reach over and pull her close. She trembles in my embrace, and I feel my heart splintering. "Did she say something to you?"

Her lips part, and her eyes blink as a singular tear rolls

out. Finally, she whispers quietly, almost as if she's afraid that someone might hear. "Yes."

My mood darkens as I tighten my embrace. *That evil old hag!* "What did she say?"

She shakes her head, fear and hurt mixing on her beautiful face. "Nothing she hasn't already said."

"That's not true, is it?"

"Don't make me say it, Konstantin." She's shivering against me now. "Please ... Just stop asking."

"The only reason I ask." I whisper into her thick wavy hair. "Is so that I can protect you from her."

"And the best way you can protect me from her," she replies, her voice quivering, "is if you forget that I said anything. Please."

There's no mistaking the quiver in her voice. As much as I love hearing her beg, I hate it when she's begging me like this.

Like she's pleading for mercy.

Whatever it is that Alla said must've been truly awful, and I suspect that it's not so much what she said, but what she might have *done*.

I intend to find out for myself.

But right now, all I care about is soothing Emily, to chase away her fears. So, I do the only thing I can do in the moment.

I kiss her.

39

KONSTANTIN

My mouth closes on hers, softly at first and then growing in intensity as I gradually lose control. I wind my fingers through her wavy hair, and when I reach the end of her dark chestnut strands, I do it again.

Her lips are stiff against mine at first, but slowly, she opens herself up until she's moaning against my lips, and leaning her weight on me onto her tiptoes to get more of my mouth.

Scooping an arm around her back, I guide her into the grapevines. The leaves welcome us like a blanket, the vines curling up, tickling my forearms. Everything around us is pure green.

But what I *see* is red—from the sunset to the flush on her cheeks—when we part, panting.

"I've been waiting to do this since I left your side this morning," I whisper.

Emily responds by kissing me harder, her fingers gripping my hair as firmly as I grip hers. There's no wildness in her anymore, but something else.

A desperation of sorts.

It compels her closer to me, makes her cling to me so hard that an army can't rip us apart. She sinks into me, giving herself to me in a way that belays her desire.

And her fear.

My cock surges to life when she rocks her hips upward. Her dress hikes up around her stomach, the blue fabric catching on grapevines so it reveals the lacy edges of her panties. I glance down, my blood racing with excitement. She ends the kiss, an unreadable twist playing at the edge of her lips.

"Is this what you want from me?"

"Yes," I say honestly.

"Then what are you waiting for?" Her eyes flash.

"I—"

She pushes her body into mine with a newfound insistence, dragging her teeth across my neck and drawing an appreciative groan from me. Her hands tug at my shirt, my belt, and the edge of my pants.

"Kitty Cat ..." I breathe, overwhelmed at the way she's whimpering against me.

This feels different somehow. Usually, I'm the one pushing *her*.

"Take it," she begs, her lips trembling. "Take what you want from me." She grabs my hands and brings them up until they slip under her dress. "Take whatever you want. Do whatever you want."

"Emily, what—"

She silences me with a kiss, moaning into my mouth as she does so. Her hips grind against mine as she shimmies out of her dress, freeing her perky breasts in the dying sun, and I breathe harder at the shadows of the leaves dancing across her nipples.

"What is the matter with you?" I ask thickly.

"Don't you want this?" She asks, her voice straining. "Isn't this what you want from me?"

"I ..."

"Isn't this what you wanted?" She arches her spine and pushes her breasts into my chest. The throbbing in my lower muscles is intense now. Each pulse makes my cock dig angrily against the front of my pants.

She parts her creamy thighs, letting her scent fill the space between us. The haze of desire overpowers my brain. My cock threatens to rip apart the fabric of my pants. The zipper will be warped if I don't let it out soon.

Pulling her panties to the side, she reveals her clit and the slit of her dripping wet pussy, whimpering softly as the sky turns a brilliant scarlet all around us.

"Don't you want me to spread my legs for you?" she moans like a beggar.

I've never wanted so *much* of one person. I don't know what to do with this desire that threatens to overwhelm me.

But this doesn't *feel* right.

Seeking release from my buzzing emotions, I nuzzle against her neck, listening to how she mewls. Her thighs squeeze around me, and she pulls me lower to force a nipple into my mouth. She envelopes me in her embrace, until I hear nothing but her pulse and my own. They merge together, a perfect, singular sound.

It's where I want to be ... But why does this feel so wrong?

Why? Because of whatever it is that Alla might've said to her? I won't let that witch hurt Emily. If I have to burn down all of Dubrovnik—no, the whole damn world—to keep Emily safe, I'll do it.

My brain tingles, warning me how crazy I'm going. I shut

it down by continuing to suck on her nipple. Her squeal of pleasure starts to erase my doubts.

"Konstantin," she whimpers. "Please ..."

"You want me to fuck you?" I whisper back, kissing the valley between her breasts.

"Yes ..."

She stares down at me, her sapphire-blue eyes practically pleading. I don't try to understand why this is happening as animal instincts start taking over my brain.

She wants me to fuck her ...

But that's not all I want.

I want to love her. To cherish her. To chase away this change that has suddenly overtaken her.

As I look into her insistent eyes, I can tell that they seem to shimmer from something else ... Something dark and foreboding.

Reaching down, I unzip my pants, releasing the painful obstruction between my cock and Emily. She stares as she watches me work, and the haze in her dilated pupils gives me what I'm after.

She sits up and wraps both her hands around the girth.

The dying sun paints the clouds in the distance a brilliant orange, and we both stare as my engorged shaft bounces into the air. Emily exhales, and licks her lips. There's heat in her blue eyes. It turns them darker and they appear more black than blue.

Licking her palm, she runs it over the pulsing vein on my shaft. I shiver and hiss like a steam engine.

She bends in half until the top of her head blocks my view, and her mouth closes around my cock.

Her tongue plays with the indentation below the engorged tip. One hand jerks me off with immense patience. Her other hand tucks stray strands of hair out of the way to let me glimpse the side of her face, and see the way her cheeks hollow as she works.

I throw my head back with a snarl. Fuck. The clouds are spinning above me, making a pastel scene of blue and gold and scarlet as the sun begins to dip below the horizon.

The world around us seems to grow still, as if we're the only things alive here. And we *are* alive. She's setting me on fire. The exhilaration makes it a struggle to breathe. Air pours into my mouth and my lungs, but it's never enough.

She's devouring my cock with reckless abandon. In a way, it's just like when I fucked her mouth in Buric's shop.

But this time, I'm not fucking her face with my cock.

She's fucking my cock with her face.

There *is* a difference.

"Stop," I pant. But all she does is go faster, and I feel my balls start to tighten.

"Emily ..." I beg. "If you don't stop, I'm going to cum."

Finally, she pulls away. The sink strand of spittle follows behind her perfect lips and dances in the wind as she dislodges herself from my cock.

In a flurry of motion, she lies back among the vines and the leaves, her dress hiked up to her waist. One hand plays with her breast. The other splays open her pussy, glistening in the sunset. Watching me without blinking, she spreads her legs wider.

"Fuck me," she commands. "Now."

And like a supplicant before a queen, I drop to my knees.

She's the only one I would kneel for.

As a packman, I'm used to ordering people around. It's a destiny I've prepared for since I was a boy. No one tells me what to do.

No one ... except her.

I brace myself over her body. A few vines overlap her shoulders; another fondles her hip, as if she's a dryad I encountered in the wild, a creature of mythical beauty. I'm entranced by her, but she doesn't need magic for that.

"Do you want me to fuck you, Kitty Cat?" I whisper.

"Stop talking about fucking me." Her cheeks glow pink, her eyes are deadly serious. "And *fuck me!*"

The final light of the sun is consumed by the sea. Emily's hands seek out my shoulders, gripping my muscles eagerly as I position myself before her entrance. Cupping her fingers on the back of my neck, she brings me down until she locks her lips to mine. Her tongue pushes into my mouth and tickles the roof of my mouth as she deepens the kiss. Blood rages through my shaft. I aim it against her slit and shove the tip in.

Her moan is hitched. She ends the kiss, biting her knuckle while waiting for me to feed her another inch of my cock. I move patiently because I want to enjoy this. I want ... no, *need* ... it to last.

"Faster!" she pants. "Harder!"

My determination is in shambles from her plea, and I obey like a slave to her command. The firm muscles of my torso grind against her soft breasts and hard nipples as I thrust myself to the hilt.

She shrieks. Her hands reach out to grip my ass, pulling me even closer.

I grunt as I rut into her, each grunt comes out deeper and hoarser than the last. But no matter how deep I thrust, it doesn't seem enough for her.

She digs her heels into my lower back, forcing me to fuck her faster, deeper, harder. I draw my hips away, but she clamps around my body and makes sure I can't escape. My strokes are fast and hard. The sound of our lovemaking echoes through the vineyard.

"Don't you stop!" Her eyes are hooded as she stares up at me. A drop of sweat falls onto her cheek, and in this light, it almost looks like a tear. "Fuck me! FUCK ME! Don't you fucking stop."

What a dangerous suggestion. I can't stop even if I want to—even if someone presses a gun to my temple and threatens to pull the trigger. My hips seem to take on a life of their own, thrusting in and out as the sun dips ever lower into the western sea.

A flock of small birds rises to the sky, startled by our cries of passion. They dart out of a nearby bush, their bodies a flurry of black blurs over the pink clouds—the same shade as Emily's nipples. I pull them into my mouth, one after the other, suckling until they harden into solid buds before I look back into her eyes.

She presses her lips against the side of my neck, and her teeth graze the sensitive skin. "Fuck me like you mean it," she whispers. "Fuck me until you ruin me."

And then, she pulls away, lips moving and voice so soft that it's almost as if she's talking to herself.

"Fuck me like I'm a whore."

The small hairs along my body rise from her warm breath. Her ragged breaths skim over my flesh, making a new ache in my lower belly. A place that yawns like a cavern wanting to be sated by something only she can give me.

Chasing the rising lust, I pound into her mercilessly. My arms hook her knees, bending her in half, with her feet by her ears. She shrieks, writhing as her pussy clenches around my cock.

Does she understand just what she's doing to me?

No … How can she, when I barely understand myself?

She screams, her nails raking against my muscles.

Tensing up, I pump my swelling cock into the depths of her wet, inviting pussy. It bounces off her softness, each ripple of her muscles squeezing me delightfully.

And then it happens.

Her orgasm flutters around me like a thunderclap, her back arches into me, and her nails dig painfully into my flesh.

The sensation pushes me over the edge, and all control shatters as thick ropey spurts of cum flood into her. Emily's legs wrap around my waist, trapping me to her as her pussy milks me for every last drop.

Whatever reason at the edge of my mind is chased away by the searing heat and bliss of my own orgasm. She holds me there, quivering, until my cock starts to soften. The breeze tickles over my skin, cooling the sweat.

Her eyes are closed, her breathing even. The sunset has turned the contrast up, giving her sharper shadows and paler skin.

"I'm a whore ..." she turns her face away from me, whimpering. "A good little whore."

My heart thuds erratically as I stare down at her. There's no mistake in my heart now. Something *is* different.

Emily opens her eyes and sits up on her elbows, adjusting her dress until it covers her breasts again.

"Are you alright?" I ask.

"I'm fine." Emily tenses up like I've slapped her. "We should go back before it gets dark."

"You don't seem fine."

"Well, I am." Fixing the hem of her dress, and hiding away her lovely legs, she folds her knees as she sits up. "When we get back, I want you to fuck me again."

Something is definitely wrong.

"Emily." I reach for her hand and she at least still permits me to do this little gesture. "If you'd just tell me what's wrong, then I can help you fix it. Please."

She casts her eyes down for a moment, and I dare to believe that she'll actually tell me. But when she returns her gaze to mine, the sadness doesn't go away.

"There's nothing for you to fix."

She doesn't say a word on the entire ride back, and my heart shreds from her refusal to answer until it's nothing but pieces.

40

KONSTANTIN
TWO DAYS LATER

"I just got an update from Zampa." Sima says as soon as he enters my office. "He has reason to believe he knows where Alisa is."

"Go on," I urge him.

"According to him, she's being held captive on Capri," Sima says.

"Capri?" I muse, rubbing my chin. "That's not too far from the Amalfi Coast."

"Seems like the Ferrata has been holding her there after they moved her from New York," Sima says. "Which means when they invited us for talks ..."

"Alisa was practically right next door," I growl. "Those bastards."

"There's more," Sima continues. "Zampa tells me that there's a *lot* of movement from Ferrata capos in the States. Important people too."

"Like who?"

"Mario Senza, for one." Sima ticks a finger. "Bastard's been running almost the whole show in New York for decades. According to Zampa, old Mario isn't exactly too fond of the way the Ferrata have been leeching off his so-called hard work and has his own bone to pick."

"Hard work." I snort with disgust. "Is that what he calls killing rivals in prison showers?"

"Either way." Sima shrugs. "Mario is visiting some tailors in Manhattan for custom suits. Not just for himself but for his wife as well."

Suits? Now *that* bit of information piques my interest. "Anyone else?"

"Bruno Merenda," Sima answers. "Alessio Spataro, and Elio Di Forno, just to name a few. Same thing. They're all getting fitted for new suits. It's nothing much if one of them is doing that. But all of them?"

"Yeah." I nod. "There's only one possibility for them."

Realization dawns on Sima's face. "You don't think it's ..."

"It has to be." I place my hand on Sima's shoulder. "They're coming to Capri for Domenico's fucking wedding. Has Zampa said anything else? Any dates?"

"Nothing yet. But if I were Domenico, I'd want it done immediately. Especially after what *you've* done."

I nod in agreement, picking at that word like it's a piece of food stuck in my teeth.

Immediately ...

Ideas are turning in my head already. As troubling as it is that the Ferrata are *all* gathering in Capri, this presents an opportunity.

I can rescue Alisa *and* deal them a heavy blow, one that can shift the balance of power enough that the war is as good as ended.

"Are the Albanians and Serbians still on our side?"

As long as the Albanians and Serbians are still on my side, then the considerable arsenal that they can bring to the table are still available ... For the right price, of course.

"They are," Sima continues as he reaches for his lighter again. "Why? Looking for a little firepower?"

"Yes," I finally say. "Reach out to the Albanians and buy up every crate of grenade they have on the market. Then do the same thing with the Serbians for their stock of rocket launchers. I want enough explosives to reduce even the thicket castle wall to rubble."

Sima scrapes his hair, a savage smile widening on his lips at the thought of impending violence. "Now we're talking, Kostya. What else?"

"Reach out to the Ukrainians, too," I say. "I want drone operators. I'm not leaving anything to chance."

"That might not be so simple." Sima sighs. "Kiev isn't exactly in a charitable mood these days."

"Tell them I'll donate two million Euros for their troubles," I say. "Four million if they can have the operators meet our brigadiers in Italy in two days."

"Two days?" Sima looks up. "You want things to move that quickly?"

"Why?" I smirk. "Are you nervous?"

"Fuck no." he chuckles grimly he pulls me in for an embrace. "I'm getting *hard* just thinking about laying waste to those Italian fucks. I'll get it done, Kostya. You can count on that."

Without another word, he gives me one more pat on the shoulder before leaving, his lighter clinking as he flips it open and closed with every step.

I turn and start making my way to the bedroom where I'm sure Emily is waiting for me. Excitement thrums through my body the closer and closer I get.

This is what triumph must feel like.

But if so, why do I feel dread rising the closer I get?

41

EMILY

I AM SO FUCKED IN THE HEAD.

That's the only thing I can think as I stare out the window, recalling the words I screamed at Konstantin in the vineyard.

But more importantly, I think about how I told him I was a whore.

And he did nothing to chase that thought from my mind.

I've never said anything like that to anyone before. Yet in the aftermath of my own terrifying encounter with Alla, and with the grapevines all around us, those words had come so naturally.

Just thinking about what we did sends a fresh shiver running through my spine. Wetness collects between my legs and I squeeze my thighs together.

I hate that he can still cause this reaction out of me, even as he proves again and again that he doesn't care about me.

He's just trying to put a baby inside of you to get that signet ring from Alla, I tell myself.

I close my eyes, recalling the way his eyes had drilled

into mine as he fucked me in the vineyard, and how his cum flooded me. I told him to fuck me again when we came home, and he did. And then one more time in the morning.

Each time, I held him close and let his cum flood my womb.

Each time, I clung to him to keep him inside, not daring to let a single drop spill out.

Because I know the consequence that awaits me if Alla were to find out that I did anything *other* than that.

My fingers fumble at the hem of my dress, tugging at it until the threads start coming loose.

You agreed to this, remember? I tell myself. *You agreed for him to use you. You agreed without realizing just what it fucking meant.*

I close my eyes as the cool night breeze kisses my brow.

Babies ...

My voice starts to change in my head until it sounds nothing like me anymore, and more like Alla.

That's all you're good for, you stupid little whore.

The door creaks open, saving me from my own spiraling thoughts. I turn and catch sight of Konstantin. There's a slight smile on his face. He's standing up just a little straighter and taller than he usually does, and his wide shoulders are squared.

He looks absolutely beautiful and perfect. But the words I heard him say through the door the other day refuse to leave my head. I have to remind myself that beauty is clearly something only skin deep even as my heart threatens to soften at the sight of him.

Silently, I touch the ring on my finger.

Just because I'm wearing this ring, doesn't make me one of them.

"He's found her," Konstantin says as soon as he closes the door. "Sima knows where Alisa is!"

"That's wonderful," I say, my voice flat and emotionless. "Is she alright?"

"I don't know yet. But it's going to be over soon, Kitty Cat." He approaches me and takes me into his arms, over-whelming me in his scent of soap and aftershave as he kisses me. As his tongue sweeps into my mouth, I smell something else. Something oddly familiar. A light scent of honeysuckle and brown sugar.

It's only when we break apart that I realize that I was tasting myself on his lips.

This is it, Emily ... I think to myself. *This is the part where he'll finally break your heart.*

"So ..." I ask. "What happens next? Are you going to rescue her?"

"Yes." He nods. "And after I rescue her, we can go back to the States. Together."

A shiver runs down my body. "What happened to you not being allowed to go?"

"That won't matter anymore." He doesn't let me go. "I plan on killing Domenico and every man of the Ferrata Mafia when I rescue Alisa. I'm going to *break* their power. Once that's done, it means I can negotiate with everyone in New York to allow me to go. Then I will give you what I promised"

Ah yes... what I want. Does that even matter anymore?

"We can avenge Olivia, together," he says.

His enthusiasm is almost believable. And for a reckless moment, I almost believe him.

"And what happens after that?" I ask softly.

"What do you mean?"

"I mean us." I continue. "What happens after you avenge her for me?"

"I ..." he hesitates as he searches my eyes. "I don't understand. We stay with each other, you and I. We're married, remember? You're my wife, Emily."

Wife ...

I can't hold it back anymore. I have to tell him. If I don't, it's going to just eat me up alive.

"What if I don't want to be your wife anymore." I tell him.

"What?" he asks harshly. "Why?"

"I *heard* you," I say before I can stop myself. "Through the door of your office that morning after Sima called you away."

His face suddenly blanches. "What did you hear?"

"I heard you tell the truth to him," I snap. "What did you say? The only way my grandmother will release my inheritance is after I put a baby in Emily's belly? That's why you asked me to be your wife, isn't it? So you won't feel guilty after you finally knock me up!"

"Emily, it's not what you think!" He rakes his fingers through his hair as he grows more agitated.

"Don't fucking lie to me!" I shout as the tears well in my eyes. "This was what you wanted for me from the very start! You and that grandmother of yours!"

"What?" His hand stops moving.

And that's the part that scares me the most.

His sudden calmness tells me that I just crossed a line.

He approaches me, like a predator stalking his prey, until he becomes the only thing that I can see. His icy blue eyes drill into mine, and suddenly, I feel my knees buckling. But he won't let me go, and I know that no matter how hard I fight him, I can't break free.

"You were conspiring with your psycho grandmother from the very beginning." I square up and tell him. "That's why you never answered my questions about babies when I first asked. This whole thing was just a good cop, bad cop routine that the two of you played to perfection."

"What the fuck are you talking about?" he snarls, and I realize I've said too much.

I can't take back those words. But I also can't tell him everything.

I can't tell him of how Alla's guards stripped me before her and held me still while she looked me over like a horse on auction.

I can't tell him of her threat to *kill* me if I don't get pregnant.

So, I settle on telling him just enough.

"She caught me listening outside your door," I snap, as I fight back the tears threatening to leak from the corners of my eyes. "And she made me confess that I heard. As once I did, she *ordered* me to march back in your bed, spread my legs like a good little whore, and keep them spread until I'm pregnant with your baby. Because that's all I am to you, right?"

"Is that why you were acting the way you have been for the last few days?" His grip relaxes just enough for me to wrench my jaw away. "Because of her?"

"Don't pretend like you didn't like it." I hug myself, and angrily wipe at my eyes. "Don't pretend like that wasn't what you wanted from the very beginning."

"Emily, that's not true!" He bellows, and I flinch from the intensity of his roar.

"LIAR!" I scream. "Stop lying to me, Konstantin, and just admit it! You never cared about me! The only thing you care about is that stupid ring and the stupid bratva!

So why don't you just drop the bullshit and tell me the truth!"

His eyes darken as anger, betrayal, and pain swirls in his eyes. He takes a step closer to me.

"Get the fuck away from me ..."

"Do you really think that I don't care about you?" He clutches my chin again; his eyes look dark and dangerous.

"That's exactly what I think." I glare at him. "So you can stop pretending and show me just who and what you really are."

A foreboding look spreads across Konstantin's handsome face. There's no smile as he closes the distance. His powerful arms trap me between the wall and himself until there's nowhere left for me to go.

And shamefully, I feel my pussy starting to grow wet.

"And what exactly am I, Kitty Cat?" he growls darkly. "Be honest."

"A monster." I breathe.

His hand moves along my thighs.

"And how are you so certain of that?"

Dread, excitement, and heartbreak mix inside of me until it comes alive in the form of a twisted creature that coils its tentacle around the entirety of my being.

I should be scared of what I'm about to say, any normal person would.

I can still stop this. I can still step back from the edge of insanity that I'm about to throw myself over.

But I don't.

"Because you have no problem hurting me to get what you want." I breathe.

A thick finger runs under the hem of my skirt, and moves over the soaked front of my panties. I shiver, hating at how easily I'm reacting to his touch.

"Do you really think I can hurt you?"

"Yes."

His palm cups my dripping hole, kneading my clit trembling with desire. The pupil of his eyes dilate until his icy-blue eyes are black as night while his hand continues to play with my swollen lips.

"Do you *want* me to hurt you?"

The answer comes easily and unexpectedly. "Yes."

He rewards my words by quickening the way he massages my soaked pussy until my knees buckle against him. Leaning in so close that his face blocks out all source of light behind him until he looks like a demon snarling in my face, he asks.

"And *how* do you want me to hurt you?"

With an impulsiveness that can only exist because of my shattered heart, I move my hand down his chest, past the ridged muscles of his abdomen into his pants, and cup his massive cock, already hard and throbbing angrily in my hand.

"With this."

He takes my hand in his and begins walking down the hall. His shoes brush lightly over the floor, silent as a bird's wing.

He isn't in any hurry. If anything, he seems to be walking slower than normal.

"Where are we going?" I ask as a heady mixture of doubt, panic, and excitement war for dominance in my head.

He stares straight ahead, his voice strained as he speaks. "You'll see."

The tension between us is thick enough to cut with a

knife. His hand holds mine tightly, and I realize that he's leading me into a section of the castle I haven't been to before. He pauses to unlock a heavy wooden door with iron framing, waving me through into another hall. This one is darker, the lamps on the wall creating strange shadows that dance on the weathered stone.

We're going down, I notice with a start. The floor slopes before becoming a stairwell. I begin to ask him where we're going, but the words die in my throat.

It doesn't matter where we're going, I decide.

The air grows colder all around us. This whole area has an unsettling air to it. With every downward step, I can't help but feel like I'm walking slowly toward the gates of hell.

Finally, we come to a stop. The door here is rectangular, the wood is faded, and missing the touch of care imbued into the rest of the castle. I have a feeling nobody comes down here much, if ever.

A shiver of dread rushes through me, followed by the most intense arousal I've ever felt.

Once upon a time, I asked him about dragging me down to a torture chamber and stringing me up until I do whatever he wants.

And just like my question about babies, he never gave me a real answer.

Something tells me he's about to do *both*.

Silently, he unlocks the door with an ancient-looking key, and looks at me expectantly.

Rubbing my arms in anticipation, I step inside. When I see what's hanging on the walls, I gasp.

Long leather strips dangle from wrapped handles tucked into wall mounts. A shelf with various angular and square blades laid out like doctor's tools turns my stomach. The space is big, but there are no windows and shadows lurk at every corner. The only light comes from an old industrial lamp dangling over a lone chair in the center of the room.

"Last chance, Kitty Cat," he whispers against my ear. "Once I close the door, there's no turning back." His large hands settle around my shoulder and his cock throbs against the small of my back. "Tell me again that this is what you want. Tell me again that you *want* me to hurt you."

My hands close into fists by my hips. *He's giving you a way out. You can still say no.*

"I don't want you to hurt me," I admit.

He stands up taller and starts to move. But instead, my own recklessness compels me to reach for his hand.

"I want you to *destroy* me."

42

EMILY

The door closes shut with an ominous *THUD*.

I flinch as the world outside the two of us disappears.

"Oh, Kitty Cat." He turns around. "You should've said no when you still had a chance."

Maybe it's the way the door locks, or the absolute *murderous* gaze in his eyes, but clarity hits me like a train and snaps me out of my madness.

"I—"

"I gave you a chance." He starts rolling his sleeves up as he approaches. "And you threw it away."

Despite my pounding heart, I'm wetter than I've ever been before.

Oh God ... Oh fuck.

His arms circle me from behind. Thrashing wildly, I struggle, but he's so much bigger than me. With a single hand, he carries me effortlessly even as I kick and thrash against him. His huge cock stabs at my back as he presses my body against his and drags me towards the chair.

He doesn't bother replying as he pushes me into the chair, knocking the wind out of me in the process. The chair is bolted to the concrete floor, four circular cuffs attached to the arms and legs. Before I can react, he presses into me, using his weight to keep me still while he attaches the cuffs.

When he finishes binding my last ankle, he steps back to observe his work.

The outline of his cock is jutting violently against his pants. A dark wet spot stains in the front. He follows my line of sight and that dark smirk on his face curls up even higher.

"What's wrong, Kitty Cat? Isn't this what you wanted?"

I respond by squeezing my legs together.

He's right ...

I *do* want this.

I *want* to surrender everything to him.

I *want* him to do whatever the fuck he wants to do to me.

I *want* him to hurt me.

Because if I can get him to hurt me, then it's easier for me to hate him.

And if I hate him, then it's easier for me to find a way to escape him.

Pacing around my chair, he begins lifting items off the wall. My pulse goes wild when he holds up a riding crop, studying it like he's judging its quality before smacking the leather tip into his opposite palm with a *thwap* that makes me jerk in my cuffs.

Sweat rolls down my spine, and my pussy is *salivating* at the thought of what he's about to do.

"Oh God ..." I whimper

"No God," he replies. "Only me."

Wandering close to me, Konstantin drags the soft ends of the crop across my chin, back, and forth, his voice unnervingly calm. "Do you know the best places to strike someone?"

I twist away, trying to escape the tool as he drags it across my lips and across my face.

"It needs to be somewhere that inflicts maximum *pain*." He drags it down my neck, drawing a shuddering gasp from my core. "A place where the skin is sensitive."

The tip of the crop starts drawing circles around my right nipple, and my eyes widen in panic.

"No, not there." He chuckles darkly. "The skin is too thin around the nipple. A single errant stroke, and you risk permanent damage."

I can't go anywhere with the cuffs holding me to the chair. My breath quickens as the whip moves down along my stomach, slips under the hem of my dress and press against my hole.

I whimper as the end of the crop pushes inside me.

"Not there either," he says. "It's the same problem as the nipple."

He withdraws the crop almost as soon as he inserts it, and slips it under my neck. The scent of my own arousal fills my nose from proximity, and the slippery wetness coats my chin as he tips my face up, forcing me to look at him.

Heaving in the chair, I wrench from side to side, not caring how it makes my wrists burn.

Yanking the crop away, he throws it unceremoniously back on the shelf.

He stands and walks slowly around my chair. I turn my head to keep him in sight, but I can only crane my neck so far. He's in my blind spot.

"You don't scare me." I taunt.

"I don't need to scare you, Kitty Cat." Konstantin's breath tickles my ear. I stiffen. "I know *all* of your weaknesses."

A tiny tremor begins in my knees. "You don't know a damn thing about me."

"I know everything about you." His fingers slip down my neck, trailing over the neckline of my thin dress.

I can't see his face, but I can *hear* his smirk as his palm brushes lightly over my chest, and his fingers tighten around my nipples to give them a hard squeeze. I can't stop myself as a yelp of pleasure punches out from my lips.

"You *love* this, don't you?"

Holding my breath, I try to distract myself from how amazing his touch feels. My lungs are screaming for oxygen as I try to keep myself from moaning in his hands. But it's not enough to cancel the sparks of desire he's stoking in my blood. My nipples firm up, eager to be played with.

Konstantin is tenacious, and his large hand works at my breasts with the expertise of someone who knows *exactly* what my body craves. He traces my nipples through the cloth, tugging gently, insistently, all the while making my clit thrum to life.

"Ah," I blurt, sucking in air when I can't hold my breath any longer.

"Did you want to say something?" he asks with faux interest as his other hand joins the mix.

I clench my jaw and hunch forward. I can't escape his large hands as they knead and massage the sensitive flesh. "Not a fucking thing."

"In that case." Fondling me, he gives both my nipples a light twist, and my lower belly jumps with maddening heat. I wriggle on the chair, thighs rubbing together and pussy growing slick with desire.

I turn my head, trying to bite his arm. He laughs and dodges the clumsy attempt. As further punishment, he tugs my nipples until I moan again. The pleasure from pain is incredible. It's overwhelming.

And suddenly, he releases me just as my pleasure starts

to crest. My hands open and close in their restraint, and I curl my toes in frustration.

I hear things clattering on the shelves, and when he returns, he takes both his hands at the neckline of my dress. Then, with a single hard motion, he rips the dress straight down the front to free my breasts.

I yelp.

"These pink nipples," he whispers as he caresses one before he gives it a light pinch. "So beautiful. So delicate. So easy to ruin."

A trickle of fear slides up my brain stem when I see him holding a pair of rubber clamps with a chain strung between them.

"Don't worry, Kitty Cat." He smiles. "I'm not a complete monster despite your accusations."

"Yes you are!" I scream at him.

He chuckles darkly. With an accuracy that leaves me breathless, he carefully pinches each nipple in a clamp and then gives the chain a slow, torturous downward tug. The weight and compression combine in the perfect dazzling mix of pain and pleasure.

I don't dare admit it, but the way it hurts is *exactly* what I want right now.

Konstantin gives the chain another tug. Pleasure ripples from my nipples to my pussy, as if they're connected.

"If I am, as you say, a monster." He murmurs as he increases the pressure, dragging a low, obscene moan from deep inside of my core. "What does that make you, Kitty Cat?"

"I ... Ah!" I whimper, pushing my knees together.

I can't escape the pressure he's creating inside of me. I hate how much I love this. I hate how wet it's making me. His absolute control of the situation wakes up a filthy part of my psyche—a dark part of my mind that's practically screaming for him to do more.

To show me just how much more he can hurt me.

To revel in the pain that he can bring me.

His hands release the chain, and I moan in simultaneous relief and frustration. My body is *screaming* for release, and I can feel the seat growing slippery from how soaked my panties and my dress have become.

Konstantin moves in front of me, and inhales deeply, licking his lips.

"I think you like this, my little slut."

He suddenly forces my knees apart and wedges his shoulders between my knees, spreading my legs so far apart that I can't close them no matter how hard I struggle.

Staring into my eyes, he brushes the remnants of my ruined dress out of the way.

"You've made a mess of my chair," he notes.

Blushing in humiliation and another flash of arousal, I try to push my legs together. All I achieve is squeezing at his upper body.

He can do whatever he wants to me and we both know it.

He hooks his finger under the soaked material of my panties, and raises his other hand. One of the knives I saw on the shelf is pinched in his grip. When the hell did he grab that?

"W-what are you going to do with that," I beg, terror growing in me again as he comes closer to me.

Ignoring my complaint, he tucks the flat side of the blade against my skin. Cold metal presses against my fevered pussy, and I shut my eyes, whimpering as I tense up.

"Relax, Kitty Cat," he chuckles harshly. "I'm not going to hurt you with this."

The knife flashes, and my panties are cut away. I'm shaking, hyperventilating, as I open my eyes. He throws the knife away into the distance, and it clatters far away in the room.

I hope I never see it again.

My naked pussy is exposed to the air. Gently, he spreads it open to reveal my swollen clit and leaking hole.

"You'd let me fuck you right here and right now, wouldn't you?" he asks. "You'd *beg* me to cum inside of you like you have been ever since our wedding."

"No," I lie.

"Liar." His smirk rends my heart apart as he runs his fingers along my slippery folds. The sensation leaves my body aching for more, aching to be filled. My legs knock together only to be blocked by his shoulders again.

"I'm not giving you that. Not yet. You haven't *earned* my cock yet."

Slowly, he inserts a finger into my hole, and then another, and another until he's slowly pulling me apart. He leans in closer, and inhales deeply again.

"I can *smell* your fear," he says. "I'm going to enjoy tasting it so much more."

My pussy flutters around his fingers as I gasp.

"Do you like it when I spread you open like this?" he taunts me. I fight to bite back the moan aching for escape from my lips. His thick digits push knuckle deep and I feel myself stretching to my limit.

"I .... I don't ..."

"No." He hisses as he starts licking along my thighs, lapping up the juices that have coated it. "Lying."

"I'm not lying!"

"Your soaked cunt tells me that you are."

He curls his fingers, their tips scraping deliciously along my sensitive insides. My pussy comes to life, buzzing with the need to orgasm, as my body spasms. Dirty wet sounds fill the air around us, and I close my eyes as I start to pant.

I'm afraid.

Not afraid of him, or what fresh tortures he has in mind for me.

I'm afraid that he won't let me come.

My mind is splitting apart.

"I hate you ..." I whimper as he tightens his other fingers around the crook where my leg meets my body, and repositions me until both my asshole and my pussy are exposed to him.

His sigh is black as a shadow. "You haven't even begun to hate me yet, Kitty Cat."

Thrashing in my restraints, I kick my legs uselessly against their restraint. He repays me by pushing his fingers even deeper in my pussy, curling them to stretch me even further while the thick knuckles move in concentric circles.

My toes curl again as my thoughts become nothing more than a haze. I'm growing dizzy from lust, and lightheaded from panting. My body becomes hypersensitive to even the lightest touch.

He continues to push and prod and tease, and I'm leaking like a ship sinking in a storm. I feel myself dripping down onto the only hole that he hasn't touched.

I moan and twist against my restraints again helplessly.

When he pulls his fingers out of me, I almost beg him to shove them back in.

But before I can speak, I feel them somewhere else.

Somewhere forbidden.

A third place that he *promised* me that he'd destroy.

Panic rises in my mouth again.

"You're so fucking tight, Kitty Cat ..." he murmurs darkly as he kisses his way along my thigh, nipping at my skin as he gets closer and closer. "So tight that I almost feel bad that I'm going to ruin it all."

That's the last warning I get as a thick finger teases my ass apart. Heat sears my mind and I cry out as it burrows deeper. Just then, he inserts two fingers in my soaked pussy and starts pumping in rapid strokes, forcing me to leak downward so that he can finger-fuck me in both my holes.

I've never felt so dirty than I do in this exact moment, and my eyes roll back inside of my head as my core tightens and spasms.

"Do you want to come, Kitty Cat?"

"Yes ..." I whimper.

My limbs are weak; they're giving up on me. The last bit of my pride is being crushed by the ever-pressing need for an orgasm. It's as if my joints, my muscles, my fibers are all being pulled in different directions. The only point of focus is my thrumming pussy, my quivering asshole, and the sensation of being filled endlessly.

His voice shrouds me, filling my ears the way his fingers fill my insides, and I never want him to stop. "Who do the filthy, greedy holes belong to?"

"You!" I sob, convulsing in the chair, desperately trying to grind his fingers deeper inside of me.

"Who do you belong to?" His voice brings me out of my own mind and back to our dark current reality.

"You!"

It's the truth.

No matter how many times I claim that I hate him, I know that in the deepest part of my core, I can't bring myself to hate him.

No matter how much I ask him to hurt me, I will never forget the way he brushed away my tears. The way his soft lips feel against my body as he whispers Kitty Cat in my ear.

He pulls his finger out of me, leaving me restless and panting. He's denied my orgasm on purpose. He adjusts his cock in his pants before pulling the zipper down. I stare as the massive length throbs in front of my face.

A single drop of precum falls silently from the tip, beads in the valley of my breasts, and slowly rolls down the length of my body.

His smile is as wicked as all seven sins combined. "Let's start with hole number one."

43

KONSTANTIN

THE MIX OF HATE AND LUST IN HER FLUSHED FACE IS DOING awful things to me. The chain dangling from clamps around her engorged nipple makes my cock rock-hard.

I've never felt such growing swell of monstrous desire that gnaws at my heart than right now.

She's afraid of you.

No. I muffle that voice with both hands, slamming it down into the depths of my soul. I'm not going to allow her to make me feel guilty.

She's the one who chose to believe the worst thing about me.

I cling to the thought like a sailor clinging to a piece of flotsam in a storm. If I don't, I'll start to loathe myself for going down this road. I have too much work left to do to give up here.

Emily's eyes widen as she stares hungrily at my cock.

"Is this how you want me to hurt you, Kitty Cat?" I ask her.

She wets her beautiful lips. "Yes ..."

I stroke along the length of my cock, mixing her arousal

with my precum. She writhes and tries to throw herself forward, her greedy mouth hungry to take my cock in her mouth.

She clearly loves this, all while she's ashamed of how easily her body is submitting.

"Please!" she whines.

"Please, what, Kitty Cat?" I continue stroking my cock lazily, filling the air with obscene wet squelching sounds. "Choose your words very carefully."

"I want your cock."

"You'll have to beg better than that." I grab a fistful of her hair and give it a hard yank. She cries out, half a moan and half a scream. "Tell me what you *really* want me to do to that filthy little mouth of yours."

She levels her gaze at me, hate and desire warring in her eyes, and takes a slow trembling breath.

"I want you to fuck my face with that cock."

There it is.

Straddling her chest, I position her face carefully, and then shove the full length of my cock inside of her mouth with one hard thrust. She cries out against my thick cock in surprise as I push myself to the depth of her throat. Her hands open and close in their restraints uselessly, and her hips rise up in her chair as she struggles to breathe.

But the muffled moans coming from her nose tells me that she fucking loves it.

"You love it when I'm stretching that dirty little mouth, don't you?"

She groans louder and sucks harder, swallowing me deeper as I punish her throat.

Spittle and drool leak from the corner of her mouth, coating her chin, her breasts, and her stomach.

My free hand reaches behind me, and tugs at the chains

attached to her nipple clamps. She cries out around my cock.

"Is this how you want me to hurt you? Do you want more?"

"Mmmm." She moans.

I yank my cock out of her mouth.

"Answer me, Kitty Cat."

She coughs as she takes one ragged breath after another. When she looks up at me with half-lidded eyes, she whispers.

"Is that all you got?"

"Good girl." I snarl, and shove my cock back inside of her throat. This time, she starts moving her head without me guiding her. Dark chestnut hair bounces in the fetid air around us. My balls slap against her chin with each vicious thrust, and I can feel my first orgasm building up.

"I'm going to cum down that throat of yours, Kitty Cat," I pant as I feel my orgasm building up.

And then with a roar, I bury myself deep in her throat, push her head against the back of the chair, and cum. Spurt after spurt of semen pour forward, and the dip at the bottom of her neck sinks rapidly as she gulps me down as quickly as she can.

But it's not fast enough.

Wrenching her head this way and that, she forces me out of her mouth and coughs, white cum dripping from her lips as she pants under me.

My hand is still in her hair, and I yank her up so that I can look into her cock-drunk eyes. The last few drops of cum dribble down her chin and join the puddle running along her body.

"That's hole number one." I chuckle. "And I'm just getting started."

Before she can react, I undo the straps holding her in the chair, and yank her to her feet. She's startled by this, but follows obediently as I drag her behind me like she's on a leash.

Pulling her to the closest wall, I raise her arms up and cuff those into straps bolted to the ceiling above her head until she's standing on the balls of her feet.

The position thrusts her chest out, exposing her breasts to me. As vulnerable as she is, I'm not done. I kick her ankles apart and tie them to straps on the floor. Her thighs tense as she balances on her toes, legs wide, and her pussy gleams pink in the light.

I stand back to appreciate my work.

"Are you ready for hole number two?"

Emily throws her head back against the wall, eyes still closed, and whispers. "Yes."

She's so slick that I push three fingers into her without any resistance. She gasps loudly, and thrusts her hips forward, rubbing her swollen clit against my palm. I watch her brows furrow from exertion and pleasure.

Two strokes, then three, and I know when I reach eight, she'll come. I can read her like a book.

Her ribs rise and fall, her neck pulsing as my cum rolls off her. The smell of sex hangs heavy between us. My cock is furious at me for holding it back from entering her. I won't let her have that yet.

Give her a taste of what she wants. That will loosen her tongue. "Go ahead, Kitty Cat. Come for me. It's right there. Go on ... That's it ... I feel how warm and wet and inviting your pussy's getting. It's practically on fire. Come for me. Do it. If you don't, I might never let you come again."

I barely finish the last word before her pussy squeezes my fingers. She bends her spine as much as she can, given the restraints, and shakes as the orgasm uproots itself from her body.

"FUCK!" she shrieks. I was telling the truth that no one would hear her in this place. But she's so loud that I wonder if she might shatter the walls with her voice.

Breathing in big gulps, she goes limp in the chains. Her eyes watch me from behind her sweaty chestnut hair and her hooded brow, and her dazzling sapphire eyes *glare* at me.

"You should be thanking me." I tell her, drawing my fingers from her pussy.

She holds my gaze quietly.

I lick my fingers clean, waiting for a reaction, but she keeps glaring. "You taste sweet for someone so dirty."

Wrapping her nipple chain in my fist, I tug it until she squeals. I feel control slipping out of my body. My cock is leaking, and I shove the tip inside of her dripping hole, stroking myself inside of her. She cries out in pleasure, louder than before, her voice cracking like she's falling down a cliffside.

"This hole was made for me to ruin." I snarl as I start to fuck her with reckless abandon, pulling back all the way before slamming myself to my full length with each thrust. She yelps each time our hips touch. "All of you is made for me to ruin. You wanted this, Kitty Cat. You *wanted* me to hurt you, and that's exactly what I'm doing."

"Yes ..." Emily pants ...

"You *like* it when I use you."

"Yes ..."

"You've *always* wanted me to use you."

"Yes ..."

There's no more insult left on her tongue, but I can still feel the fight in her body.

Savageness fills me as I fuck her with the tempo of an automatic rifle, I feel my own anger rising. How *dare* she agree that I was always going to use her.

I told you that this marriage was real!

I swore to you!

I loved you!

The last thought hits me like a clap of thunder, and for a moment, I nearly think about pulling out of her. I nearly think about freeing her from her restraints, to hold her in my arms and kiss away the pain that I'm inflicting on her body.

But I'm in too deep now. I'm too far gone to do anything other than fulfill her command for me to hurt her.

To destroy her.

I reach up to squeeze her breasts. My teeth nip at the sensitive skin along her neck. Her pussy squeezes me with every thrust, and slowly, her voice comes back to life as one moan after another punch out of her throat.

She's on the edge of shattering, and the temptation to tip her over it is powerful. I can rip her apart if I want to ... but I can't, even as the darkest corner of my mind urges me to do exactly that.

What's stopping me?

Because I love her ...

Emily ... My beautiful, perfect Emily. The girl I pulled from a lake. The one I chose to be my wife, to share my world, to risk opening myself up to in a way I've never done with anybody.

And I'm destroying her.

Roaring, I cum inside of her pussy. I pull my cock out and slump against the wall beside her. My seed drips down silently onto the floor. Her rib cage shifts near my ear. I can hear her ragged breathing ... and the furious racing beat of her exhausted heart.

"Is this what you wanted?" I whisper. "Have I hurt you enough?"

Whether it's a question or a plea ... I don't even know anymore.

Emily opens her eyes, and the fire in those dazzling sapphire-blue eyes remain unextinguished.

"No ...." she whispers and shakes her head, her chestnut hair sticking to her sweaty neck. "Not even a little bit."

"Stop lying," I beg.

She goes quiet, her breathing faltering. A small, strange smile plays over her tired face.

"You're right. I was lying."

I knew it. I knew it! Grabbing her by her jaw, I bring her lips an inch from mine. The way she flinches makes me think she *wants* me to kiss her.

Because I want nothing more than to do exactly that.

I want to kiss away the pain I caused her, I want to tell her I'm sorry for bringing her down here, and I want to tell her that it's not the bratva that's important but her.

"You haven't even *started* to hurt me," she snarls.

Her sapphire eyes shine with a strength she has no right to. It leaks from her as if she were crying, but no tears stain her cheeks.

"Do you want this to end?" I ask, my heart begging her to say yes.

"No," she hisses. "I told you to destroy me. And that's exactly what you're going to fucking do."

44

EMILY

Konstantin laughs in disbelief. "Don't play games with me, Kitty Cat."

Instead of answering, I look to the side. It's too much to stare straight into his face while he clutches my chin, our lips close to kissing while our hearts travel further apart.

I wish I *was* playing games.

But I'm not.

He asked if I've had enough. Maybe I have, but the pain feels too good for him to stop *now*. Maybe on some level, I crave the pain because it's the easiest way to punish myself for being a pushover my whole life.

Maybe if I had a bigger backbone, I wouldn't have been expelled from vet school.

Maybe if I did more, my sister might still be alive.

Maybe if I hadn't picked up the phone call from Mom, I wouldn't be here like this.

Maybe, maybe, maybe.

But no amount of maybes will ever change the lone thought that keeps echoing in my head.

That this is the only place I want to be.

I want to be here because this is the only place where I can be honest about who I am and what I want.

And only *he* can give that to me.

"That look on your face," he growls, interrupting my thoughts. "I fucking hate it."

"What look?"

"Like you know something I don't."

That gets a shallow laugh out of me. "It must drive you crazy to know that you can't break me."

"I *am* breaking you!" His teeth glint like sun-bleached bone. He pushes my knees further apart, sending another delicious ache of need through my body.

I shake my head weakly. "No, you're not."

His smirk tilts higher on one side, like a bridge ready to collapse. "Let's test your restraint."

Despair and a terrible, insatiable lust wash through my core. *Can I even survive another round?*

Nuzzling the crease that divides my breasts, he takes the chain in his teeth. A tug draws a whimper of pleasure from me as he undoes the clips. All the cells in my body are centering on my nipples as relief ripples through my body.

His tongue rolls over my left nipple, then the right, taking turns and never leaving one alone for long.

"Fuck ..." I sob.

God, yes! my body screams.

"Were you always this filthy?" he asks me. "Was this what you always wanted from me?"

Yes!

"Look at how wet your dirty pussy is." He runs his fingers through my slit, showing me how they glisten as he pulls a string between his knuckles. "Do you even remember how many times you came?"

I shudder as he starts smearing the mixture of our arousal against my asshole.

"Is this what you've been dying for me to do?" His cock is pressed against my asshole, and the massive head—aided by my dripping hole—pushes into the impossibly tight entrance. "Is this what you mean when you told me to *destroy* you?"

My chest rattles with every breath as the searing heat rushes up my body, but I manage to level a hard glare down at him where he's wedged between my breasts.

"You tell me, *Kostya.*"

He closes his mouth on a nipple, his tongue drawing harsh circles around the sensitive bud. I point my toes and squeal when I feel his cock push deeper into my ass.

"I can *feel* your clit swelling up in front of me." He drops his hand between my legs, gripping me so I can't budge an inch while he continues pushing his huge cock inside of my ass.

His low, primal murmur of pleasure against my ear has my eyes rolling into the back of my head. He touches a finger to my clit and I moan, straining against the cuffs.

"Just that little bit of pressure and you're already on the verge of shattering."

I cry out again. My voice is hoarse from all my shouting. I worry I'll lose it entirely before he's done here.

I suck my bottom lip inward, working through how to answer, but the lusty fog clouding my brain ruins every sensible thought. His fingers enter my pussy, bit by bit, as his cock pushes deeper in my ass. I'm so turned on that I can't talk, can't think, can't focus on anything other than the sensation of him filling me.

"Is this enough for you?" he asks, snarling.

But it doesn't sound like that.

"Tell me, Kitty Cat!" He begs.

I clench my jaw, and refuse to answer. Because if I say anything, this will stop.

And I'm not ready for it to stop just yet.

Konstantin has gone oddly quiet. I open my eyes and look as he stares at me with fierce yet curious eyes. My arousal is off the charts. I'm hot all over. My inner thighs are slick. My chest and belly is coated in saliva and cum. The cock and fingers inside of me are doing wicked things, even as the two of us stand still.

I take a big breath. "Please ...."

"Greedy girl," he shakes his head as he suddenly pulls out of me and reaches up.

A second later, my arms are free of my restraints, and I collapse forward into him. He bends down and does the same around my ankles.

"What are you, Kitty Cat?" He asks as he holds me. "Tell me."

I know the answer I want to say, but I can't say it.

He turns me around and falls to his knees, bringing me down with him. "Are you my wife?"

I squeeze my eyes shut and turn my face away from him.

He spins me around, pushes my face into the cold hard ground, and I feel his massive cock throbbing against my sensitive ass.

"Are you my whore?"

My mouth opens. Wicked heat torments me the longer he rubs his cock head against my entrance. I'm losing myself.

I shift my ass toward him, but he stays out of reach.

"No," he taunts, leaning away, depriving me again. "You get *nothing* until you answer me."

"Say what?" I groan.

"What you are!" He snarls as he holds my head to the ground and leans down to my ear, pleading. "Which one are you? My wife or my whore? Tell me!"

I know which answer *I* want. But I don't know if that's the answer *he* wants.

So, I tell him the convenient lie instead of the inconvenient truth.

I buck my hips under his powerful body, throwing my back into his muscular chest, and scream.

"Your whore! I'm your fucking whore!"

He closes his lips around my shoulder, then my neck, his teeth scraping the sensitive skin as he shoves his cock in my ass and his fingers in my pussy. I thrust my hips back into him, grinding helplessly as he ruts into me.

He fucks me with a terrifying new resolve, an anger that I can hardly comprehend. And in that moment, I realize that what I wanted and what he wanted are the same thing.

Stupid! Stupid! Stupid!

He *wants* me to be his wife!

He *begged* me to tell him that I'm his wife.

But instead, I convinced myself to lie and tell him that I'm his whore.

His free hand grabs my chin and turns my face so that his mouth can conquer mine. His tongue brushes across my tastebuds as he deepens our kiss. Fingers digs deeper into my pussy and his palm rasps against my clit, driving me higher and higher as his cock opens my ass.

Keening in the terrible mix of pain and delight, I throw away all control of my body, squeezing every muscle to hold him inside as he plugs all of my holes.

I've said terrible, reckless things.

Every single one of them was wrong.

And now I'm facing the consequences.

Konstantin embraces me tightly, kissing me as he fucks me without mercy. He swallows my screams, and once he's sure that I won't pull my mouth from him, he moves his free hand down until it seizes my breast and squeezes.

I allow myself to be swallowed by the overwhelming sensations.

I allow him to drive all thoughts out of my mind.

Because it's the only way I can keep my own heart from shattering.

I can feel his heart race through his cock buried in my ass, his fingers in my pussy, and his tongue down my throat. They match the thunderous beat from my own.

Robbed of every form of escapism, I sink further into the black pit of erotic nothingness. My muscles flex and squeeze all over, my belly tightening as waves of desire wash over me.

He fills me to the root. Every motion sends an unbelievable burst of pleasure ripping through my body. Fire blooms inside of me. A delicious, head-swimming fire that burns away every part of my being.

My lower belly tingles. *I'm going to come*, I realize. My legs go taut. I reach out and grip his legs as I pull him closer to me, my fingers digging into the iron hard bands of muscle. With a pathetic, wanton moan, I convulse on his cock and fingers and tongue as I come, screaming.

As one throat-breaking scream after rips out of me, Konstantin pulls me close to him, enveloping me in his powerful body and his warmth.

And then it happens.

Searing wet heat surges into me, and I feel him fill me from the impossible depth he's buried within me. With one ropy spurt after another, his cum flows forth and leaks out around his cock buried in my ass, running down my hips and thighs.

Roaring, he pulls out of me and falls backwards, still cumming. I turn just in time for a few more errant drops to splash on my belly, my breasts, my face, and even my hair. The hot, sticky liquid beads and rolls along my skin. The salty musky scent—his scent—hangs heavy in the air, marking me as *his*.

I fight the urge to reach out with my tongue and lick away the salty pearly drop at the corner of my mouth.

Shuddering, he backs away and observes me at a distance. His cock is red and swollen. His seed puddles on the floor. We stare at each other, both breathing raggedly as if we've finished a marathon at full sprint.

I am leaking from every hole. Cum plasters my hair, covers my body, and leaks out of my pussy, mouth, and ass.

I begged him to destroy me, I think. *And he did.*

The air around us hangs heavy with the scent of sweat and sex and guilt. I'm quivering on the ground, limbs twitching as I convulse from even the lightest touch.

I don't know how long we stay like this before Konstantin finally rises to his feet, sweeps me up in his arms, unlatches the door, and carries me up the steps.

He deposits me gingerly in our bed, and I feel my lips trembling at the gentleness of his touch. There's no mistaking the self-loathing in his eyes at the thought of what he just did to me.

No, I correct myself. At what I *made* him to do to me.

This is who he really is. Not the monster he pretends to be in that dungeon. But this. The man who will reach up to wipe the tears away from my eyes. The man who chose me over the bratva when both came under threat in a hail of bullets. The man who would burn down the world for me if I just ask him to.

He showed me his heart, begged me to choose it, and I ripped it to shreds.

I made him believe that I can only see him as a monster.

Don't cry. I plead silently. *Don't you fucking cry.*

But just who am I pleading to? Him? Or myself?

I don't know.

And it doesn't fucking matter.

Without another word, he walks away, quietly closing the door behind him as he does so. And only when I'm alone, do I dare let myself cry.

Marrying Konstantin Siderov was supposed to be a ruse.

It was supposed to be nothing more than a game.

And games aren't supposed to break your heart.

45

KONSTANTIN

Anguish tastes a lot like broken glass.

No, it's worse.

I'd rather eat a mouthful of shattered bottles, and let the shards cut my tongue and gums until I'm gurgling blood, than know that I did this to her.

To Emily.

Falling to my knees, I listen outside the door as she cries, and feel shame overwhelm me.

"There you are." Alla says in Russian, as she turns the corner of the hallway, flanked by her bodyguards. Her hands are folded in front of her.

I turn to face her, and my anguish transforms to rage the closer she approaches.

"You bitch." I refuse to answer her in Russian. I *want* Emily to hear.

I *need* Emily to hear.

"Have you done what is necessary?" Alla's eyes narrow as she levels a frosty gaze at me and continues speaking in Russian. "Have you impregnated the whore?"

I rise to my feet and walk towards her. Her bodyguards

immediately move between us, but part at a single wave of her hand.

"I asked you a question, Kostya."

"And I told you," I growl, "to stop calling her that."

"Congratulations." Her lips shift, and they look like two skinny wriggling worms twisting as she smiles. "This was your final test, Kostya."

What the hell is she talking about?

She raises her left hand, and I gasp when I see that she's wearing the signet ring engraved with the Siderov family emblem. I haven't seen it in years, not since father's death. *This* is what I was after by marrying Emily.

This is what I hurt her for ...

I should feel victorious. But instead, the sight of it only compounds my guilt.

"Final test?" I ask.

For the first time in my life, she looks uneasy. Taking a deep breath, as if gathering herself, she reaches over and slowly works the ring off her finger until it is free. A metallic tang spreads over my tongue.

Anticipation? Excitement? Or dread?

I can't tell anymore.

Not that it matters.

Because all of those emotions inevitably give way to the same result: guilt.

"I needed to know if you could be ruthless." Now she switches to English. "I needed to know that I was about to hand over control to a worthy pakhan. I needed you to show me that you were willing to do whatever was necessary for the bratva."

Sick realization pits in my stomach. "You *wanted* me to hurt her ..."

"Of course, my darling Kostya," Alla says sweetly. Her

worm-like smile spreads wider. "I had to know for certain, after you abandoned *me* for *her* when those Ferrata dogs invaded the wedding. Could I really have trusted the future of the bratva to you when you were so ready to abandon it in that moment?"

"You devious old bitch."

"Careful now, Kostya." She withdraws her hand and the ring. "This ring isn't yours yet."

"And if I were to take it from you?" I glare at her. "By force?"

She shrinks back slightly, and her bodyguards immediately move to my flanks.

My hand moves before I can stop myself, and I seize her by her throat. Alla gasps in surprise and the ring tumbles from her fingers, where it clatters on the ground in a soft clink. Quick as lightning, I feel something cold press against my forehead.

A gun.

"You dare point a gun at your pakhan?" I growl at the bodyguard.

The man remains still as a statue, but the gun doesn't waver.

"Think about your wife, Kostya," Alla strains against my hand. I tighten my grip, but she continues to speak. "My guards will keep any child in her belly safe should both of us die, but their allegiance is to the *heir*. To the bratva. Not to *her*. What do you think they'll do to *her* once that child is born?"

My hand shakes. As much as I want to tighten my fingers and snap her neck, I don't.

I can't.

Because I know that she's right.

If I die, then Emily will suffer the consequences.

She's already suffered enough because of me.

Slowly, one finger after another, I release Alla. She falls to her knees, gasping.

I take a step back, and the gun is removed from my temple.

Rising to her feet again, Alla regains her composure as she massages her neck. The angry red marks are visible on her papery skin, and I know that by morning, those red marks will turn to bruises.

Slowly, she picks up the ring, and holds it out for me to accept. And when I do, she drops it into my palm.

It can't weigh more than a chestnut, but my hand wavers as if it's a boulder.

"Our future is in your hands now, Konstantin Yurevich."

I don't dare close my palm, half thinking that she'll yank it away as soon as I do to shame me. Finally, her hand withdraws, and I start to close my fist.

That's when she grabs my wrist with both her hands. Her grip is like iron as she scrutinizes me the way she has always done since I was old enough to walk.

"Now," she says. "Do what you must, and bring my granddaughter back to me."

My eyes narrow suspiciously. "I thought you wanted to use her to end this pointless war? What changed?"

"*You* proved that you will do what is necessary to ensure the family's survival," she says. "For the bratva. And now that I know our future is secure, I will not allow my darling little Aliska to languish in the grips of the same people who murdered my son."

"You devious bitch." My hands ball into fists.

"Call me what you like, Kostya," she muses. "But *never* doubt that everything I do, I do for the family. As a woman, I cannot lead men to war." She raises her hands and cups my cheeks, her single good eye drilling into mine. "Therefore, I must do what I can to position the family for the best possible outcome. It's what I've always done. When will you depart?"

"The men will be ready in two days."

"Good." She smiles. "I trust you to do what boys do best."

"And while I'm gone," I tell her as my fist tightens around the signet ring. "You will stay away from my wife. Understand?"

She stares back at me with both of her eyes so that I can see her defiance.

"Of course," she says softly.

I give her one final look before I start walking away. My fingers are already tapping at my phone to inform Sima of what is to come.

Because this next part is shockingly simple.

After all, there's only one *real* rule in a Mafia war.

Your enemies have to die.

46

EMILY
TWO DAYS LATER

THE CLAP OF THUNDER AWAKENS ME BUT I CLING TO THE FINAL remnants of sleep. The darkness outside of the window is oppressive from the thunderclouds that rumble outside of it.

Konstantin hasn't returned to bed with me after what we've done in the dungeon.

For two days, I've stayed in bed, leaving it only to use the attached bathroom or accept the food that Ivica brings to me. All attempts at finding out what is happening beyond the bedroom door is met with nothing but stony silence.

It's almost as if I'm being *purposefully* kept in the dark by everyone around me.

Not that it matters.

I heard enough through the door the other night to know that I will always be a prisoner here.

Hours after Alla and Konstantin had their argument, I finally found enough strength in my rubbery legs to make my way to the bathroom. I had stripped down to run the water at the hottest temperature possible.

Under the searing hot water, I washed away all traces of our furious coupling from my body.

To my own great shame, when the steam enveloped me inside of its warm embrace, I longed for Konstantin to come in and join me.

I *prayed* that he would walk in during that moment, open my legs, and use me the way he had in the dungeons below.

But when he never did, I reached between my legs, and brought myself to one whimpering climax after another.

I wished then that I could vanish into the steam, to change into something vast, merge with the millions of water molecules outside, and never return to my body.

Konstantin had embedded himself in my mind, my body, and my soul.

And *nothing* can wash him out.

The door creaks open, and I don't look over. It's probably just Ivica. But when I hear the heavy footstep, my heart starts racing with elation, and my pussy—shamefully—grows slick with want.

He's back!

"Konstantin?" I murmur as I slowly sit up.

But the massive hand suddenly closing around my mouth is decidedly not Konstantin's. The foul smell of cigarettes and alcohol stabs at my nose, and I feel a revulsion punch its way down into my stomach.

A fork of lightning briefly illuminates the world around me, and I see *her* materialize, like a demon taking shape in the night.

Alla.

I cling to the sheets desperately, but it's no use. Rough hands rip them away to expose my body, and hold me down by my wrists and my ankles. Blinking, I realize that I am *surrounded* by Alla's stone-faced bodyguards. Their hands burn against my skin as if they're covered in acid, and the metallic tang of fear rushes through my mouth.

"My grandson has left," she speaks from the darkness. "And he won't be back for some time. Perhaps never, if this plan of his goes to shit like all of his other plans have."

Dread snakes its way through my mouth, but I can't speak, not with the hand holding my mouth shut.

"I warned you, didn't I, little whore?" She leans down towards me and her cloudy eye is somehow more visible in the dark. "I warned you that I'll remember the mockery you helped him make of this family. I warned you that I will make you hurt in ways you cannot possibly even begin to imagine."

Dread turns into full blown panic and I thrash under the hands holding me down. But all it does is draw a ring of dark chuckles rising up around me.

I can feel their hungry lecherous gazes raking my body, and I can't stop the tears flowing uselessly down my face in fear as I recall Alla's strained words through the door.

Do you think they'll carry her gently in their arms from the dungeons below when they're done, and put her in a bed up here? Or do you think they'll keep her down there for their amusement until they've had their fun?

Oh god... is she about to make her threat come true?

Alla leans in closer and I see something flash in her hand as another bolt of lightning zigzags across the sky.

"Oh, no, no, no, little whore," she coos as she strokes my hair. "Until I am certain that a Siderov lives in your belly, I will keep my guards away from your tantalizing little cunt. But the instant that I know ..." She smiles as she lets the implications linger in the dark. "In the meantime, there are other ways to make you hurt. Ways that leave neither scars nor draw a single drop of blood."

She brings her hand closer and that's when I see what she's holding in them.

Sewing needles.

Each one is filed down so impossibly sharp that they seem almost invisible, were it not for the way they glimmer each time from the lightning.

My hand is yanked up before her, and I shake my head against the hands keeping me immobilized in bed.

A shriek bubbles from the depth my gut, but never make it past the hand clamped around my mouth. My heart hammers like a piston against my ribcage while tears fill my eyes in anticipation of the pain.

Panicking, I beg her with my eyes to not do this.

But there's no stopping her now.

"Poor naïve little whore," Alla whispers, her one good eye glinting in the night as she places the sharp tip of a needle in front of my finger. "Nobody is coming to save you."

Then, she starts to push.

47

EMILY
MORNING

I HUG MY KNEES TO MY CHEST, AND PAIN STABS THROUGH ME from my fingertips, to my palms, my arms, along my legs, and down to the soles of my feet. But I don't dare let go.

After Alla left with her guards, I stayed awake, my heart racing with terror until the sun chased away the storm clouds at daybreak.

At first light, I held up my trembling hands and searched them for any signs of damage.

Alla was right.

Those needles left neither scars nor drew any drops of blood.

All except one.

At the end of my torture, Alla had one of her body-guards bring out a single syringe. She expertly inserted it into my arm and drew out a full measure of blood. Smirking, she told me that she'll have an answer for her questions soon enough.

Afterwards, she leaned down, and whispered in my ear that she'll be back tonight to let me know the results.

I shudder against myself. I don't think I can survive another night of this.

Especially if I *am* pregnant.

The door creaks open, and I look over with a start only to find Ivica entering with a plate of pancakes and tea. She looks away immediately when she sees me, and my heart hurts at how she's ignoring me.

"Ivica ..." My voice cracks. I just want to hear someone say something to me. Anything. "Ivica, please."

She blinks harshly as she continues to avoid my gaze and lays the tray of food and tea on the table beside me. Then, wordlessly, she starts making her way back to the door.

"Stay," I plead. "Please ..."

Her hand stays at the doorknob for just a moment. For just a moment, I dare to imagine that she might stay—that she might turn around and ask me what is wrong.

But all she offers is a single lone sniffle, the frame of her body shaking as she grabs the doorknob.

"Stay!" Desperate, I reach for a familiar phrase that I've heard from Konstantin in Buric's shop. "*Eto moi prikaz!*"

Whatever the phrase means, it achieves the effect I want. Her head rises, she turns around to face me, and my heart breaks when I see that her eyes are brimming with tears.

And then, she speaks—so soft and quiet that I almost thought I imagined it—from her trembling lips.

"Yes, dear?"

I blink, and my own vision grows blurry and hazy. "Please stay with me for just a few minutes," I beg in a small voice. "Please talk to me. Please don't leave me alone in this place."

Casting one final, furtive look at the door, she gives me a

quick nod, and then strides over beside me. I look up at her when she arrives, my hands still wrapped around my knees as pain stabs throughout my body.

"I can't stay for long, dear," she whispers. "Alla Antonovna ... She'll ..."

"I know." I nod. "Please, can you just sit with me?"

Nodding, Ivica sits down on the edge of the bed and looks at me with her kind eyes brimming with tears, and I feel the pinpricks of pain from Alla's cruel needles again.

Slowly, she reaches out with a single hand and I wince from pain when she brushes my arms. She quickly withdraws, but I grab her hand in mine before she can, biting back the urge to cry out.

If I scream, Alla will hear, and then it won't just be me that she hurts.

Ivica scoots a little closer and then suddenly, she pulls me into a hug like a mother. Not my mother, but the mother I wish I had. I wrap my arms around her, ignoring the searing pain overwhelming my body as I hug her back, unable to stop the tears overwhelming my eyes.

"Where did he go, Ivica?" I whisper, and I feel her embrace tighten at my question.

"He left with Gerasim Petrovich, and the best killers of the bratva," she replies. "They're going to go save Alisa Yurevna."

His sister ... I think. Of course that's why he left. That's the only reason why he'd leave.

I don't blame him for that. If our roles were switched, I would've done the same thing.

But does he know just what kind of monster he left me with?

Did he even have a choice?

"I'm scared, Ivica," I confess. "I'm scared of what she'll do to me when she comes back tonight."

Ivica breaks the hug, holding my shoulders gently in her hands, and asks. "Did she use her needles?"

Tears well in my eyes. Just how many other people have suffered at the hands of that cruel woman? Slowly, I muster a tiny nod. Almost as if I'm afraid that somehow, Alla is watching.

"Oh, Emily Samovna ..." a single tear rolls out from Ivica's eyes. "She shouldn't have. You are Konstantin Yurevich's *wife*."

"Not to Alla, I'm not." I shake my head. Then, with a trembling breath, I say, "I can't stay here, Ivica. I won't survive if I do."

Ivica recoils when I say those words. Her kind eyes are shimmering in the morning light. I can pick out the fear in them. Slowly, the fear gives way to sympathy, sympathy shifts into understanding, and finally, understanding transforms into something else.

Something that makes me feel safe.

Something that tells me that she'll *never* hurt me.

"Where will you go?" she asks me.

"Home," I say. "To America."

I can always go back to New York and stay with Nadia for a little while. But eventually I have to go and face the reality of my expulsion, of Olivia's death, and of my parents demanding information so they can get the money from her life insurance.

But those are problems that I can handle.

Anything is better than the hell that awaits me tonight when Alla returns with her needles.

Or once she confirms that I am *pregnant with Konstantin's child* ... I shudder.

I can't think about it.

Ivica chews her lip.

"Take the boat to the other side of the lake," she says. "From there, through the trees, it's an hour-long walk in a straight line north until you reach a road. Every day, a delivery truck from the castle will travel along there two hours after sundown towards Dubrovnik."

My heart thunders at my throat. I know just how dangerous it can be for her to tell me all of these things. But I don't dare interrupt her, and listen intently as she continues.

"Once you flag the driver down, tell them *ya trebam pomoch*," she says. "That means I need help. Then tell them *ya sam Amerikanka*. That means I am an American. They should be able to figure out where to take you from that point on. And don't worry, the drivers won't know who you are. They *only* ever interact with the kitchen staff. They won't sell you out. Any questions?"

I blink and stare at her, shocked that she is offering up all of this information to me. Was she always willing to do that? Or does she also realize that should Konstantin fail to rescue Alisa, the fate that awaits me is one worse than death?

"I need to hear you repeat those two phrases, dear."

Slowly, I do. She asks me to do it again, and then one final time until the words are practically seared inside of my mind. Finally, when she's satisfied, she tells me.

"I will lace Alla Antonovna's meal later tonight with just enough sleeping medication so that she will go to bed at sunset. I can have some of the girls distract the guards. There's a service corridor on the left side of the hallway. Go through there once the sun has set and I will take you to the boat myself."

She gingerly takes my hands in hers. I can tell she wants to squeeze them to reassure me, but she doesn't out of fear that she might hurt me. Gritting my teeth against the pain stabbing at me, I squeeze her hands tightly in mine as tears of gratitude rolls down my face.

"Thank you, Ivica. For everything."

48

EMILY

Ivica comes to fetch me exactly when she said she would. She also brings me a pair of sturdy shoes, a compass, the old clothes that I had arrived at the castle in, and even my phone.

It takes me no more than a few minutes to change completely, my body stinging from the pain the entire time.

When I'm done, I stare at my reflection in the mirror, and my eyes travel down to the rings on my finger, both the engagement ring with its massive diamond and the wedding band.

Both of them tie me to Konstantin, and I move my hand to remove them when Ivica stops me.

"I have no money to give you," she explains. "So you may need to sell those for a ticket home. Now come."

Realizing she has a point, I give her a quick nod, and follow her out the door.

True to her word, she leads me all the way to the boat. When we finally reach it, she helps me in and pushes it silently over the darkening lake.

"Good luck, dear," she tells me.

"Ivica, wait." I tell her.

"There's no time!" she hisses as she continues pushing. "You need to go now!"

I reach forward and place my hand on hers, and she stops.

Even in the dying sun, I can see the tears in her eyes.

"I just need to know," I say. "Why did you choose to help me? If Konstantin finds out that you did this for me. If Alla finds out ..."

"Because you needed help." She stops me from speaking and gives the boat one final shove until it's gliding on the glassy surface. "Now go!"

TWO HOURS LATER, I am sitting in the back of the truck as it makes its way towards Dubrovnik. Everything went exactly as Ivica said. The ride is bumpy, and the driver chatters with the man in the passenger side in Croatian the entire time.

Neither of them spares me another glance as I sit quietly in the back.

As far as they're concerned, I'm a nobody.

Which is exactly what I wanted.

I start twisting the rings on my finger again. I had turned the massive diamond inside to hide it, and now, the immense weight of the rings seems to grow heavier with each mile the truck puts between me and the distant castle.

My mind is focused on Ivica.

And Konstantin.

Will Ivica have a chance to tell Konstantin the truth before Alla gets to her? Will Alla be furious when she finds me missing?

And what about Konstantin?

Will he get a chance to find out just what his grand-mother had done to me?

I stare down at the rings on my finger, giving them another twist, and feel a familiar sting in my nose. Ugh ... the last thing I want to do right now is to cry more, but once the tears start, I can't stop myself anymore.

The driver peers at me in the center mirror, and he asks me something in Croatian as he offers up a sympathetic smile. When I don't say anything, he exchanges a quick concerned look with his passenger before resuming the drive in silence.

I wish I could've seen Konstantin one final time ... I think. *I wish I could hear his voice calling me Kitty Cat one last time.*

But that's impossible.

There's a vast canyon between that happy ending and where I am now. We haven't gone all that far away from the castle yet. For all I know, Alla is rallying her bodyguards to drag me back there, kicking and screaming, so that she can torture me some more before Konstantin comes back.

I shudder as I touch my sensitive skin, still raw and prickling from her needles.

Slowly, my hand moves down to my belly, and I wonder if maybe I *am* already pregnant.

The thought of Konstantin's baby growing inside of me sends another burst of tears pouring from my eyes.

He might never know.

Maybe there'll be a way I can get in touch with him ...

The driver looks back at me. The concerned expression in his eyes helps chase away some of the nervous clouds swarming my heart. He asks me something again, and I do the only thing I can, which is shake my head at whatever it is he's saying and mustering up a fake smile to assure him that I'm alright.

He sighs. Whether to himself or for me, I will never know.

Because that's the exact moment when the glass shatters beside his head.

Blood sprays across the car. Shards rake the passenger's seat, and both men cry out in pain. Loud thuds slam into the body of the car, one after another. Spiderweb cracks blossom into white balls in the windshield and I huddle myself into the space behind the driver's seat.

The last thing I see is the passenger's body convulsing as his shirt changes color from a light blue to a deep crimson. The coppery scent of blood fills the air, and I scream in shock.

The driver tries to yell something at me. But his word is cut short and he collapses forward, honking a single long note as the truck barrels full speed ahead.

He's dead!

Scrambling upwards, I grab the handbrake and give it a hard pull. The truck starts slowing down immediately, but momentum carries it forward until it slams through the guardrail separating the curving road and straight into a thick olive tree.

The front of the truck is twisted against the bent metal guardrail. Green leaves and fresh olives clatter on the hood like hailstones.

I clamber backwards, and tug at the handle of the door. Adrenaline chases away all sensation of prickling pain still coursing through my body. Time seems to move in slow motion, and I breathe a silent prayer of thanks that the door still works.

I stumble outside, collapsing immediately on my knees from disorientation, and try to get back up.

I reach for my phone, but as soon as I have it, I realize I

don't know what number I can even dial. That's when I notice the red smears on the glass surface.

When did I get blood on me? I try to wipe it away, but it's playing hell with the touch-screen's functions.

"No! No! No!" I groan in frustration. Each time I scrub the screen, it only gets worse.

I need to dial—

Glass crunches, drawing my attention to the sound of boots heading my way. Fear rises in my throat as I imagine Alla's bodyguards stalking towards me. Getting up on wobbly feet, I start to move, only to collapse onto my back.

The thin man who looms towards me is framed by light. Instantly, I know he's far too small to be one of Alla's bodyguards. I see the gun in his hand and my eyes widen in panic. But he doesn't raise it as he continues to walk calmly towards me.

Once he's closer, I see that he's wearing black leather gloves that match his long jacket. They practically gleam as he grabs the front of my left hand and yank me up to see him.

Another man, much fatter than his companion, comes to join him. He points at my hand. That's when I realize he's staring at my rings. The thin man looks at him, then back to me, and the two of them excitedly exchanges a few words.

Their words sound musical, almost as if they're singing.

And then it hits me.

They're not speaking Croatian or Russian.

They're speaking *Italian*.

The thin man holding me by my hand turns his face towards me, the sight of his sharp eyes and crooked smile— like a starving animal suffering a long winter that's finally found something to eat—turns my skin cold.

"*La puttanella di Siderov,*" he says, grinning. "*L'Americana.*"

It doesn't take a genius for me to know exactly what he's talking about.

Run, please, run! I beg my body. I try to make a move towards the guardrail. I don't know just how high up we are or what is on the other side. But I know that it can't be worse than what will happen to me in their hands.

If I can just get free ...

Maybe someone will help me. Someone will save me.

A hard object presses into my ribs, and chases all thought of escape out of my mind. "Don't move, *puttana*," he whispers in my ear.

His voice is rusted nails and candy. It turns my stomach.

He rubs the gun along my side. It's small and stiff, scraping my skin through my shirt. He uses it like it's a third hand and inhales deeply, making it obvious he's enjoying the smell of my hair. Revulsion climbs up in me.

And this time, Konstantin isn't here to save me.

With a hard yank, the two of them drag me back towards their waiting car.

Each step forward is heavy, and my feet drags. The lingering pain in the soles of my feet from Alla's needles return, stinging me with every step. Strangely enough, it doesn't seem like their car is getting any closer.

Just as I think it'll take an hour to reach it, suddenly I see my own reflection staring back at me in the tinted backseat window.

They shove me inside, and the memory of the same action by a different man who I wish was here right now hits me hard enough to leave me dazed.

The thin man gets into the driver's seat while his fat companion slides into the seat next to me. With his gun pointed at me, he starts leaning in close.

Icicles form on my spine as his thick sausage-like fingers reach for me ...

... and rips the phone—still covered in the blood of the truck driver and his passenger—out of my hand.

With a single swift motion, he throws it on the ground, and shuts the door.

Konstantin won't know where I am.

And I can't even contact him if I wanted to.

The car starts, and the driver gives me one last look through the rearview mirror, his eyes staring greedily at my chest.

And without warning, the car speeds away from the violent scene.

END OF BOOK 1
Emily and Konstantin's story continues in Book 2:
VENGEFUL PROMISES

Made in the USA
Las Vegas, NV
25 October 2024